The Hush

William R. Flowers
January 18, 2009

All scriptural references and quotations are taken from:
<u>The Holy Bible, The Revised Standard Version</u>. New York: William Collins Sons, 1952.

Time references are based on ancient Hebrew reckoning, which began the day at six o'clock a.m. (first hour) and divided the night into four watches. The first watch was from six to nine o'clock p.m., the second from nine o'clock p.m. to midnight, the third from midnight to three o'clock a.m., and the fourth from three to six o'clock a.m.
The Sabbath was observed from sunset on Friday evening to sunset on Saturday.

Friday, fifth hour

Close your eyes.

But before you close them, try to bring to mind the most splendid morning that you can remember. Think Hard.

Now close your eyes.

Was there a spectacular sunrise, with deep colors of fiery crimson and purple? Was there gentle surf, calm and smooth like a sheet of crystal? Or, was there a quiet mountain stream with a swirling mist rising into clear, cold air? Were there birds singing in the background? Was there a smell of fresh cut grass?

In order to fully comprehend what happen on that dreadful day, it is first necessary to appreciate the kind of day on which it happened.

From all appearances, this particular day had seemed to be shaping up as one of the best days ever, if such a thing were possible. The sun had been shining all morning; the air had been fresh and cool, and the golden remains of winter wheat had been swaying gently in the soft breeze. From the first moment it had been a gorgeous daybreak, blinking softly to life with a shimmering glow, while birds everywhere responded with noisy delight, announcing the arrival of a fresh new day. By the second hour, the sky was a deep indigo, and the distant highlands were visible and breathtaking on the horizon.

But appearances too often deceive; sometimes, keener observation is required.

Walking along the road just outside the city, an observer might have noticed the early evidence of spring: fig trees were not yet blooming, but they were softening and just beginning to produce tender green buds; and though the nearby wheat fields were still a dry golden brown, weeds were already hard at work, beginning to spread and invade, little islands of green getting a head start in the race to cover the neglected landscape. Heavy dew had covered the landscape overnight, but had eventually burned off with the rising sun. Nothing unusual here.

By the fourth hour, the road was nearly deserted; but a keen observer would have seen evidence that there had been brisk traffic earlier in the morning traveling westward into the city: the freshly trampled grass, the occasional remains of a half-eaten breakfast or bit of fruit, the heavy tread of footprints and wheels and hooves, all heading in one direction.

Still, there was nothing remarkable about any of this.

Now, at the fifth hour of the day, the road was still and quiet. The only noise to be heard was an occasional call from a lone hawk circling high overhead and the rustling of the dry wheat stirred up by the light breeze. It was the kind of day that should have been spent with a pleasant nap in the warm sunlight, or on a stroll across the face of God's green earth, as white clouds floated silently across the deep blue sky, casting long, soft shadows on the rolling hills beneath them. A more marvelous day would have been hard to imagine, with all of God's handiwork fully awake and on display in stunning, vibrant glory.

But on this day, at this hour, God's handiwork was bracing for the hush.

This moment had been anticipated by creation for a very long time – or to be more precise, it had been anticipated by all of creation outside of mankind from nearly the beginning. Of all the living, breathing creatures that God had placed on the face of the earth, only man had chosen to rebel, and as a result, only man was unable to recognize the mounting, horrific consequences all around him, or to see where his now altered history was clearly headed.

The fox knew; the cattle in the field and the beasts in the wilderness saw and understood that something was not right all around them, and that whatever it was would some day require a resolution. And worse yet, mankind had not been entirely alone in his madness. There had been others.

Rebellion, in fact, had originally found a place outside of creation, in the spiritual realm - among the inhabitants of heaven. Then, as the trouble spread, the first man and woman joined in the sad folly, and God's fresh new creation witnessed firsthand the devastating effect of the revolt: death began its shocking rule; pristine gardens, lush with fruit and colors suffered the first decay of autumn and barrenness of winter; violence became the norm as man killed man and animal devoured animal. Years turned into centuries and centuries became millennia, while the vast army of fallen angels, warped with unrestrained deceit and thoroughly evil motives, waged war with the host of heaven; the battles raged continuously in mankinds blinded though clearly affected presence, and the rest of creation silently observed it all. Sadly, humans learned very little through the years regarding this warfare or the fall or his part in it; Outside of man, however, creation quietly watched and learned dependence on its creator, and developed a deep longing for renewal, for liberation from the mad cycle of death and destruction. But without man's ability to voice this longing, the entire universe has been patiently waiting for the day when history, marred and stained by the fall, will finally come to an end, and all things will be made new.

But today would not be that day.

The prospect of a major confrontation had been building pressure for many generations, and of course man was entirely unaware of the mounting tension. He rarely noticed the evidence for what it was: a goat would suddenly raise its head and flee for no apparent reason; a donkey would halt in the middle of the road, refusing to proceed; a sudden, chilling wind would pick up, scattering birds and debris in a cloud of dust, and just as suddenly it was gone. To human senses, these events were commonplace and meant nothing. But to the goats in man's fields, to the donkeys upon which he rode, to the sheep he led from pasture to pasture, the clashing of forces, the fierce, mounting combat was obvious and real and would someday have to come to a climax.

It should not be surprising then, that with his fallen, stunted vision mankind was unable to recognize the stage slowly being set in his presence. And neither should it be surprising that when the final countdown began in earnest, it caught no human attention.

It happened in a little, out of the way stable in the presence of a handful of animals. We all know the story, or at least we think we know it: a baby boy was born to a virgin, and the little family was visited by some shepherds and some wise men from the east. To our ears, the story sounds sweet, with warm, familiar characters playing in front of makeshift props in lonely obscurity.

The advent was nothing of the sort.

The night that the baby was born brought more sharp attention, more widespread clamor, more panic throughout the worldwide kingdom of darkness than any event history had ever produced. There was no way to hide the human birth of the Creator himself; every angel and every fallen spirit knew exactly who he was; every living creature, every single member of created life outside of mankind knew without a doubt the child's identity. No spot on earth held more attention, commanded so much respect, created such enormous battle lines.

The manger that held the infant amidst the straw was surrounded by a handful of deeply honored guests from the animal kingdom; the animals were surrounded by a growing circle of men, who were surrounded by thousands upon thousands of spirits, engulfing the entire valley. All of creation held its breath as the author of life blinked his little eyes and inhaled his own first breath. After a moment of profound silence, the heavens erupted in a thunderous roar, a deafening mixture of demonic chaos and panic with angelic praise and celebration. Attacks were launched and repelled; huge forces were suddenly locked in fierce, unseen combat all around the stable, while the handful of unsuspecting men and women gazed at the beautiful child in silent, rapt attention. The shepherds quietly paid their respects, and the demons exploded in a massive attack. The wise men from the East humbly presented their gifts, and the angels mounted a tremendous counter-attack. The night eventually turned into day, and the day turned into weeks. The furious combat at length began to weaken, but the danger did not. A sense of urgency now pervaded both sides.

Troubled by the inquiry from the mysterious, foreign magi, Herod the Great became an easy target; his sleep was tormented by repeated, frightening visions of a baby who would destroy his lineage and his name. In response, he gathered what information he could and dispatched assassins to seek out and destroy the potential rival, while at the same time the father of the child was warned by an angel in a dream to take the mother and child and flee immediately to Egypt. The standoff continued.

Years raced by, with battles and skirmishes building with every step. The infant became a little boy, the boy a teen, and all eyes were focused in his direction. With each year, each change of season, and each conflict, the tension grew.

Suddenly, Jesus stepped into the River Jordan to be baptized, and the wait was over. The cool, swirling water, fed by the Sea of Galilee sixty miles to the north, now touched and encircled the feet of the MASTER, and paused for just a moment, reluctant to pass on by. The grass along the bank rejoiced at his presence. The stones below the water refused to let him stumble. The air shimmered, the clouds retreated, and the sun shone in brilliant glory as the pure white dove lightly descended, touching his head for just an instant. All of God's creatures, great and small, heard the welcome, tender, voice of the Almighty declare to the universe: "This is my son, whom I love; with him I am well pleased." The ground shook in glad response. The trees raised their limbs in the sudden breeze, the angels roared in approval, and the wicked spirits, too numerous to count, fled in terror. Jesus the Christ, Son of God, Son of Man, entirely in control of the moment, stepped out of the water, and headed into the wilderness alone. It was time for round one: eye to eye, face to face.

The trap was set.

Jesus had come alone with no food and no water. He carried nothing in his hands, wore no protection on his head.

A week passed and he was still alone. Two weeks. Twenty days. Thirty days, and still he continued in prayer and fasting, wandering the wilderness with no hint anywhere of protection. The ancient foe, Satan the adversary, ventured out of his own protection in baffled curiosity, watching him, waiting for a sign of weakness. This was a moment he never dreamed he would see. Forty days, and it was clear that Jesus was exhausted, in need of rest, and hungry.

Satan stepped into the trap; he couldn't help himself. The God-man was here at his very doorstep, weak, vulnerable, and he had to take his shot. He hesitated, looked around once more, and then stepped in front of the weary human figure, fully aware that those were a pair of human eyes that could see him.

"If you are the Son of God, tell these stones to become bread," he whispered, while the aroma of roasting lamb and savory vegetables wafted on the air around them.

Deep hunger flashed, then passed.

The stones smiled as Jesus deflected the blow.

"If you are the Son of God, throw yourself down," he chided as they stood atop the pinnacle of the temple, towering high above the crowded streets of Jerusalem. "Isn't it written 'He will give his angels charge of you,'" he mocked, "and, 'On their hands they will bear you up, lest you strike your foot against a stone;' unless, of course, these do not apply to you."

Temptation to prove him wrong rose, along with a sudden desire to retreat to the comfort and care of his Father, but the winds rejoiced as Jesus overcame them both and rallied.

Then they flashed around the globe in a dizzying tour of all of his carefully managed kingdoms with their fabulous riches and powerful rulers and beautiful glory; and the devil, unable to control himself any longer, raised his voice to a shout and laid bare once again his ancient, desperate passion: "ALL THIS I WILL GIVE YOU, IF YOU WILL BOW DOWN AND **WORSHIP ME!**"

The sound echoed through the canyons, spreading out in all directions, slowly dying out to a whisper, and then there was deep, profound, heavy silence. Nothing moved. Nothing breathed. The devil seemed suddenly very small and frightened. He was exposed and helpless, drawn out in the open before his powerful enemy by his own wicked desires. He had seldom done anything more foolish.

"Away from me, Satan."

It was barely above a whisper.

"As it is written, worship the Lord your God, and serve Him only."

And Satan was gone.

Two more years elapsed, years filled with advances into the kingdom of darkness. Blind men were healed. Demons were cast out. A woman's son was raised from the dead. Five loaves of bread and a few fish were miraculously multiplied to feed thousands. Huge crowds were following him everywhere he went.

Then came the news that the Baptist was in prison.

Though Jesus and John were cousins, they had seen each other only twice over the years, just once prior to the baptism. The first time they had been young boys, and had been introduced during a trip to Jerusalem for Passover. Few words had been exchanged; but years later, when the moment was repeated at the baptism, both of them remembered that brief moment in front of the temple, staring into each other's eyes. They had never experienced any other contact. Life had moved on in two different families, two different directions. This lack of personal contact, however, did not soften the blow when John was arrested; for both of these men, and only them, knew from the beginning where the road would eventually lead.

When the time had come, John followed his calling, stepped into the wilderness, and obediently played his part. He was the first to appear on the stage, and the first to leave. His role had been to introduce the Savior, nothing more, and that role was quickly completed. As Jesus had risen in prominence, John had been satisfied, even happy to slip into the shadows after so fiery and brief a ministry. He did not look back. But with the crowds and attention gone, he became easy prey. He surrendered quietly, aware that he would never again see his cousin, his savior.

After his arrest, sitting alone in the dark prison, doubt and despair had slipped in, as unseen and unhindered spirits gathered all around him, pouncing with fury, confusing his mind and shaking his faith. Hope was a fading light, and clinging to it became difficult.

Round two was well under way.

The spiritual assault was brutal, thorough, and effective. Few men have ever endured what happened in that lonely, forgotten cell. His brief life had been spent preparing for one brief moment, and now that the moment was gone, he faced a barrage of doubt that it had all been in vain. At his lowest moment, John sent a message to Jesus through friends: "Are you he who is to come, or shall we look for another?"

Jesus received the message from John's disciples with great compassion. He gently brought the messengers into the midst of the massive crowd, and showed them the men and women and children who had been healed and restored and made well. He instructed the disciples to return to John, and to report to him what they had heard, and had witnessed with their own eyes: "The blind receive their sight and the lame walk, lepers are cleansed and the deaf hear, and the dead are raised up, and the poor have the good news preached to them."

The road ahead would become even more difficult for John before it reached its end, but this message had been exactly what he needed. Upon hearing the words, chained in a corner of his dark, oppressive cell, he remembered a promise he had memorized long ago about the days of Messiah, recorded by the prophet Isaiah: *"Then the eyes of the blind shall be opened, and the ears of the deaf unstopped; then shall the lame man leap like a hart, and the tongue of the dumb sing for joy...and a highway shall be there, and it shall be called the Holy Way."*

Suddenly John's mind cleared; and recalling another poignant memory, his spirit began to soar: he saw himself on the mountain top that first day, standing in the dazzling afternoon sun, with the fresh breeze touching his face, where he had stepped forward from the wilderness and proclaimed with all of his might, "The voice of one crying in the wilderness: Prepare the Way of the Lord!"

In spite of the oppression, filth and gloom storming down on him from all sides, the Baptist had been restored. They had taken his freedom, they had taken his dignity, and soon they would violently take his life; but they could not take from him his confirmed belief, his freshly reassured knowledge that God had come in the flesh, and that he, John, the cousin of Jesus, had seen him with his own eyes, and had prepared his way.

Come what may, he was ready.

The daughter danced, the mother schemed, and the depraved king was caught in the trap. Wickedness was exalted, millions of evil spirits around the globe rejoiced, and the earth shuddered as the severed, bloody head of the Baptist was lifted up.

The conflict was now truly engaged.

Battle lines were drawn everywhere as Jesus moved deliberately about the Galilean countryside, challenging customs and regulations and strongholds, breaking sacred (and misguided) codes of conduct, rebuking and terrorizing demons, lifting up the downcast, restoring the wayward, healing the sick, shaming the proud, strengthening the weak, and proclaiming freedom to those trapped in slavery to sin.

By the time Jesus turned his eyes one last time toward Jerusalem, the air around him was charged with danger and storm warnings. The religious leaders in the city were plotting openly against him. Spies were afoot, infiltrating the crowds, attempting to infiltrate the disciples. Roman legions were mobilized and ready for trouble. Jesus himself spoke often about his looming death. Spirits swarmed around him, clashing and challenging, pushing and defending. The atmosphere was ripe for disaster.

In the kingdom of darkness, it was time to do

something, anything, before it was too late. Plans were hatched and discarded. Ideas were floated and shot down. After a long, frustrating and fruitless debate, it became painfully clear that their playbook of successful tactics was thin - very thin. Finally, this secret assembly of the most powerful and deadly rulers from around the spiritual universe reluctantly settled on the obvious: *They had successfully eliminated his fore-runner, the Baptist; could they do it again? Could they take out one of his followers? Could they take them all out? What about his friends?*

The illness of Lazarus was no fluke. He had been singled out, attacked, and brought down by the enemy of our souls. The illness grew worse, the physicians gave up, and an urgent message was sent to Jesus that his dear friend was dying.

And of course invisible eyes followed the progress of this messenger as he left Bethany, headed for the wilderness. After all, this wasn't just an acquaintance; Jesus had spent as much time with Lazarus and his two sisters as he had with anyone, even his own family. No one, save his disciples, was closer to the Galilean. Surely he would rush back to his aid. Surely he would come back to Judea, back to their turf, back to the battleground that he had so recently fled.

So they settled in and waited.

Two nights later, Lazarus passed away. He had been pushed too hard, and his frail body hadn't been able to take any more. His sisters spent the night in anguished mourning, alone in a silent house with the body of their dead brother, for they had given strict orders that no one else was permitted to enter the premises until daybreak. It was a very long night.

By morning, word had reached nearby Jerusalem that Lazarus was dead. The news was shocking, for not only had he been a healthy man, he had been a close friend of the Galilean healer. His sudden death stirred something among his friends and acquaintances, and before noon, the road to Bethany was filled with travelers dressed in black. So when the doors to the house were finally opened, Mary and Martha were confronted with a flood of well-wishers and mourners, friends and family, cousins and distant relatives, all of whom had a word or a tear for the dead, and many of whom came to stay for the burial. And it was clear to them all that Martha and Mary were stunned at their sudden loss; they seemed to be lost in denial, unable to accept the fact that he was gone.

But by mid afternoon, the body had been embalmed, the grave site had been prepared, and the young men were in the process of laying their brother to rest. The sisters, supported by a noisy crowd of mourners, watched as the stone was rolled into place.

Lazarus was dead and buried.

For the remainder of the day, Martha sat quietly and stoically in her favorite chair, her face fixed on the door, as if she were waiting for her brother to change his mind and come back to her. Mary retreated to her room, where she wept quietly, surrounded by a number of women who were less restrained in their sobbing, doing their best to assist her in her grieving. All evening, and well into the night, men and women came and went, bringing food and offering condolences, and shuffling their feet, and struggling with what to say, and leaving distressed at their helplessness in the face of such great loss.

On the morning of the fourth day, two days after they had buried their brother, Martha heard familiar footsteps outside of the door. She leapt from her chair and threw the door open: it was indeed the servant that they had sent to fetch the master, but he was alone. Martha looked up and down the road, saw no one, and then slowly looked into the eyes of the young man. He could not return the gaze. He lowered his eyes, and shook his head. Her shoulders slumped, her eyes hardened, and she returned to her chair.

Another morning and another evening of smothering despair, and the house again grew dark and silent; the only sound that could be heard was the subdued voices of grieving women crying out in dismal, repetitious chanting.

The fifth day came and went, and still Jesus did not come.

By the time Jesus and his disciples drew within sight of the town of Bethany on the sixth day, news of his approach had already reached the grieving family. His late and unexpected arrival was initially a shock, but shock quickly gave way to frustration, which just as quickly became anger. Martha stood again, leaving her post for only the second time in four days; this time, however, she moved deliberately. She had no idea what she was going to say, but she would face him and say it to his face. But not here, not in this room where they had shared so many happy moments, where she and Mary and Lazarus had welcomed him and his twelve followers as if they had been family. She smoothed her cloak, straightened her hair, and walked out of the house. She would meet him outside – outside of town if she moved quickly and headed him off.

The confrontation didn't even need any prompting. The invisible spirits gathered around closely as the woman stepped into the roadway in front of the weary travelers. There were no greetings, no hugs, no effort at decorum. Martha crossed her arms.

"If you had been here, my brother would not have died."

The words were not delivered with fire, but there was clearly a warmth of emotion behind them, and it wouldn't take much of a spark to ignite it. The gaggle of wicked spirits exploded in delight; they giggled and roared and slapped each other, screaming in circles around and around the little crowd of humans. This was exactly what they had hoped for: the enemy had returned, his friends were clearly alienated from him, and the sky was beginning to grow thick with more of their invisible comrades. IN fact, their commotion grew so loud and unruly that most of them were unable to hear the conversation between the woman and their enemy. When they were finally able to refocus their attention, the woman was fleeing back into town. Confusion ensued, orders were dispatched, and the forces of darkness, suddenly too close to Him for their own comfort, withdrew some distance until the situation was understood better.

Presently, the other sister emerged from town, accompanied not only by Martha, but also with a small crowd of friends and supporters.

Mary ran ahead of them and fell at his feet weeping; between sobs, she quietly repeated her sister's words spoken just a few moments before: "If you had been here, my brother would not have died."

In the painful moments that followed, Jesus saw with human eyes and felt with a beating, human heart a complicated tangle of emotions: a deep sympathy for these two grieving friends; tender compassion for their lack of understanding at what was really going on; profound sadness over the accumulated misery and sorrow brought on by sin and death; heaviness over the looming ordeal he himself would be facing in a matter of mere days; and sorrow at the sense of hopelessness so evident in their tears. He heart was full, it was heavy, and it spilled out, overwhelmed.

Jesus wept.

Had they been on better footing, the three of them might have embraced at that moment, but neither Martha nor Mary was yet willing to soften so far. Instead, Mary rose to her feet and stepped back beside her sister and waited for him to say something. In a voice choked with emotion, he asked to see where they had buried Lazarus.

The sisters glanced quickly at each other, then nodded and turned back toward town. Jesus again joined those who were weeping as they headed for the tomb. This fact was not lost on the crowd accompanying them, mortal and immortal. Murmuring spread, speculation as to the cause of his weeping.

Nor was the sight of his tears lost on his faithful creation all around him. The flowers planted along the roadway wept with him, and the sloping hillside trembled in sympathy at the touch of his feet. Step by step, the mourners made their way slowly through the streets of Bethany, the procession growing rapidly as they went.

And finally, he was standing at the mouth of the cave.

"Take away the stone."

It was a simple command, but it shocked and confused

everyone.

Martha recovered first. She clutched his sleeve, and whispered, "Rabi, by this time there will be an odor, for he has been dead four days."

Four days.

If he had only come when he had been asked, he might have prevented the death, or at least have revived him if he had come within the first day or two. But after four days...everyone knew that after four days the spirit has left the body and decay has set in. His request was difficult to understand; the tomb was defiled because of the decay.

Was he going to enter and defile himself?

Jesus looked into her eyes, and returned the whisper, "Did I not tell you that if you would believe you would see the glory of God?"

Martha stepped back, a new emotion trembling deep within her: was it...hope? Her mouth was suddenly dry and her heart was pounding. She glanced at the young men nearby and nodded.

Among the demons circling the area, there was sheer panic. They didn't know what he was up to, but they knew by now that it couldn't be anything good. As the men stepped up to roll the stone back, the shocked and silent crowd of mourning men and women drew back in horror, while the smothering cloud of dark spirits pressed forward in morbid, fearful fascination.

Jesus stepped near the open grave, and closing his eyes, he raised his face to heaven, his expression now bright with anticipation.

Every noise of every kind withered into absolute silence. The wind died. The birds in the trees grew still. Even the sound of weeping ceased. For a moment, it seemed that the very earth itself had been stopped in its rotation, and all its color had been drained.

No one moved.

No one even blinked.

Every living creature in that region held its collective breath, straining to hear what he would say.

"Father, I thank you that you have heard me," he said

quietly but clearly.

Suddenly, he raised both hands to the sky, and shouted with unrestrained joy:

"Lazarus, come out!"

The world instantly sprang back to life as the dead man stepped out of the tomb. His family and friends raced up the hill to him, bursting out in a frenzy of joy, hugging and weeping, while the children began to dance, and the cloudless sky thundered its praise. The ground quaked its approval, the wind sang through the limbs of the happy trees, and all around them the birds of the air, the sheep in the fields and the foxes in their dens lifted their voices, all of them rejoicing together in one big noisy chorus.

Jesus stepped back from the clamor around his dear friend, as his family unwound the grave clothes and extracted him from its clutches. He looked at the skies and watched as his enemy fled in terror; no one else present had yet comprehended that the Master of the universe had just reversed the inevitable, fearful, universal process of decay and death.

Jesus finally left the crowded celebration at his friend's home as the sun was setting. He and Lazarus walked quietly in the gloom out to the barren street. There were thoughts that Lazarus wanted to express, but he didn't know how to put them into words: he was struggling mightily over his recent departure from this life and subsequent return. He loved his family and friends, but he wasn't sure if he was glad to be back or sorry to have left his new home. There were glimpses of wonders he could not describe swirling around in his mind, memories and experiences that humans were not intended to have to keep to themselves. But he knew that he would. There just weren't any words he could use.

He stopped at length, and as the two faced each other, Lazarus finally spoke up.

"I'm homesick," he said softly, tears glistening on his cheeks.

Jesus nodded, and struggling with his own emotions,

gave him an understanding smile and wrapped his arms around him. They said their good-byes, hugged again, and then they parted. Jesus had sent his disciples on into town, and needed to join them. The Passover was fast approaching, and with it would come the greatest conflict yet.

Saturday, six days previous

"What can be done, then?" No one responded. It was nearly noon; they had been debating for hours, and this ground had been covered repeatedly.

The rest of the nation of Israel was in the process of observing the Sabbath, as their fathers had done, and as their fathers and grandfathers for many generations back had done. There was to be no work performed on the Sabbath. There were thirty-nine categories of work specifically proscribed in their written tradition: sowing, plowing, reaping, binding sheaves, threshing, winnowing, selecting, grinding, sifting, kneading, baking, shearing wool, washing wool, beating wool, dyeing wool, spinning, weaving, making two loops, weaving two threads, separating two threads, tying, untying, sewing stitches, tearing, trapping, slaughtering, flaying, tanning, scraping hide, marking hides, cutting hide to shape, writing two or more letters, erasing two or more letters, building, demolishing, extinguishing a fire, kindling a fire, putting the finishing touch on an object and transporting an object between the private domain and the public domain, or for a distance of ten feet within the public domain. In addition, there were thousands of more specific rules added over the years in an attempt to close loopholes that had been discovered by the more industrious. For instance, a letter written with the left hand and one written with the right on the same day constituted two letters and was a violation.

Through successive generations, the religious leaders and scribes and lawyers had developed a tradition which spent six days of the week discovering and categorizing and emphasizing what could not be done on the seventh. But on this particular Sabbath, tradition had been temporarily set aside among the highest religious leaders of the land, who were gathered together for a highly unusual meeting.

"Well, what can be done?" The question had become obnoxious. Though all of them knew something had to be done, none of them had any supportable solutions. After six meetings in ten days, nerves were beginning to show. The issue, what to do with the Galilean, was not new; but the sharp sense of urgency was new, prompted by reports that had come from the town of Bethany regarding Lazarus. The Galilean had already been systematically destroying their world, and now he was reportedly raising the dead. The Romans would soon step in to take control if they couldn't, a prospect that none of them wished to think about. Time was quickly running out.

They had dealt with trouble-makers before, many times; there were the routine criminals, the religious zealots, the patriotic anti-Romans, and those who were simply ruthless madmen, thirsty for blood. The problem wasn't the lack of will to take action, the problem was his popularity. From the very beginning, nearly three years ago when he stormed into Jerusalem, his outlandish behavior and scandalous rhetoric appealed immediately and broadly to the street rabble. His tricks and magic had made him an overnight hero. Since that time, he had toured the countryside, dragging an ever-increasing mob with him, undermining and openly challenging proper authority everywhere he went. Something had to be done, a conclusion that had been reached in their midst long ago, but what and how it was to be done continued to elude them.

"Did you hear about the ointment?" an older fellow by the name of Manaseh near the end of the table said in a conspiratorial tone. The usual pause followed, no one willing to answer, and no one really in the mood for another one of his dubious reports. The man was a regular rumor-mill, claiming to know something about everything.

"He was in Bethany again last night, eating a fabulous meal with his dear friends..."

"With Lazarus?"

It was a sharp response from the high priest. His headpiece fluttered and danced slightly on his broad forehead as he spoke, an annoying mannerism the rest of them tried to ignore.

"Yes, with Lazarus, your eminence. There was the family, some relatives, his closest followers…"

"Why do we need a list of guests?"

"I am simply trying to explain the circumstances in which the ointment was wasted. It was in front of a number of reliable witnesses."

The entire group of men, the most powerful leaders in Israel, looked around at one another in dismay, some of them actually rolling their eyes. Did they really need to endure this?

"Who cares about some wasted ointment? What are you prattling on about, old fool?"

"What is your point, father Manaseh?" said a younger, more diplomatic member to his left. It took the old man a moment to regain his dignity before he was ready to continue.

"I will tell you the point if you would all be so kind as to hear me out. There are two points, actually. First, the ointment, a full pound of expensive perfume, was poured over his feet and onto the floor. Naturally, this created a stir among the guests."

"And?"

"And the woman who wasted the mixture was rebuked sharply by one of his followers; division, my friends, a clear sign of division."

They were paying attention now.

The high priest tipped his head to the side, studied the old man for a moment, and decided the incident may be worth pursuing.

"You said there were two points. What else did your reliable source tell you?"

A snicker escaped from across the table - the old man's sources were anything but reliable. His face blanched just a shade, but he proceeded as if he didn't notice the jab.

"After the dispute about the nard was over, the Galilean spoke of his burial."

"His what?" The ornamental tassels slapped his round cheek as the high priest turned abruptly to face the old man.

With a smile of satisfaction on his lips, Manaseh

repeated the unexpected words: "His burial."

Uproar spread across the gathering, as everyone jumped in, speculating and arguing.

"Hold it, Hold it!" The red face of the high priest warned them all that he was in no mood for squabbling. Once silence was restored, he turned again to the smiling, smug old man. He stared at him for a long moment, but Manaseh didn't flinch.

"Do you have anything else to report? Did he explain himself?" urged the high priest.

"He said only that the ointment was better used as a preparation for his burial than given to the poor. 'The poor you always have with you, but you do not always have me,' he said. After this, he rose from the meal, led his followers out, and disappeared into the night. A huge crowd had been waiting outside the house, and most of them left with him. I think many of them had come to catch a glimpse of Lazarus as well."

"Preparation for his burial did he say? Why, this is fascinating."

Murmurs of agreement spread around the table.

"Perhaps we can assist him in this preparation. And while we are about it, it seems to me that we must prepare something for his friend Lazarus as well. He is becoming as troublesome as the Galilean."

The high priest looked around the table, saw the consensus, and nodded once more for effect. "Yes indeed. We must find the means to bring about his burial." He rose ceremoniously, and the rest of the assembly rose in response. "Until tomorrow, then; we will meet once again after morning prayers."

The room emptied without another word, and the last to leave was a stray dark shadow, wearing an unseen smile, eager to report to his superiors.

Finally, some good news.

□□□□□

The disciples spent a long, difficult day traveling to Jericho. By now, everyone knew that something had changed, that something big and ominous and dreadful was just beyond the horizon. Jesus was still ministering, still healing, still telling stories to the ever-growing crowds in his wake; but there was now a distant look in his eyes. His smile was genuine, his grip and embrace strong and sure, but his mind was clearly wrestling with something big, and that something lay ahead of them.

At one point early in the day, he had pulled the twelve aside along the road, apart from the rest of the crowd. The twelve relaxed in the shade of a huge tree, anticipating yet another parable that none of them would understand. In the quiet of the moment, they could hear insects buzzing nearby and the distant sound of sheep bleating in the pastures above them. After a long, uncomfortable pause, Jesus had spoken quietly: "We are going up to Jerusalem, and everything that is written of the Son of man by the prophets will be accomplished."

The twelve glanced around at each other, sensing his distress, but were unable to understand his point. He walked slowly about the circle of his closest friends, looking each one directly in the eyes.

"He will be delivered to the Gentiles, and will be mocked and shamefully treated and spit upon; they will scourge him and kill him."

Now they were completely lost.

Peter scratched his ear and glanced out at the restless crowds keeping a respectful distance, milling around in the warm sunlight, each of them longing to be a part of this intimate conversation.

Who was he talking about? Who would try to kill the Son of man?

No one in his right mind would even think of trying to harm Jesus. The disciples believed that they could defend him; if not, then certainly the crowds could. Besides, he was doing nothing but good.

This was just crazy. He was making no sense.

But there it had been: something just ahead of them, something none of the rest of them could see or sense was looming, casting a long shadow over their Master. He had then slowly turned, his shoulders sagging slightly, and continued on the road, making his way to the gates of Jericho. As the street ahead had crowded before him with buzzing and chattering residents of the city, a blind man sitting by the gate had cried out, asking what was happening.

"The rabbi is here," answered an old woman standing nearby, watching the procession.

"The rabbi? Which rabbi?" he asked the familiar voice.

"The one from Nazareth, you blind old fool. Jesus of Nazareth is passing by."

The blind man suddenly stood to his feet and began crying out at the top of his voice, "Jesus, Son of David, have mercy on me! Jesus, Son of David, have mercy on me!"

The old woman swatted him on the back of his head and told him to be quiet, embarrassed by his ridiculous display, but he instead increased the volume, "Son of David, Have mercy on me!"

By this point, the Master had come near at hand, and a crowd of locals had gathered around the blind old man, trying to shut him up forcibly by dragging him to the ground and muffling his cries with their hands. Hearing the scuffling, Jesus had stopped and asked the crowd to part. As they stepped back reluctantly, one by one, the blind man was released. He stood again, pulled his stretched and rumpled cloak back about himself, and stepped forward, trembling. The crowd pressed in on all sides, eager to see what would happen.

Looking intently at the man, whose eyes were a milky haze of ruin from some long ago accident or disease, Jesus was moved with compassion. "What do you want me to do for you?" he asked tenderly, aware of the obvious nature of his own question.

The man fell to his knees, still trembling, and shedding tears from his useless eyes; he grasped the Rabbi's cloak and pleaded softly, in a voice broken by years of abuse and pain, "Lord, let me receive my sight."

Jesus knelt down in the dirt with the man, touched his chin and raised his face to the sunlight; and again looking intently into his eyes, he replied, "Receive your sight; your faith has made you well."

The first thing he had seen was the Son of God kneeling in the dirt, gazing deeply into his eyes.

The man stood, and a loud cheer erupted, sending waves of celebrating up and down the road. He raised his hands before his clear eyes, and then jumped up and down, looking all around him at the wonderful sights and colors, drinking in the details with his perfectly restored vision.

As the celebration continued, Jesus resumed his journey. When he finally entered the city, he suddenly looked up, above the crowds lining both sides of the street into a huge old Sycamore tree and spotted a strange little man laying on his stomach across a low-hanging branch, just a few feet above his head. The Master laughed, and calling the tax-collector Zacchaeus by name, was quickly gone with him to his house for the evening meal, for it was sundown, the Sabbath was now over. A few moments later, amidst the thinning crowd, the dark little shadow emerged and began to make his way carefully, at a great distance, behind the tax collector and his diner guest.

☐☐☐☐☐☐

Every lantern, candlestick and oil lamp that the tax-collector owned was burning brightly, and could be seen from a long way off. He had planned a huge banquet for this very night weeks ago, unaware of how fortuitous that planning had been.

Amazing!

He had been squeezing extra coins out of the Jews for months for this event, and had arranged for the best food, the best wine and the best company anyone in the city could buy.

Astonishing that the Galilean would pick this night of all nights to pay a visit!

His heart still pounded as he thought about that moment, now just over an hour ago. He had been standing in the street with the curious crowd - no - he had been climbing up in the tree because of the crowd, trying to gain a glimpse of the teacher as he passed by. As the teacher and his followers approached, the crowd thickened; so he leaned forward, straining to see over all of the shoulders and heads. And then, he had heard his name and his heart leaped; not because he had heard his name, but because of the way in which it had been spoken.

For as long as he could remember, his name had been a joke, a rhyme, a weapon, or a curse in the mouths of others. As a child, he was scolded for being too slow. As an adolescent, he had been tormented for being short. As an adult, well... adults were the worst. There was no clever turn of phrase, no ugly remark, no obscene reference, no cruel mockery that had not been hurled at him. He had heard it all: Zacchaeus the short, or Zacchaeus the filthy tax gatherer, or Zacchaeus the traitor. He was so accustomed to it, that he no longer paid attention to what he was called or how the name was delivered.

Until today.

For the first time since he was a child, he had heard someone call him by name without any malice. The voice had not been overly loud, and now that he thought about it, he wasn't sure why he had heard it at all amidst the clamoring and jabbering of the crowd. No one else seemed to notice. But he had heard his name, and he had jumped down into the street, stumbling among angry and offended people who didn't want to have anything to do with him, and fumbled his way forward until the crowd parted and he stood face to face with the Galilean.

Incredible!

Jesus had known his name, known where he lived, and wanted to eat with him in his own home.

He had said so in front of everybody!

Zacchaeus looked out of the little window at the front of his house, wondering again when the Rabbi would arrive, then checked with the hired servants to make sure everything was ready. A few guests were already seated, but none of them were important enough to demand attention. They murmured to themselves in low tones, occasionally glancing up in mild humor as the comical, distracted little host paced back and forth at the front of the house, oblivious to their presence.

And then he heard the distant, echoing sound of feet. He raced to the window, saw nothing, and then stepped out onto the front portico. Sure enough, there was a small crowd headed his way. His heart again pounding, he was suddenly unsure of himself.

What if this was all a big ruse? What if the rabbi now refused to come into his house, and mocked him in front of his guests?

Trembling slightly, he bowed low as the teacher stepped into his courtyard; but instead of hearing cold words in response, he felt a warm hand on his shoulder, someone actually touching his shoulder. Choked and unable to speak, he gazed up into the warm, friendly eyes, and felt something deep down inside begin to thaw. Zacchaeus was being transformed, and no words had yet been spoken.

Among those standing around in the crowd outside the house were a few local residents, and these were silently offended that not only had the rabbi come to this place, but he compounded the outrage by touching and befriending the ruthless, mercenary tool of the Roman tax system. Everyone knew who Zacchaeus was, and everyone hated this little cheat who enriched himself with the aid of the enemy. There was no one in Jewish society more hated than a tax-gatherer, and Zacchaeus was their chief.

Also among the crowd mingled a number of dark spirits, busily fanning the burning embers of hatred all around them. So when the rabbi turned to go inside the house, arm in arm with this man, a wave of murmuring surged across the crowd, a disrespectful, unclean spray of ugly words that immediately changed the atmosphere among those who had come as curious would-be followers. A handful waited about, in hopes of seeing the rabbi again when he emerged later from the banquet; others drifted off in small groups, whispering and shaking their heads as they went. One went his way alone, a tall silent man with a cloak over his head, who smiled to himself as he made his way toward the road to Jerusalem.

Inside the house, the atmosphere was very different. The fabulous meal – roasted and boiled meats, huge baskets of fruit, a wide array of exotic vegetables and cheeses, bundles of warm bread, and dozens of varieties of expensive wine – having been laid before the guests, the feasting began, and before long satisfied appetites gave way to a rather merry mood, with chattering and toasting and easy dialogue.

In the past, Zacchaeus had watched such moments with a jaded eye, aware that the moment the food and wine gave out, the strained, trivial conversation would wear off, the bloated guests would excuse themselves, and he would find himself alone again. But tonight something was different. The conversation was anything but trivial, as the initial surface-level communication gave way to something deeper, with the Rabbi at the center of attention. Other conversations slowly dried up, and eventually everyone in the room became interested in the frank, probing questions he was being asked by two or three men, and they were fascinated with his honest, direct answers. Zacchaeus forgot about the time; he listened intently to the disarming words of the Galilean, and began struggling with memories and emotions that had long ago been stuffed away and nearly forgotten. Years of abuse and resentment and hidden pain rose to the surface, shook him violently and threatened to burst him open. But then his eyes met the Rabbi's, and as he continued to speak about forgiveness and mercy, the terrible burden quietly melted away. The Master's words of life had penetrated his soul, and he was free.

With that feeling of freedom, however, Zacchaeus also felt shame over many years of his own selfishness, cold-hearted cheating and stealing, and a sinful, indulgent lifestyle. Overflowing with remorse and joy at the same time, Zacchaeus stepped suddenly into the middle of the room, weeping and laughing, and declared his freedom: half of his sizeable wealth would go to the poor, and to all those he could find that he had cheated over the years, he would repay at double the rate of recompense required by the Law of Moses. Having delivered this astonishing message, he hugged the nearest person, setting off a wave of celebration that led to other confessions and other declarations. In the midst of the happy commotion, the Rabbi rose to his feet, approached Zacchaeus, wrapped him tightly in his arms, and made a declaration of his own: "Today, salvation has come to this house."

"And who was this little man?"

The tall quiet man, his face still shrouded, responded in a low rumbling voice, "He is a tax collector, my lord. For some reason, the rabbi sought him out, invited himself to his house, and went in to spend the evening meal with him."

Flinching just a little at the sound of his abrasive voice, the other said "Do not refer to this man as a rabbi. He has no training, and is a dangerous, misguided menace; but you were right to bring this report to me. News of his movements indicates that he is heading this way, and we suspect that he intends to show up in the city during Passover week. This meeting with the tax collector may tell us something about his organization and funding; I will need a list of everyone who attended the banquet, and anything you can find out about the little tax collector."

"Yes, my lord. Is there anything else?"

"You heard nothing of the conversation yourself?"

"Only what I have already related to you."

"Very well, then. Here. Take this message to the high priest, and wait for a response. I must see him tonight at all cost."

"Yes, my lord."

"And why could you not get into the house?"

The dark little shadow flitted around the chamber, uneasy about repeating the obvious.

"My lord, as I said, there were too many enemy warriors. The house was surrounded by thousands of them."

"But this is our territory; this is our house!"

True. At least it was true until this evening. Now he wasn't so sure. He decided to try to shift the blame.

"I had no prior warning, my lord. As soon as I heard the report, I went to see for myself. There were locals there, but none of them were helpful at all. They were all caught completely off guard; no one seems to have suspected any connection between the enemy and the tax collector."

"Then get back out there and find something out! He is headed this way, and I need to know why. I am expected to report our situation tonight, and it would help if I knew our situation. Do whatever it takes, use any resources necessary, and get me some answers! If you fail this time, don't bother to come back. Now get out of here!"

As the last of the guests were leaving, a wealthy merchant turned to the Master, and asked a question: "Rabbi, I have heard rumors that you intend to go to Jerusalem this week. Do you go to celebrate the Passover... or is there something else?"

There was a noticeable pause in the room as everyone within earshot turned to hear his response. Instinctively, Peter moved to step in and challenge the implication, but the merchant quickly retreated, saying "I'm sorry, I simply meant...well, the rumors...I do not believe these things myself, you see...but the rumors say that you intend to set up a new kingdom."

The air snapped with electricity; sensing trouble, Zacchaeus also stepped forward to rescue his honored guest, but before he could speak, Jesus responded:

"A nobleman went into a far country to receive a kingdom and then return."

As he spoke, he stepped out into the courtyard, and was immediately surrounded by a crowd of Jews, and an even larger crowd of spirits, both friendly and hostile. All eyes and ears were glued to him as he continued.

"Calling ten of his servants, he gave them thirty months wages and said to them, 'Trade with these till I come.' But his citizens hated him and sent an embassy after him, saying 'We do not want this man to reign over us.'"

Murmurs rippled through the crowd, which had by now grown even larger.

"When he returned, having received the kingdom, he commanded these servants, to whom he had given the money, to be called to him, to know what they had gained by trading."

The Jews were bewildered:

Is he a king, then?

Where will he go to receive this kingdom?

How will he overpower the Romans?

Why is he talking about money?

The disciples had heard this parable before; he had explained to them that the kingdom would come, but not immediately. They had different questions:

What was this new twist about his citizens hating him?

Am I the one who will return thirty months wages from three?

Will he tell me – 'Well done, good servant'?

Who is the one that will fail?

He continued the story, finishing with the wicked servant who refused to participate, instead hiding his share of the money in the ground, but then He added something that he had never spoken before:

"But as for these enemies of mine, who did not want me to reign over them, bring them here and slay them before me." He looked around at the stunned faces, one at a time. No one moved.

And suddenly the Rabbi turned and walked away, while murmured questions rose to the surface behind him, and the murmuring quickly swelled to a roar. His disciples moved with him into the darkness, fending off the crowd as Jesus continued to walk away, seemingly oblivious to their questions and shouting.

It was a privilege to be appointed high priest. It was a privilege and an honor that very few men in Jewish society ever attained. Of the millions of Jews scattered throughout Palestine, only thousands were Levites. Of these Levites, only hundreds were appointed as priests. Of the priests, only one – just one – was given the prestige and honor that came with the appointment as high priest. It was a long, rich tradition, dating all the way back to Aaron, who had served with Moses. The name of Joseph Caiaphas was not as well known as that of Aaron, but he held the same position, and he felt that someday perhaps he would be remembered for his service as well.

The meeting at the house of his father-in-law had been arranged hastily, in response to rapidly changing news, which was a source of irritation for Caiaphas. He liked order, he liked discipline, and he did not like surprises. A sudden knock at his door in the late evening was not something he welcomed, and was not usually tolerated. Upon receiving the message, however, he had fought off his initial urge to discipline the messenger, and instead thought for a moment, sighed, and then reluctantly put together a return message. Caiaphas was powerful, he was the high priest appointed by the Roman governor himself, but he was not Annas. When Annas insisted on a meeting, even when it was the middle of a comfortable evening at home, it was not wise to argue.

The two of them had met many years ago, when they were both young disciples of unknown rabbis, scrabbling around for a little recognition in the backwaters of minor Jewish affairs. But Caiaphas had seen something in Annas: a hunger, a determination that told him that this was a man with a future. They became friends, and eventually Caiaphas had married one of the man's daughters. And Caiaphas had been right; Annas had climbed into power rapidly, developing an uncanny ability to make quick decisions that always led to his benefit. And then suddenly one day Annas was high priest, appointed by Quirinius, the Roman governor of Syria. He then served in that esteemed capacity for nine years until he stumbled into a power struggle with Valerius Gratus, the governor of Judea. By that time, Annas wielded incredible authority and influence, far more than any of his predecessors, and had become incredibly wealthy through a money exchange program he had initiated at the temple grounds. This money program was where the problem began. The new governor of Judea had come directly from Rome, was not accustomed to local Jewish ways, and enjoyed enormous liberty in his position. He could do nearly anything he wanted, but was given very little financial resources. So when he noticed the money piling up over in the Jewish temple, he decided to take some of it to finance an aqueduct he had planned.

Thus the battle began. Annas strongly resisted, but of course he was no match for the Roman army. Instead, he began a campaign of complaining to the one person in his world more powerful that the Roman governor: the Roman emperor. Messages and threats were sent back and forth to Rome, and in the end Annas stopped the outflow of cash, but found himself at odds with the governor, who though he had lost, still ruled in Palestine, and still had the authority to appoint anyone whom he chose as high priest. In a move of retribution, he un-appointed Annas, an unprecedented slap in the face, and appointed his much more compliant son-in-law in his place as high priest. Annas quietly stepped aside, but not very far. Though Caiaphas now wore the robes, everyone in Jerusalem knew who continued to wear the power.

So, with another sigh, Caiaphas dressed himself to go out into the night, called to an urgent meeting with his father-in-law and whomever else he chose to summon.

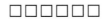

Shortly before the arrival of the priestly council, the holy little meeting chamber near the temple was surrounded, secured and then occupied by a sizeable group of invisible residents of that region, deceiving spirits who were accustomed to these clandestine meetings and seemed to feel quite at home.

"If you would please all calm down, I have a suggestion." Caiaphas gazed at each face around the chamber until order finally returned. Once everyone sat down and it was again quiet, he proceeded to explain the plan he and his father-in-law had worked out only minutes before their arrival. They had argued for over an hour before coming to the agreement, and once the others had arrived, they let the discussion drift down its inevitable and well worn path before bringing it up. Now, it was time.

"We have debated the issue long enough. It is time to take decisive action," said Caiaphas, his official high priestly tassels swaying in rhythm as his head shook slowly from left to right.

"But I still don't see what can be done," whined someone down the table to his left. Several others began to murmur again.

"Silence!" he roared. Shock and disbelief settled in heavily as the red-faced priest rose to his feet. "Don't any of you see it? Does no one understand where this will all lead? The Romans are on the verge of stepping in. We have been in communication with officers of the Praetorian Guard, and they are making preparations as we speak, all around the city, in expectation of an uprising."

Caiaphas let his words linger for a moment. None of them had forgotten the gruesome spectacle just last year when hundreds of young Jewish men were nailed to Roman crosses, lining both sides of the road leading to the Holy City. The last uprising had ended as they all did, in blood - Jewish blood. The young, brave Zealots with sticks and rocks were no match for Roman armor.

"Need I remind you that another uprising would be all the excuse the Emperor would need to move in and wipe us all out? We are in a precarious position, my friends. If we do not take control, now, we will not get another opportunity. Simply put, the Galilean must die. We have a sacred duty to our people, a duty passed down from the patriarchs and prophets, to keep the nation safe from those who would lead them astray or worse yet, lead them into terrible danger."

All around the room, recognition of the gravity of his words sank in. There were no words of response, no one moved or flinched, and every wide and unblinking eye was fastened on the high priest.

No longer needing to raise his voice, he continued, barely above a whisper: "It is expedient that one man...ONE MAN...should die for the people, and that the whole nation should not perish."

He gently sat down, and as the rest of those present eventually found their voices and began debating about how the Galilean should be put to death, Caiaphas glanced across the long table and nodded once at his father-in-law, who sniffed, brushed his hand across the sleeve of his immaculate tunic, looked around the room, and returned the nod.

In a remote, desolate part of the Judean highlands, far away from the calm of this solemn meeting, and at about the same time, a man's neck was quietly severed. The man had done nothing more than speak carelessly to a friend about his concern over the rising violence among the Jewish renegades, or Zealots. He had made the mistake of commenting negatively about their leader, or at least saying something that could have been regarded as a negative comment. The brutal outlaw, who refused to identify himself by name - known only as 'son-of-my-father' – bent down and looked into the terrified eyes of the dying man without pity and quietly cursed him as a traitor to the Jewish nation. Rising to his feet to leave, he wiped his bloody knife on a tunic laying nearby and slowly looked around the room for anything of value; but finding none he silently crept to the door where he suddenly froze: outside the little shack of the poor shepherd he heard the unmistakable sound of a horse's hoof.

"Again!" the unseen spirit demanded.

The plan had been laid out, challenged, changed, and perfected over the last seven days. They had been rehearsing roles each unit would play, and each commander had long since memorized their various responsibilities. The kingdom of darkness lacked wisdom, but there was no lack of determination. Over the thousands of years of exile, they had experienced every imaginable form of defeat, setback, division, failure, and shame, and yet they were every bit as driven on that day as they were at the outset. No amount of loss, no embarrassment, no hindrance wore away the black varnish of hatred and rage that colored everything and impelled the host of wickedness like a moth to a flame. They couldn't help themselves; it had become their very nature to press on, no matter the cost.

So, they pressed on. The spirits around the commander spread out and barked the orders to repeat the whole plan once more. And while the maneuvers resumed, myriad scouts flitted back and forth, and groups of important officers took council, and positions all around the mountain were strengthened. By the time the enemy arrived at the city, they would be ready. This time, the target wouldn't be a single old man, but all of his friends; all twelve.

Sunday

Long before daybreak, the Rabbi had risen and gone out into the early morning darkness alone. The disciples had become used to this; early in their relationship, some of them had tried to keep up with him, but those efforts had faded quickly as the fatigue of constant travel and ministry and confrontation had taken its toll. It wasn't easy being a disciple of someone with such endless passion and commitment. As the weeks turned into years with no break, the twelve had found it more and more necessary to seek opportunities to nap, even in broad daylight. So when it was still dark, during the third watch of the night, it was difficult to make enough noise to rouse any of them.

In these nightly seasons of solitude, Jesus found resolve and strength to continue the march toward the end. He missed the sleep; in his human body, the lack of rest was certainly taking a toll, but without the regular refreshment of spirit these hours alone with his Father and his creation afforded him, sleep would have made no difference. And since every waking moment of every day was now spoken for, his only chance for this necessary union came while the rest of the world still slept. So each day for at least two hours, he communed in the quiet, dark moments before dawn with his Father, speaking rarely, listening intently, and sensing the beauty and pleasure of his handiwork all around him. He was never alone; guardian spirits were always nearby, of course, but he was also always surrounded by silent creatures, large and small, who patiently and reverently watched the hours with him, always in numbers that wouldn't attract attention.

On this particular morning, the first day of his last week, a sense of urgency accompanied him, an atmosphere surrounding him that affected everything – the grass that his feet touched, the still, cool air all around him, the lone fox sitting quietly on the hillside across the valley. The birds in the trees began their chorus early that morning, affected by his presence and his countenance. The refrain was picked up by the fox – a long, mournful sounding howl that carried on the soft new breeze wafting down the valley, into the city. A few of the disciples stirred for a moment, but never came fully awake. The Master stood to his feet, stretched, and began pacing slowly around the little garden. It was obvious by the condition of the plants and lack of weeds that someone had spent a lot of time and care in this place. He bent over, and touched a vine, looking for fruit. It was there, hidden among the lush leaves, but not yet ripened. He smiled his approval. But even in his smile, there was the same evidence of urgency, of weight, of...dread?

On the eastern horizon, the first trace of morning began to sparkle, bringing with it a steadier breeze and a stronger chorus of music from his winged friends. Somewhere in the distance a cock crowed heartily and repeatedly. The disciples would be rousing now, and normally the Master would have turned to go, but this morning he was reluctant to leave the beauty and comfort of the little garden. He looked around once more, touching the plants, observing the short wall around the perimeter, and then lifted his head once more to the slowly vanishing stars. They were all his; he had formed every one of them, and he knew exactly where to look for them even when they were obscured by daylight. The plants, the stones, the mighty mountains in the distance, they were all his. The earth itself, with its seasons and seas, its wonders and dangers, its colors, and sounds, and smells, and life, was his. At no point in history was this fact more important, more profound, and dearer to creation that at this moment, at daybreak of the day when the Master would fulfill the promise he had made four hundred and eighty-three years ago to his prophet Daniel. After this quiet moment alone, one of his very last, he would have little time left to walk among and enjoy his surroundings, and all of creation knew it.

By the time he returned to the place where he and his friends had stayed that night, there was a bustle of activity: a morning meal in preparation, housekeeping by several young women, children playing games, and a rather noisy discussion between Peter and the sons of Zebedee. Upon hearing the heated debate, Jesus felt the urge to turn around and run back to the quiet peace of the garden, but instead he stopped to listen, and was immediately confronted by the three of them. But before any of them could speak, a stout woman pushed her way through, knelt before him and spoke first; "Rabbi, may I ask you to do something for me? I have seen you heal many, and I know that you are the anointed one, sent by God."

The three men exchanged nervous glances.

"What do you want?" he asked softly in response to the woman, but his eyes were on the disciples as he spoke. The three of them avoided eye contact with him.

The woman, delighted with the opportunity to speak, rose, and clutched at his sleeve. "Command that these two sons of mine may sit, one at your right hand and one at your left, in your kingdom."

There it was. The words were out; the debate that had been secretly raging for weeks now among the disciples had finally been brought out into the open. The rest of the disciples surged forward, crowding in, voicing their opinions and their objections to the mother's request:

"Pick me! Rabbi!"

"Don't listen to her! Why should they be the ones?"

"I was with you longer!"

"Quit shoving! Get your hands off..."

"Master!"

With a look of sadness clouding his face, Jesus raised his hand for silence, and the clamoring slowly died away. After a moment, an uneasy, embarrassed quiet settled around the ring of followers.

"You do not know what you are asking."

The mother, who had been squeezed to the fringe, tried to step forward and speak up once again, but her younger son John stepped in the way and shook his head fiercely at her.

"Are you able to drink the cup that I am to drink?"

Again, the clamoring broke out:

"We are able!"

"I will follow you anywhere!"

"You can count on us, Master!"

The cup: none of them could comprehend it.

He raised his hand yet again, and when silence resumed, he declared, barely above a whisper, "You will drink my cup."

THE CUP.

He was suddenly struck by a scorching glimpse of unbelievable pain and loneliness, like a sudden flash of lightning, which took his breath away.

His hands were trembling slightly and his voice strained as he continued "But to sit at my right hand and at my left is not mine to grant, but it is for those for whom it has been prepared by my father."

He turned and walked away, a bead of sweat trickling down his flushed cheek. He fought to shake the terrifying images from his mind, focusing instead on the debate that he knew wasn't over. Before the end of the week, he would have to face this issue of ambition again. But for now, he took a deep breath and moved on. It was going to be a big day.

"Here they come."

The news had been expected for hours. The enemy and his entourage had been seen leaving Bethany early in the morning, but for some reason they hadn't traveled directly along the road from Bethany as expected. At a small grove of trees, they had stopped, and a handful of men had gone ahead into the city alone. For several hours, there was no movement, and it had become apparent that they were waiting for something. Meanwhile the oppressive sun had inched its way high in the bare open sky, the still air thick and hot, and the spooked animals nearby had raised their voices in objection to the presence of the huge demonic army hidden all along the route into the city. The ranks of dark spirits had grown restless and irritated; waiting was not something at which they excelled.

But now the enemy was coming, and the waiting was

about to pay off.

The invisible armies moved quickly and silently into position, the battle front took shape as planned. But when the command to attack was about to be issued, the little band of men came suddenly around a bend behind them, returning from the city, towing something behind them.

"What is that?" shrieked the senior commanding officer, squinting in the brilliant sunlight. "Who was in charge of the rear flank?"

There was a mad scramble for a better view all around him, as aides tried to identify the object. "Well? What do you see?"

"It's..."

"It's what?" demanded the impatient commander.

"Well, it looks like a donkey."

The dumbfounded spirits looked at one another for a moment, embarrassed that a donkey had created confusion.

The commander, shuddering with rage, blurted out one word: "ATTACK!"

The hillsides surrounding the road from Bethany suddenly came alive with motion. Thousands upon thousands of foul spirits descended like bats from the roof of a cave, from three directions, sealing the enemy and his friends in from behind and on both sides. A fourth and far more massive force took to the air above them, prepared to fight off the angelic warriors that they knew would come to his rescue. Everything was proceeding as planned until the forward flanks, with their backs to the city, noticed panic among the forces closing in behind the enemy. Stopping for a moment, they heard a commotion behind them. Turning to face the threat, they were confronted with a surging mob of humans, pouring out of the city, waving branches and cloaks above their heads.

This wasn't in the battle plan.

Why were they coming out of the city?

Why were there so many of them?

Why were they acting so strangely?

The commanding demons had no answers to these questions, and the crowd was growing larger by the minute, with hundreds, perhaps thousands of men, women and children racing out of the city and lining the roadway right in front of them, cheering and yelling and worshipping at the top of their voices. None of them had ever witnessed anything like it before.

"What do we do, my lord?" shouted a frightened aide, trying to be heard above the deafening commotion.

"What?"

"What is your command? Do we proceed anyway?" he shouted back even louder.

They stood for another moment, transfixed by the unbelievable scene before them. The dark commander looked around, studying the reaction of his troops, thinking through contingencies, and trying to give attention to something nagging at him behind all the noise and distraction generated by the unexpected mob. And then looking up, it suddenly hit him.

"Withdraw," he said finally, as he looked once again at the empty sky above him. The moment was gone, but he knew that there would be another, and the next time they would make sure that no humans were around to interfere. That was the easy part. What he had not expected, what none of them had even dreamed about, was this glaring absence of their ancient foes, the heavenly host. They were nowhere to be seen. This wasn't in the battle plan either. Watching his troops turn back and reform in the distance, the invisible commander of darkness smiled an unseen smile.

"I am sorry, your eminence. I did not wish to disturb you. However..."

"What is it now?" roared the high priest, rising quickly from his bed, in no mood for intrusions of any kind. He had left strict instructions that he should not be disturbed before at least midday, due to the late night he had just spent filled with intrigue and secret meetings.

"Your esteemed father-in-law has sent word that there is a commotion just outside of the city that requires immediate attention."

"What was that? What do you mean by 'a commotion'?" Though he was by now fully awake, he was not ready to face yet another confrontation simply because Annas sent word. He was tired of the whole thing, and wished that someone else would deal with whatever it was, and let him go back to sleep.

"There is some form of...disturbance in the streets. Master Annas suggested that I mention the prophet Zechariah to you."

As Caiaphas rose and began clothing himself for yet another day in the holy vestments of the high priest for the Nation of Israel, his mind was racing, recalling his days as a young scribe, when he had spent hour upon hour memorizing the law, the books of wisdom, and the prophets. At some point in the foggy past, he had committed the entire book of Zechariah to memory. But now, fumbling distractedly with the clothes, he was having trouble placing it, and turning back to his servant he asked, "Are you sure that it was Zechariah?"

"Yes, your eminence."

Woe to those who go down to Egypt for help and rely on horses...no that's not it.

Therefore thus says the Lord God: Behold, my servants shall eat...?

Prophesy to theses bones...?

King Nebuchadnezzar made an image of gold...?

He paused, thought for a moment, carefully placing the ornate headpiece atop his furrowed brow, and then shook his head, fluttering the tassels. "I do not understand. What can he possibly mean by this?"

"I'm not sure..."

"Mind your impudence; I was not addressing you. Of course you do not understand. Now, leave me. And send word back to my 'esteemed father-in-law' that I will join him presently."

"Yes, your eminence."

□□□□□□

"Why are they doing this, Peter? What has come over

them?" Nathaniel roared.

It was difficult for Peter to hear the question over the unbelievable noise from the crowd. None of them had ever seen anything like it.

They had been traveling toward the city for the Passover, the morning sun high in the sky behind them, when the two disciples had returned with the colt, chattering about something regarding its owner. Jesus had smiled, but not a happy smile. He had stood completely still, the only motion in their midst created by the slight breeze that gently moved his hair. He had looked at the young donkey for a long moment, looked at his disciples, drawn in a deep breath, and then turned toward Jerusalem, leading the donkey beside him. After a few steps, Peter had come alongside of him, they had spoken a few words, and Jesus had mounted the donkey. The whole thing had been curious. When he had sent the two into the city to ask for a colt, the rest of the disciples responded in mute surprise, for Jesus had rarely ridden, and by now they were close enough to the city that it made no sense. He hadn't seemed tired; at least not tired of walking. They had been within a few minutes walk when they had stopped to wait for the animal.

And then the crowd had come. How had they known that he was coming? Had the two disciples spread word of his approach? It was the first day of Passover, and instead of any of the normal activities one might engage in to prepare for the holy week, the entire city, it seemed had decided instead to come out to watch the Rabbi ride a donkey into the city.

"What did you say?" Peter roared back.

Nathaniel leaned closer, and shouted into his ear "What is going on?"

Peter simply shrugged his shoulders. It was hot, the air was now heavy with dust from the crowd, and Peter wiped his forehead with a sleeve as he trudged along holding the short rope lead to the donkey. He had never seen or heard of anything like this before. The crowd, growing larger by the minute, swelled ahead of them, dancing, singing, shouting praises, and dropping cloaks and tunics and tree branches on the road before them. Some of the other disciples had by now joined in, shouting at the top of their lungs, but not Peter. He was worried about the young colt, expecting it to react to the strange activity in fear, since they had been told it had never yet been ridden. Peter kept the reign short, ready to intervene if the donkey were to try to throw the Master off, but the unusually calm animal kept plodding forward, unaffected by the seething tumult all around. And the crowd continued to grow.

As they drew within a few hundred feet of the city wall, Peter noticed a commotion ahead and to the left. The crowd was growing louder, and there seemed to be a new edge to the noise. He looked closely, trying to see what was causing the change, when he spotted the tassels. He turned to warn Jesus, who simply shook his head and indicated for him to be still. Within moments, they were confronted with the red-faced priest, pushing and shoving his way along, shouting something in great anger, but the roar of the crowd made it impossible for them to understand him. It occurred to Peter that he had never seen the high priest touch anyone before, and certainly had never seen him so stirred up, so sweaty, so...normal. Predictably, a number of lesser priests and Pharisees popped up behind him out of the crowd. They were all red-faced, uncomfortable looking, and trying desperately to create some room for their leader amidst the dense crowd, now noisier than ever, stirred up by their presence. Having waited a few moments for the tumult to die down, and then realizing that this was not going to happen, Caiaphas looked directly at the rabbi for the very first time in his life, and exploded in rage.

"Teacher, rebuke your disciples!"

All of the disciples heard the sarcasm and hatred in his voice when he spoke the words 'teacher' and 'disciples'. Jesus looked at the high priest, and then looked at Peter. Peter smiled, tilted his head back, and roared with all of his might "Hosanna to the Son of David! Blessed is he who comes in the name of the Lord!"

The high priest tried to match him in volume, but Peter closed his eyes in joyous defiance, and proclaimed even louder "Hosanna in the highest! Peace in heaven and glory in the highest!" A deafening concussion of praises erupted from the crowd in response, and it was clear that there was no end to the noise in sight. The outraged high priest, sweating profusely and vibrating in fury looked once again at the face of Jesus.

"I tell you", the Master said in a firm voice, loud enough for Caiaphas to hear above the ear-splitting din, "if these were silent, the very stones would cry out."

And the stones beneath his feet did indeed rejoice, and as if on cue the donkey began moving again, heading for the Eastern, or Beautiful Gate, which led to the temple area within the city of Jerusalem. The high priest, cast aside in the backwash of the procession, took hold of his headpiece with both hands to keep it from flying off and getting trampled in the dirt.

□□□□□□

Watching the entire episode, from beginning to end from a great distance, the archangel grumbled loudly: "I still don't get it. Why? Why must we sit here on our hands and watch? And why must we stay so far away? This is the moment that we have all anticipated for a long, long time – and we can't even be there. I would love to get my hands around...

"I know it would be great sport, my friend, but now is not the time, and you know that. Be patient, Michael. As hard as this moment is, there will be other opportunities that...well I can't even begin to comprehend. We have our orders."

A long silence ensued as they watched the growing cloud of demons become a thick, black canopy above the valley, undulating and boiling and blocking out the sunlight, then suddenly spread out in every direction as the enemy prepared to strike in the classic enclosure battle plan. They had seen it hundreds of times over the centuries; their unseen enemies were ferocious, bloodthirsty warriors, but they were not very creative. Their preferred approach relied heavily on overwhelming numbers, with very little regard for finesse or skill.

"Watch closely now," commented Michael's senior lieutenant to the ranks of heavenly warriors. As they looked on with close attention, the filthy black canopy suddenly ripped and disintegrated into millions of fluttering specs, spreading out in every direction. One moment it was descending in the familiar, suffocating enclosure, the next it had exploded and evaporated. In the aftermath, the sunlight returned and the sky slowly cleared as the fleeing demonic hoard became just a smudge on the horizon.

"What happened? Why did they flee?"

"There is only one thing that causes such panic among our enemy, and it is not *us*. Tell them, Michael," urged the big angel Gabriel, with a hint of a smile on his face.

A bit chagrined by the mild rebuke, Michael was once again amazed at his own lack of wisdom. There had been only a few moments like this since the fall, but the moments had occurred, and somehow it always caught him by surprise. He drew in a deep breath, and then explained:

"He is right, of course. Our enemy will fight when he is faced with the host of heaven, even when he is outnumbered. It is not the battle that causes him to retreat so hastily. In this case, he wasn't even aware of our presence. No, what caused him to panic had nothing to do with us at all. It was them," he declared as he pointed at the crowd surrounding the Master.

They all watched with a new sense of wonder as the donkey slowly made its way up the last incline into the city, amidst the roar and celebration of unrestrained, unrehearsed, spontaneous *worship*. None of the angels spoke again until the last of the crowd had disappeared into the city, and the roadway was once again barren and all that could be heard was the mild breeze stirring the Judean hillside.

Michael turned to face his troops. They had all been affected by what they had seen, and the glow of approval still shone on their faces. "Remember this moment," he said. "We will not see it again for...we will not see it again." And then remembering his orders, he looked once more at the place where his sovereign had disappeared, and said with a heavy sigh, "Order the troops to withdraw."

Just before entering the city, still riding on the donkey,

Jesus looked up at the towering walls gleaming in the sunlight and the eastern gate looming high above his head. And then he entered. The moment came and went quickly; no one else noticed, for no one else understood its importance. They all could have understood, it was all there for them to see; but it had now been many generations since the promise had been made, and no one remembered. Daniel, the beloved servant of exile, had been given a vision over five hundred years ago that predicted the coming of the anointed one ON THIS VERY DAY, after sixty-nine weeks of years, dating from a decree given by Artaxerxes, king of Babylon, the historic decree to rebuild Jerusalem. Someone, anyone familiar with the book of Daniel could have done the math recorded in the prophecy, and could have anticipated the moment, but no one had. True, the crowds had come to meet him, a fulfillment of another prophecy, but none of the shepherds of Israel had been ready. They were all asleep, and it was time for him to wake them.

In a low voice, trembling with emotion, Jesus declared:

"If you, even you, had only known on this day what would bring you peace," and sweeping his gaze along the enormous stone wall leading off in the distance to the south, he breathed, "but now it is hidden from your eyes. The days will come upon you when your enemies will build an embankment against you and encircle you and hem you in on every side." He looked down at the massive foundation, stones so large it was inconceivable that they could be moved. "They will dash you to the ground, you and the children within your walls. They will not leave one stone on another, because you did not recognize the time of God's coming to you."

And the donkey stepped through the gate.

As the great door closed behind them, the gathering crowd rapidly swelled to a mob, choking the narrow streets of Jerusalem. Since it was the week of Passover, the city was full of guests and travelers from all over the world, all of them curious and most of them with too much time on their hands. News of a teacher entering the city on a donkey spread like wildfire, and the already clogged, noisy streets became unbearable as waves of humanity condensed from every direction, packing, pushing, shouting, gawking, and straining to see what the commotion was all about. By the time Jesus reached the temple, the entire city was in an uproar, and the fireworks hadn't even begun yet.

"What is it now?" demanded the captain of the Jerusalem cohort, weary of Jews and weary of uproars. He had been in Judea for only two years now, and had already requested a new assignment. He was a soldier; he understood warfare and he knew how to deal with an enemy attack, or how to motivate his men for battle, or how to maximize his resources during a siege. But this endless parade of local misfits and unpredictable zealots and religious troublemakers: how could anyone ever learn to cope with them? No matter how many you nailed to a cross, the parade never seemed to end.

"A teacher, sir; a Galilean, I understand. He is reported to have swept into the city upon a sea of adoration."

Rolling his eyes at the ridiculous use of imagery, he replied rather deliberately "Find this teacher, and put an end to the adoration. I want no news of this reaching the procurator. Passover will be quiet if I have to kill them all. If you meet any resistance at all, you have my authority to use whatever force necessary."

By the time Jesus stepped down from the donkey, it was late in the afternoon, and the crowd had grown so large that there was no way to proceed any farther. He looked up, and the crowd around him looked with him: the temple. He had been here only once before, and his presence had created a stir, even then. The temple was an inspiring sight, still flashing brilliantly, even in the late afternoon sun; It sat atop the highest hill in Jerusalem, was flanked on the north by the opulent Roman Fortress Antonia, on the south by the deep Kidron Valley, on the west by the city itself, and of course on the east side the city wall and the eastern gate. This side of the temple, the eastern side, was covered completely in gold plate to create a dazzling effect with the morning sunlight. The structure was built largely by priests, with massive slabs of white marble pieced together without any mortar or tools. Even now, it was still uncompleted, though it had been under continuous construction for over forty years. The walls around the massive, twenty-six acre courtyards were high, the columns and towers higher, and the temple itself, set atop a steep rise of stairs was higher still. Its beauty and grandeur was stunning, a sight that took the breath away; nothing in the Jewish world was more revered or more holy.

On this day, however, as Jesus gazed around, it didn't look very revered and holy. Everywhere he looked, he saw the taint of corruption: merchants boldly hawking their wares, right in the temple; tax gatherers harassing the crowd for the temple tax; soldiers and guards intimidating and looting shamelessly from the helpless crowd. And everywhere, *everywhere*, the smell of animals, the bleating of sheep, the shouting of vendors and money changers. The temple had turned into quite a money making racket for those who ran the place: the merchants and vendors were allowed on the temple grounds, for a fee; the temple tax had to be paid in Jewish coins rather than the common Roman or Greek currency, available for purchase only at the temple, for an excessive exchange fee; worshippers who came with their own sheep or doves for sacrifice were turned away, unless they purchased (with Jewish coins only) "pure and spotless" animals that just happened to be available from the vendors and acceptable to the temple leaders for an inflated fee; the "impure" or "spotted" animals were then given to the temple workers to dispose of, for yet another fee. The place built to house the Glory of God now housed instead ruthless, wealthy businessmen dressed in long, priestly robes.

Filled with emotion, Jesus stepped forward, bent over a small table loaded with coins and looked into the eyes of the nearest merchant. As he gripped the edges of the table, he declared "It is written: 'My house shall be a house of prayer for all the nations'; but you have made it a den of robbers!" And he flipped the table over, sending the pile of coins clattering to the stone pavement. The air was suddenly charged with astonishment as those closest to the spectacle let out a collective gasp. But this was just the beginning. The Rabbi grabbed the next table and did the same, and then the next and the next...then he turned suddenly and strode into the midst of the animal cages, kicking gates open and flinging ropes and nets loose, creating a tidal wave of sheep and birds and astonished men and women fluttering and trampling in his wake. As the crowd caught on, a roar of approval rang in the streets, and a surge of eager young men stepped forward to join in; before long the court of the Gentiles became a war zone from one end of the temple to the other, while the merchants and moneychangers and animal keepers and temple officials abandoned their posts and ran for their lives. Within minutes an entire Roman cohort had showed up in full battle gear, but by then every coin, every scrap of cloth, every feather, every shred of evidence that money had ever changed hands in this place was gone. And so was the Rabbi.

There it is, he thought. His heart raced as he gazed at the carefully recorded words. He had been up all night, poring over the scroll. He was not as familiar with it as he would have wished, but in the end, perseverance had pain off:

> "Rejoice greatly, O daughter of Zion! Shout aloud O daughter of Jerusalem! Lo, your king comes to you; triumphant and victorious is he, humble and riding on an ass, on a colt the foal of an ass."

Could it be? Was the teacher from Galilee the one?

> "I will cut off the chariot from Ephraim and the war horse from Jerusalem; and the battle bow shall be cut off, and he shall command peace to the nations; his dominion shall be from sea to sea, and from the River to the ends of the earth."

Could it be any clearer? Surely God was on the move, and his long awaited Messiah was standing at this very moment within the city.

> "As for you also, because of the blood of my covenant with you, I WILL SET YOUR CAPTIVES FREE."

His hands trembled as he slowly, carefully rolled the scroll. He paused for a few minutes to slow his racing heartbeat, and then checked the corridor. No one was stirring. He moved quietly, with no light, and found his way by memory. He kissed the scroll, then laid it back in its dusty place where it had laid undisturbed for many years. He had never before been interested in the prophet Zechariah, and it was clear that his master wasn't either. He checked the corridor again. He was sure that everyone in the house was fast asleep, but he knew that he would be in grave trouble if it was discovered that the high priest's servant had been rummaging around in his sacred books.

Monday

When the eastern horizon began to show traces of the coming dawn, John was already awake, restless and irritated from another night of poor sleep. He rose, looked around in envy at his slumbering friends, and walked out onto the cool, dark portico. He yawned and stretched, and looking to his left could just make out a lone figure at the other end leaning on his elbows, illuminated by the soft, waning moonlight. It was the Rabbi. John hesitated, wondering if he was praying or just thinking. The Rabbi turned and motioned for him to join him. Three years ago, John would have marveled at the timing, wondering if the Master had read his thoughts; but by now he had come to accept the fact that Jesus was always aware of everything around him, always ready for the moment, and never taken by surprise. He quietly walked over and stood beside him. For several moments, neither of them spoke. The early morning was still and quiet and John enjoyed his little slice of it alone with the Master. The frustration he had felt only minutes before over his sleeplessness quickly melted away. It looked like it was going to be a beautiful morning.

Jesus gently turned to John, titling his head, and asked quietly "Did you hear that?"

John listened carefully for a moment with a puzzled look on his face, shaking his head. After a few seconds of silence, however, he heard it, way off in the distance.

"Ah yes, the cock: the early riser, announcing the arrival of morning." John began to stretch again, but the Rabbi put his hand on his outstretched arm and motioned for him to be still.

"Once more...there it is." He turned around, leaned back on the rail, and gazed into the thick darkness of the portico. "Do you remember what I said about the shepherd and the sheep? 'He who is a hireling and not a shepherd, whose own sheep they are not, sees the wolf coming and leaves the sheep and flees; and the wolf snatches them and scatters them.'"

"I remember, Lord."

"The good shepherd lays down his life for the sheep. He doesn't flee when the wolf comes."

Again, there was a long moment of silence. John yawned once again, and began to move toward the door of the house.

"Stay with me, John."

The words were beautiful in his ears, and John smiled in the darkness as he turned and leaned back against the rail next to the Master. It was going to be a beautiful morning.

All around the house, invisible clouds were slowly forming as demonic spirits from every corner of creation gathered in this one place, to participate in the approaching confrontation. They could sense it; the time was growing short, and still there was no sign of the angelic enemy. Confidence was on the rise in their midst; for without the host of heaven to support them, the humans would provide *him* with no protection when the time came, and the time was rapidly approaching.

As the morning came alive in earnest, there was commotion all over the house as the disciples and the rest of their company prepared for the day: washing of faces, removing of bed clothing, preparation of breakfast, feeding of animals, arrangement of supplies, shooing of children, mending of sandals. The routine was hectic, but well rehearsed after so many mornings together, even while staying in a fine home in Bethany. By the time the last of them were finished and out of the door, the sun was high and it was beginning to grow warm.

Along the road from Bethany, there were olive and fig

groves. The olive trees were slow to leaf, and the harvest was still months away, so they were as yet still only budding; normally this was true of fig trees also, but as the company passed on, Jesus pointed out to his disciples a lone fig tree off in the distance, already in full leaf. It was luxurious and healthy looking, in rather stark contrast with the rest of the figs nearby which were still tender with smaller, lighter green leaves.

Peter remarked that he would enjoy a handful of fresh figs this early in the season, since everyone knew that full leaves meant fruit. Jesus was hungry as well, and agreed with the sentiment, but he cautioned him not to get his hopes up – "Don't always believe what you see. Looks will often fool you." And sure enough, as Jesus approached the tree, there were no fruit whatsoever to be found anywhere in its branches.

"Master, how can a tree look so healthy, so much better than its neighbors, and yield no fruit?" asked someone.

"Lord – I remember what you said on the hillside in Galilee, the day I met you; you said something then about good fruit and bad trees..."

Jesus smiled at the memory. "'Beware of false prophets,' I said 'who come to you in sheep's clothing but inwardly are ravenous wolves. You will know them by their fruits. A sound tree cannot bear evil fruit, nor can a bad tree bear good fruit. Every tree that does not bear good fruit is cut down and thrown into the fire. Thus, you will know them by their fruits.'" He looked around at his friends, who were all staring intently up into the lush branches, as if hoping to spot some sign of good. "They are accursed trees."

Jesus also looked up a last time into the branches and stated "This is an accursed tree." And then barely above a whisper, yet loud enough in the still moment for all to hear, he spoke a chilling curse: "May no one ever eat fruit from you again," and he moved on.

The walk wasn't long, only about two miles, but it was all uphill and with so many in the company, it took nearly an hour before they again reached the city gates. Today, there was no celebration, but there was already a crowd awaiting them, eager to pick up where things had left of the previous evening.

As Jesus came into view, a buzzing of voices spread the news. Once inside the gate, the buzz suddenly jumped in volume to a noisy cackle as the crowds quickly compressed around the Rabbi. Peter and Andrew took charge of crowd control, pushing back a clearing as Jesus made his way toward the temple.

☐☐☐☐☐☐

There had been little sleep in the house of Annas that night. The high priest and his father-in-law, along with all the rest of the rulers of the temple had been caught entirely off guard by the uproar outside the city gates, followed by the shocking behavior within the temple itself. They had expected to have an opportunity to arrest the Galilean quietly once he arrived in the city, but his surprising offensive moves had changed things. The situation was rapidly escalating and the leaders of Israel had convened once more to try to formulate a plan to defuse it before it was too late and the Roman governor stepped in. For hours they debated, whined, accused, denied, screamed in rage at one another, and still they had no clear plan of action. Now that the crowds had grown so large, simply arresting him on the street in broad daylight would be difficult. And according to witnesses, the rabbi had simply disappeared when it was over, and no one knew where he had gone for the night. In the end, spies and temple guards were dispatched with orders to find out where he was staying at night, and they were given a great deal of money, along with the liberty to use it in any way necessary. The message was clear: find a way to arrest him quietly and bring him in, or find a way to kill him.

Now that it was morning, the common assumption was that he would be back in the temple, surrounded once more by the ignorant, accursed mob. Fine; they couldn't stop him from entering the temple grounds since he was a Jew, but they didn't have to let him run the show. Today would be different; today he would find adversaries less easily frightened than the filthy moneychangers he had faced yesterday. It was time to see just what this rabbi from Galilee was made of, face to face.

Kill him? Was this idea even possible?
The dark spirits held a hasty conference to develop plans of their own; Lucifer himself would be in the city within hours, and they desperately needed a plan to present to him. Over the millennia of their struggle, they had found it difficult to destroy humans devoted to the enemy; they had even less success against those with significant angelic protection, and they had never had any success at all in destroying one of the heavenly host. This fact was plain to them all, but it was never discussed, and never acknowledged. Throughout the centuries of warfare, they had always entered battle with the hope of seeing an angelic warrior fall, but with the unspoken expectation that it would not happen. Though lying to themselves had long since become a way of life, some lies were just too hard to believe. The prospect that one day they would kill an angel was one of those lies.
So how could it be possible that they could kill him?

Here they come, thought Peter. Glancing across the sun filled courtyard, he could see the bulge form in the crowd over toward the north end of the court of Gentiles. It had been almost an hour since the Rabbi had sat down and begun teaching, and Peter had been watching for them ever since. He knew they would come – *like moths attracted to a flame* he thought. The bulge grew as people gave way, until the crowd finally split, and Peter could see the all-too-familiar headpieces and tassels bobbing their way carefully through the crowd toward the Master. He counted six, but he didn't see the high priest. *This is going to be fun.*
The little band of Pharisees were accompanied by twelve armed temple guards, but these were just for show; the temple guards had no intention of raising their arms, and everyone knew it. Roman law forbade it. So into the middle of the crowd they came, trying for all they were worth to appear

intimidating and failing miserably. The crowd was most uncooperative, stepping aside just enough to let the temple party squeeze through one painful step at a time. Most of those in the crowd had never been this close to a Pharisee before; in uncharacteristic defiance, many of them stared openly as they passed, and some of them actually leaned in to give the finely tailored linen robes an elbow or a shoulder. The process took several minutes, and by the time they finally came to a stop in front of the Rabbi, they were quite ruffled, more than a little embarrassed, and very angry.

"Rabbi, we have been ...authority...if you please?" The question was muffled by the noise of the crowd, who were pressing in from all sides, eager to claim a good view for the confrontation they knew they were about to witness. The Pharisee, who was rather young looking, but appeared to be a spokesman, raised his voice and tried again, with no better results. His face flushed bright red, and as he drew in a deep breath to support his third attempt, the Rabbi held up a hand to still the noise. In the sudden stillness, his bellowing voice rang out loud and clear, reverberating all around the temple courtyard: "By what authority are you doing these things, and who gave you this authority?"

The response from the crowd was quick and negative: authority – it always came back to that. The Roman governor exercised authority. King Herod exercised authority. The tax collectors exercised authority. The scribes, the priests, the Pharisees, the Sadducees, the soldiers, the centurions, the jailers, and the gate-keepers all exercised authority. It was written, it was spoken, it was transferred, and it was enforced, all on the backs of those with no authority. The last thing that any of them wanted to hear on this particular morning was a reminder of the enormous pile of layers of authority they suffered under. Ugly comments and angry murmuring spread throughout the crowd until Jesus again called for silence.

"I also will ask you a question; and if you tell me the answer, then I will also tell you by what authority I 'do these things'".

Peter smiled. He recognized that there was a trap

coming, and he turned to watch their faces as it was set.

All around the courtyard, unseen faces of demonic spirits swirling overhead all broke out into smiles. The protected one, their ancient enemy hidden in a human body was falling for the trap.

From his carefully concealed vantage point high up in the rafters of the temple, Michael smiled as well, seeing the whole picture, and chuckling at the foolishness of a debate with the creator of the universe about his authority to take action within his creation.

"John's baptism" he asked, "where did it come from? Was it from heaven, or from men?"

Foreheads furrowed. Eyebrows arched. One of them began to say something, and then he reconsidered. This was not a subject they had anticipated. They huddled up and conferred in private. A minute went by, then two, and they continued to debate amongst themselves. It became obvious to all around them that the mighty Pharisees had made a mistake by allowing the Rabbi to ask them a question. He had turned the tables, asking *them* a very sticky question about authority. There were only two possible answers, and neither answer would do:

    a) If they answered 'from heaven,' then the Rabbi could easily chastise them for opposing the Baptist, failing to recognize the authority given to him by God and for not heeding his teachings.

    b) If they answered 'from men,' they would deny he had such authority, but they would be insulting a recent martyr who was very popular with the crowds, and by doing so they could in fact spark the public riot that they were trying desperately to prevent.

It was clearly a no-win situation. In the end, the well-dressed, well groomed, well-educated leaders of Israel decided to hedge, and said simply "we do not know." This was not the sort of position they often found themselves in, and the crowd enjoyed the response immensely, as bursts of laughter spread around the courtyard.

With a warm smile on his face, Jesus stepped forward, put a gentle hand on the shoulder of the nearest Pharisee, and said "then neither will I tell you by what authority I do these things." The laughter this time was loud and long.

"What do you think?" Jesus continued with his hand still on the Pharisee's shoulder. He turned in a slow arc, looking at the expectant faces packed closely all around him. His eyes came to rest on a withered old man. He beckoned for him to step forward, and as the frail, thin old fellow stepped within reach, Jesus stretched out his other hand and placed it on his boney shoulder. "A man had two sons; and he went to the first and said, 'Son, go and work in the vineyard today.' And he answered 'I will not'; but afterward he repented and went. And he went to the second and said the same; and he answered, 'I go, sir,' but did not go."

Jesus looked to his left at the richly clad Pharisee, who was by now growing indignant, then turned to his right and looked at the nervous, trembling old man who was obviously very poor. Addressing the Pharisees again, he asked "Which of the two did the will of his father?"

Seeing no way to avoid the obvious answer, one of them blurted out rather peevishly "The first one, of course."

Jesus released the two men, and stepped around directly in front of the holy little entourage, coming uncomfortably close. With a steady, clear voice and unblinking eyes he continued "Truly I say to you, the tax collectors and the harlots go into the kingdom of God before you."

Shocked silence; the only sound was the cheerful chirping of a bird nearby. A young Pharisee who happened to be within reach of the Rabbi began sputtering with the clear intention of responding to the outrageous statement, but he wasn't quick enough.

"For John came to you in the way of righteousness, and you did not believe him, but the tax collectors and the harlots believed him;" His voice was now a little stronger, but there was still no heat to it. "And even when you saw it, you did not afterward repent and believe him.

"Hear another parable. There was a householder who planted a vineyard, and set a hedge around it, and dug a wine press in it, and built a tower, and let it out to tenants, and went into another country."

Andrew nudged his brother and smiled; they had both heard this one before. Jesus was becoming more animated, and stepping back from the temple gang he turned to include the crowd and pressed on.

"When the season of fruit drew near, he sent his servants to the tenants, to get his fruit; and the tenants took his servants and beat one, killed another, and stoned another."

A series of boos and hisses went up from the crowd.

"Again he sent other servants, more than the first; and they did the same to them."

More response erupted from the crowd, this time louder and longer.

"Afterward he sent his son to them, saying 'They will respect my son.' Here Jesus turned back toward the same indignant scribe, who had been inching away, trying to hide behind one of the older Pharisees. He pulled him gently out into the open, placed his hand on his shoulder once more, and softly repeated the words "They will respect my son." He paused for just a moment, gazing into the eyes of the young man, and apparently not finding what he was looking for.

He whirled away, and raised his voice "But when the tenants saw the son, they said to themselves, 'This is the heir; come, let us kill him and have his inheritance.'" Above the angry shouts from the crowd he finished "And they took him and cast him out of the vineyard, and killed him!"

Bedlam erupted, the enormous crowd now seething and boiling with anger. They didn't understand just how, but they had all come to the conclusion that the Pharisees standing in their midst were personally responsible, and at that moment it wouldn't have taken much nudging to spur them to violence.

"When therefore the owner of the vineyard comes, what will he do to those tenants?"

The roar in response was deafening, but he could hear snatches here and there:

"He will put those wretches to a miserable death..."

"...let out the vineyard to other tenants..."

"...give him the fruits in their seasons."

Jesus turned his back to the terrified huddle of religious leaders, raised his hands to still the crowd, and said to them, "Have you never read the scriptures:

> 'The very stone which the builders rejected has become the head of the corner; this was the Lord's doing, and it is marvelous in our eyes'?

"Therefore I tell you, the kingdom of God will be taken away from you and given to a nation producing the fruits of it!"

Who was he talking about?

There was absolutely no sound by this time, as the crowd looked on in stunned disbelief.

Was he talking about them?

No one moved, no one looked around, and it seemed as if no one dared to breathe. Suddenly, the Pharisees found their courage at last, and in the vacuum tried to mobilize the temple guards to arrest Jesus. But the moment was quickly gone, as the crowd surged forward with hundreds of questions and comments and pushed the puny little party of religious leaders aside. As Jesus fielded questions from those in the crowd closest to him, the disciples closed ranks, and the frustrated Pharisees slipped out, all but unnoticed.

Who was the son?

Who were the tenants?

Is there any way to save the poor son?

Why did the owner send his son without protection?

Jesus sat down to teach, and the crowd sat down as well, the motion rippling away from him in a sea of robes and sandals settling in relief to the temple pavement. The sun was by now high above them, and it was good to sit down.

"The kingdom of heaven may be compared to a king who gave a marriage feast for his son, and sent his servants to call those who were invited to the marriage feast; but they would not come."

Murmurs spread once again: *Is this the same son?*

"Again, he sent other servants, saying, 'Tell those who

are invited, Behold, I have made ready my dinner, my oxen and my fat calves are killed, and everything is ready; come to the marriage feast.' But they made light of it and went off, one to his farm, another to his business, while the rest seized his servants, treated them shamefully, and killed them."

Outrage rumbled around the crowd for a second time, as they began asking each other questions: *How could these people be so wicked? Who would do such a thing? Who is he talking about? What did the king do?*

"The king was angry, and he sent his troops and destroyed those murderers and burned their city. Then he said to his servants, 'Go therefore to the thoroughfares, and invite to the marriage feast as many as you can find.' And those servants went out into the streets and gathered whom they found, both good and bad; so the wedding hall was filled with guests."

Peter was sitting next to John, and looking over at him he noticed a perplexed look on his face. "What is it?" he said.

"The guests invited to the wedding feast. I don't think I have understood until now who they are."

Peter waited a moment, but when John failed to continue, he prompted him, asking "Well, who are they?"

"When he has spoken this parable before, I have always assumed that the guests were the religious leaders, you know, the scribes and Pharisees. I don't think that is what he means."

"Why not?"

Jesus was speaking again, so John leaned in closer and lowered his voice. "In the parable of the vineyard, he speaks of a son killed by the tenants. In the wedding story, the invited guests reject the invitation and show disrespect for the king's son. Tell me Peter, if the tenants and the invited guests are the leaders, where are the followers? Where are we?"

Peter stared at him with a blank look on his face.

John continued, "He said that the kingdom of God would be taken away from 'you', looking at the crowd. Didn't you see their reaction? He said that the kingdom would be given to another nation 'which produces the fruits of the kingdom.' I think he means us, Peter."

"Now that is just stupid. How could we..."

"And the fig tree, Peter; the fig tree which produces no fruit."

Peter scratched his cheek.

What was John implying?

Sitting in counsel once again, the leaders of the Nation of Israel debated what to do. They had tried to arrest him, and that had failed; the crowds were too large. They had tried to speak to him directly, asking him to back down, and that had failed; they had dispatched soldiers and spies and even some of their own members in an attempt to find a way to bring him in or silence him, but so far nothing was working.

"I think it is time to speak to the governor, your eminence," said a crusty old scribe sitting near the high priest. "We must move now, before he does," he wheezed.

"And what will we offer him?" responded Caiaphas with a sharp edge to his voice. "We must have the Galilean in hand before we approach the Romans, you know that. If we ask them to move now, we are asking for a bloodbath. No, we must get our hands on him first, and we must find a way to do it now."

The face of the high priest was by now flushed and wet with perspiration. They had been wrangling for nearly two hours and had nothing to show for it. "Has no one in this room anything better to offer?" he bellowed.

Someone near the other end of the long, ornate table coughed.

"Yes?"

"It seems to me, my esteemed brethren that we have yet to use our full resources in this matter." It was his old rival, Eliab, the chief priest from Bethlehem. They rarely spoke to one another, and when they did, it was only out of necessity, and usually indirectly. Over the years, there had been a quiet struggle in the background for control of the seat of the high priest, and the family of Caiaphas held on to it with only the slimmest of handles. Both families knew that a mistake, any mistake, could shift power in a moment.

Before Caiaphas could blurt out something he would later regret Annas spoke in response, "Does our friend from the house of David have something to offer?"

"I intend no disrespect to the capable young men that have been sent on our behalf to speak directly with the rabbi, but they are in fact young. Perhaps we should ask the high priest if we should not send someone with...shall we say someone with more experience in such matters; someone who would not get tangled up in the Galilean's clever speech."

It was a masterful stroke, delivered with no obvious malice; in one statement, he had insulted the high priest's judgment, the Pharisee's whom he had sent (most of the powerful men at the table were Sadducees), and the entire province of Galilee (Galileans were never characterized as clever).

"Does our friend have someone in mind that he would recommend for such a noble task?" Annas replied.

"In my humble opinion, we could have no greater representative than the high priest himself. Who among us is better qualified to handle such a delicate situation?"

The suggestion caught them all by surprise, for no one at the table would agree with this assessment of Caiaphas' abilities at all; he was a strong man, yes, but he was anything but qualified to handle delicate situations. He had a fierce temper, and it took very little to ignite it.

Annas noted the pleased look on the face of the high priest. Apparently he was the only one in the room fooled by the suggestion. Coming to his aid once again, he spoke up before Caiaphas could step into the trap. "We all appreciate the suggestion, and agree with our friend's good opinion of our high priest. However, we must be careful with the message that this would send to the crowd. A public debate with the high priest himself would send a signal that we consider the rabbi to be an equal; it would attach too great of importance to his words. I agree that we must send someone capable to handle such a challenge, but we must consider carefully just whom we should send."

Another member of the family of the high priest sitting across the table from Annas recognized the cue, and asked the question: "Does our brother Annas have a suggestion as to whom we should send?"

"Considering the crowd, the situation with the Romans, and the clever tactics of the Galilean, I believe we could have no better spokesman than our dear friend from Bethlehem."

Everyone in the room turned to look at the chief priest from Bethlehem, whose expression was inscrutable. Annas couldn't tell if he was surprised or if this was in fact what he wanted all along.

"Very well then; it is decided," Caiaphas concluded. "Our friend from Bethlehem will select a team to assist him, and he will approach the rabbi in the morning. His object will be to expose the man as a fraud before the crowd and take him into custody. I will expect a full report by the end of the day describing his arrest or failing that a complete explanation by our friend as to why he was unable to complete the task. We are adjourned."

□□□□□□

Leaving the city late in the evening through the Eastern Gate, the disciples filtered out with the waning crowd. It had been a big day, filled with teaching and ministering among the crowds, and they were all exhausted. But instead of continuing with the crowd eastward along the dusty road back to Bethany, Jesus suddenly turned to the south into an obscure path which skirted the far side of the Kidron Valley, and which eventually led up the slope toward the Mount of Olives. There were a few puzzled glances among the disciples, and someone muttered softly, but they all turned and followed him on the narrow pathway up the hill. They walked on in silence for some time; by the time they reached the summit, many of them were panting from the exertion. Stepping out of the olive grove into a small clearing, Jesus sat down on a large stone and rested for a few moments.

"Rabbi, why are we here?" inquired Thomas, still breathing heavily.

Nathaniel sat down next to Jesus and added "Are we not returning to Bethany to meet the rest?"

Peter could see the troubled look in his Master's eyes, and stepped in. "Let him catch his breath, will you? It's been a long day and we need no more questions." He looked at Nathaniel until he reluctantly rose to his feet and moved off to join the rest of the twelve, who were spread out against the gnarled, ancient tree trunks a few paces down the slope. Peter sat down next to Jesus and settled in, saying nothing. He had a few questions of his own, but he knew that now was not the time to pursue them. A few more quiet minutes went by, until Peter finally realized that Jesus had fixed his gaze on something off in the distance, to the west. Peter squinted and peered in the same direction, and seeing nothing in particular in the deepening gloom, he looked again at Jesus. And then he remembered where he was, and looked again, this time a little lower and a little farther north. And there it was: a ghostly, black silhouette of the temple against a nearly black horizon. From this vantage point on the top of the Mount of Olives, they were at an elevation nearly two hundred and fifty feet higher than the Temple Mount. Jesus suddenly flinched, then shivered for just a moment.

What was he seeing?

Peter wanted to say something soothing and helpful, something wise; but nothing came to him so he continued to sit silently next to his Master, waiting. A few more long moments passed, and Peter could see that the rest of the twelve were growing restless. He glanced once more into Jesus face, and the Rabbi finally returned the look, with a mixture of apprehension and kindness written into his features. He leaned close and patted Peter on the arm, and smiled. He shivered again. Peter removed his outer tunic and placed it around the Rabbi's shoulders; within moments Jesus was nodding off. Peter gently eased him to the ground where he curled up and was soon fast asleep. After a moment of watching the Master's breathing relax into a deep, regular pace, Peter stood and walked quietly toward his friends.

"I believe we will be staying here for the night. Quiet – I don't want to hear it. I know it has been a long day, and tomorrow will be here soon, another long day. Try to get some sleep."

The grumbling continued for awhile until one by one they all succumbed to fatigue and fell asleep; all of them except for one.

Tuesday

At daybreak, the Master was nowhere to be found. This in itself was no cause for alarm, for everyone was familiar with his habit of rising early for solitude and prayer. But on this morning, on the lonely Mount of Olives, the disciples were waking up grumpy, sore, and hungry. None of them had slept well on the hard ground, and now they were facing the day with no breakfast. The grumbling picked right up where it had left off the night before, and now there was no reason to be quiet about it. Peter looked over at his brother, who had a worried look on his face; when Andrew returned the gaze, a question clearly showing in his body language, Peter merely shrugged. But then it occurred to him that Jesus wasn't the only one who was missing. Someone else...he counted heads: nine, ten, and he himself made eleven. Who was missing? Nathaniel, James, John, Philip...and as he arrived at the name, he saw Judas emerge from the olive grove carrying two baskets. There was a sudden clamoring among the twelve to see what he had brought with him, and the atmosphere brightened instantly when they began passing around fruit and bread, plenty for everyone.

"Where did you get all of this food?" asked John, his mouth crammed with bread and a broad smile on his face.

Judas replied simply "I know some people."

The disciples spread out with their breakfasts in a vastly improved mood, and several conversations began between bites.

"Do you miss it?" Andrew asked his former partners, James and John, referring to the life on their boats that they had left behind. The three of them had drifted over and sat down beneath a particularly large, very old olive tree, perhaps a thousand years old.

"What? Getting up in the middle of the night to go to work, or the wonderful smell of rotting fish?" replied James between bites without looking up.

"Do you miss the sea," Andrew clarified, long since used to James' sarcasm.

"I haven't thought much about it."

"What about you, John? Have you ever thought about the boats, our boats?"

"I have; I have often thought about that moment alone on a sea of glass, with no one around, when the sun is just starting to peak up over the horizon and the sky is on fire – there is nothing like it."

They all reflected quietly for a little while as they ate, all of them remembering many such moments on the Sea of Galilee.

"Why do you ask, Andrew?" John finally inquired. "Are you thinking about going back?"

"No, I was just wondering. Sometimes I just miss the..." Here he struggled for words: "...well, sometimes I miss the pace of life on the sea."

"It has been rather hectic, these last few years, I'll have to admit that," observed James, munching on a piece of dried fruit.

"How is your father doing without you?" asked Andrew. "I mean, Peter and I had no one else who depended on us; well, that's not really true, I guess – Peter's wife had to move home to Capernaum to live with her parents while he is gone."

John stood up and stretched. "Father is making it without us. He hired a couple of young men to take our place in the boat with him. Of course, he is still angry about us leaving; he has never understood."

James grunted his agreement on that account.

"I don't think anyone understands," Andrew added. "That's what makes it so hard. But...I don't think I would trade what we are doing with anything else in the world."

Nathaniel and Philip were also reflecting on the past, remembering the day they had met Jesus.

"You should have seen the look on your face, Nathaniel.

I have never seen you so rattled."

"Well, what did you expect? You asked me to come with you to see a new prophet from Nazareth. Since he was from Galilee, my expectations were rather low," Nathaniel said with a grin.

"He showed you, I guess," answered Philip, who was also grinning, his cheeks puffed up with food like a squirrel.

Thomas, who was sitting with them asked, "Why? What happened?"

"This guy," said Philip, gesturing at Nathaniel, "had to be bribed to come with me. He said 'Can anything good come out of Nazareth?' like he was some kind of expert on prophets. So I promised him that if he wasn't impressed the way I was when I first met the Master, that I would do his chores for a week."

"Did you ever have to do his chores?"

The two looked at each other and laughed.

"No, I didn't. Actually, as it turned out, neither of us went back to Bethsaida. When I brought him out to meet Jesus, Nathaniel concluded on the spot that he was the Son of God, the King of Israel."

"What did the Master do?"

"It was what he said that impressed Nathaniel so; as we approached him, Jesus called out from a distance, 'Behold, an Israelite indeed, in whom is no guile.' Flattery has always worked on him."

"No, no, that wasn't what impressed me at all," said Nathaniel good-naturedly, "though he was very observant with that comment. After he said that, I asked him how he knew me so well, and he said, 'Before Philip called you, when you were under the fig tree, I saw you.'"

Still smiling, Philip added, "I never mentioned the fig tree. Jesus was over a day's walk away when I met Nathaniel by the fig tree."

The men continued to chatter pleasantly as they ate, and Peter watched and listened thoughtfully from his perch on the rock. Something was bothering him, but he couldn't place what it was. As the last remnants of breakfast were finally consumed, they heard a slight rustling of branches, and Jesus stepped into the clearing, his face bright and pleasant. Chagrinned, a few of them glanced uneasily at the empty baskets until Peter stepped forward and offered the Master a handful of dried figs and a piece of bread he had saved. Jesus took them, gave thanks and ate while everyone stood around in a circle, watching. When he was finished, he looked around the circle, smiling into each face, and then asked "Shall we go?"

□□□□□□

The morning hadn't gone as smoothly for Eliab and the party he had chosen to accompany him to the temple. One of his best Sadducees had come down ill in the night, the squad of temple soldiers he had requested had yet to show up, the five or six Pharisees who did show up were too young and he had just received a hand written message from Annas that was polite but insulting at the same time, wishing him success in the days' activities. Fuming, he paced around the room, counted his Sadducee brethren, eight in all, and surveyed the dozen or so scribes and lawyers lounging on the terrace; at least these men would prove useful. They were among the best experts on the law in Jerusalem.

Where are the soldiers?

The morning was racing by, the rabbi was probably already working the mob in the temple courtyard, and here they sat waiting on soldiers.

They are probably all nursing hangovers, the vulgar, drunken bunch of them.

How had he gotten himself into this position? Eliab Ben Zadok from Bethlehem, one of the most powerful men in Israel, was reduced to waiting on common temple guards. He was tempted to proceed without them, but he knew it would be unwise to enter a large crowd without means of security, without a way to clear a pathway through the sea of sweaty, stinking humanity. He shuddered at the thought of making contact, of *touching* unclean peasants. No, he would wait for his escort. But they would pay for their tardiness.

The day was overcast and heavy; rain was threatening – which would normally be a good thing, but not for a massive crowd in an open courtyard. Even so, the numbers were swelling by the hour. Travelers from outside the city had begun arriving before daylight, having heard the stories racing around the Judean countryside about the skirmishes between the Galilean and the temple rulers. A showdown was coming, everyone was sure of it, and no one wanted to miss it. So when Jesus and his disciples entered the courtyard, an enormous cheer erupted. He moved slowly through the crowd, touching, smiling, speaking, blessing and healing. And finally, after a long, unhurried season of personal contact, Jesus sat down once again on the steps leading up to the inner court and began to teach.

Peter stepped back and relaxed against the massive stone wall, and noticed the empty tables and booths where only two days ago there had been merchants and money-changers operating a thriving business. They had not returned. He continued to gaze around the huge Court of the Gentiles as he listened to the familiar stories, taking in the details of the magnificent structure, with its soaring towers and gleaming white walls built on hand-chiseled sandstone foundation blocks the size of a house. He was suddenly happy and proud to be here in this place at this time, a follower of this man. He could think of nowhere he would rather be. But still something nagged at the back of his mind; something was out of place...his thoughts were interrupted by a commotion at the doorway into the temple. He didn't even have to look to know what it meant: the temple rulers were back.

The soldiers came out first, pushing their way into the crowd and setting up a clearing; more soldiers took up security positions, and still more soldiers descended the steps just ahead of the richly clad entourage. The young Pharisees in their long flowing robes came first, followed by the scribes and lawyers, followed by the Sadducees in their distinctively trimmed white cloaks. In their midst was a quite round man with a large, elaborate headpiece and flashing, brilliant jewelry on his chest. With all of the decoration, he looked like the High Priest himself, but he was too short and too wide to be Caiaphas. It was clear, however, that this was someone important.

The interruption was not welcomed. The crowd, emboldened by the events of the previous couple of days, didn't hesitate to hiss and boo as the religious leaders made their way toward the Rabbi, though the much stronger presence of soldiers made it difficult for them to impede their progress. The robes fluttered down the cleared space unruffled and implacable until the rather large party finally arrived at the bottom of the steps where the Rabbi continued to sit. They stood there calmly as the unruly noise from the crowd continued for several moments, and when the din finally began to subside, one of the lawyers stepped forward to speak. But as soon as he raised his voice, the clamoring broke out again, this time with more heat, and he was easily drowned out. He tried again a few minutes later, but with the same result. Finally, with a smile on his face, the Rabbi raised his hand to the crowd, and when there was peace, he asked the gentleman if he wished to speak.

The lawyer cleared his throat, paused for effect, and then began in his most charming and disarming voice, just loud enough for those nearby to hear "Teacher, we know that you are true, and teach the way of God truthfully, and care for no man; for you do not regard the position of men. Tell us then what you think. Is it lawful to pay taxes to Caesar, or not?"

The question sounded reasonable. His delivery made it sound as if they were old friends and that they were sure to agree on his answer, no matter what it was. He smiled broadly, waiting for the answer.

The crowd, at least those who could hear the question, was immediately buzzing with opinions. Peter turned to his brother, who was standing at his elbow, and commented, "Lawyers: they are all alike. They ask such stupid questions."

Andrew thought for a moment. "Oh, I don't know; the man is a Herodian. The Herodians back the Roman government. They are probably on the Roman payroll."

Peter persisted, "Then why didn't a Pharisee ask him this question instead? They hate the Romans and consider foreign taxes an affront to God. If they are trying to trick him into saying something subversive to the Romans, wouldn't the question come better from someone who..."

"There is more than one trap here, brother. Listen."

The lawyer was still smiling, confident that he had outsmarted the uneducated rabbi from Galilee. He knew that a yes answer to his question would be as damaging as a no. Obviously, payment of taxes to the Romans *was* unlawful in Israel, but no one in his right mind would actually say so in public; refusal to pay had cost thousands of Jews their lives over the years. On the other hand, no Jew could hope to remain popular with the common man while openly supporting Roman taxation. The Herodians tried (rather unsuccessfully) to walk a fine line of supporting the Romans, but without the appearance of doing so. This question was designed not only to trap Jesus in a no-win situation, but to also validate the Herodian position; thus the smile.

Jesus had been smiling in return. He glanced around the faces of the crowd, still smiling, and asked with the same disarming manner his own question: "Why put me to the test, you hypocrites?" Though his smile, genuine in every way remained, the lawyer's had suddenly vanished. "Show me the money for the tax."

Naturally, the lawyer had no money on his person. Religious leaders did not carry something so common, so defiling with them. With a puzzled look, he turned to face his brethren, who were scrambling to produce a coin. The crowd began to titter at the unusual sight – Pharisees and Scribes begging one another for a simple coin. Finally, one of the temple guards reluctantly gave up a denarius, which was passed hastily to the lawyer who was by now visibly uneasy. He stepped forward to hand it to Jesus.

Without hesitating, and with a smile still on his face, Jesus asked yet another question: "Whose likeness and inscription is this?"

Did he not recognize the image of the ruler of the entire world?

Is the rabbi so poor that he has never seen a Roman Denarius?

"Why...Caesar's, of course," replied the confused lawyer. The crowd was again buzzing. *Was he missing something?*

"Render therefore to Caesar the things that are Caesar's, and to God the things that are God's."

The crowd burst into a roar of approval at the masterful response, and the cluster of religious experts wilted into a hasty retreat. The circle closed around him, and Jesus resumed his teaching, a smile still on his face.

They formed a perfectly straight line along the hillside overlooking the Fortress Antonia on the north side of the city, impervious to the gathering storm. Lightning flashed all around them, the quickening wind howled in vain to move them. Dark and gloomy though it was, it was still daytime; nevertheless light seemed to flee from these immovable figures, leaving no shadows, reflecting no image. These were the fiercest, the darkest spirits in the universe, nine individuals who had long evaded destruction at the hands of the heavenly host. They were evil beyond human imagination; they were brutality and corruption incarnate. Any form of greed, any form of intimidation, any form of sheer terror could trace its roots back to one or all of these individuals. There were no rules, there were no boundaries that they had not tested or broken. They were far and away the most fearsome and loathsome demons, yet here they stood awaiting the arrival of one who inspired fear in them. Behind them, arranged in perfect ranks stood row after row of filthy spirits, the most despicable and gruesome on earth, gathered from the four corners of the globe. Not a word was spoken, not a muscle twitched. Together in one place for only the second time in centuries, they waited in silence for the arrival of the prince of darkness.

The Holy Father from Bethlehem was not going to give up easily – there was simply too much at stake. After a quick conference to plan the next move, they were back, and once again they stood aloof from the crowd as one of their best Sadducees proceeded with their best line of attack: the controversial issue of bodily resurrection. The Sadducees scoffed at the idea, while the Pharisees defended it. The confused children of Israel didn't know what to think.

"Teacher, Moses said: 'If a man dies, having no children, his brother must marry the widow, and raise up children for his brother.' Now there were seven brothers among us; the first married, and died, and having no children left his wife to his brother."

James snickered, and leaning over to John, whispered, "This is so old. I have heard this stupid story for years. They argue over it in the synagogues as if any one believes there ever were such seven brothers."

The Sadducee was just warming up. "So too the second and third died, down to the seventh. After them all, the woman died. In the *resurrection"* (he spoke the word with the slightest hint of amusement), "therefore, to which of the seven will she be wife? For they all had her." He stepped back with a smug look on his face, waiting for the rabbi's response. He ignored the chuckling among the crowd, unaware of how absurd the scenario sounded to ears unaccustomed to a regular diet of theoretical posturing and discourse. He instead focused on the rabbi's face, trying to sense a clue as to what direction he might take. He had heard every possible argument, every line of reasoning in defense of resurrection, and he was prepared to rebut them all; he was confident he could easily demonstrate how silly and illogical the whole notion proved to be when examined by an expert in the matter. And of course the rabbi believed in the resurrection...

The answer, however, was not one he expected.

Jesus began evenly and without heat, "You are wrong, because you know neither the scriptures nor the power of God."

The statement hit the huddle of scribes and lawyers,

Pharisees and Sadducees, life long students of scripture all, like a blow to the head. There wasn't a notion conceivable by man that would have stunned them more: between them there was a combined 730 years of scholarship, of studying the scriptures; over 480 years among the lawyers and scribes alone.

We don't know the scriptures?

"For in the resurrection they neither marry nor are given in marriage, but are like angels in heaven."

Fury was brimming among the scholars, but Jesus raised his voice a notch to preempt the angry response that was obviously coming, for he was not yet finished:

"And as for the resurrection of the dead, *have you not read what was said to you by God,* 'I AM the God of Abraham...'"

His voice climbed yet higher in volume:

"'...and the God of Isaac...'"

The walls at the far end of the temple courtyard now resonated with his echo:

"'...and the God of Jacob?' He is NOT the God of the dead, but of the living!"

After a brief moment of stunned silence, the huge crowd discharged an enormous concussion of approval and glee. No one among them had ever heard such powerful teaching, such clear authority, and against so many teachers of the law! The cheering and celebrating drowned out any response, so the humiliated leaders of Israel huddled together once more in an attempt to find a way to salvage the effort. At last, as the uproar was finally dying to a bearable level, an old lawyer, perhaps the oldest present, stepped forward. He bowed before the rabbi, a gesture none of them had previously offered. Though his colleagues were offended by this obnoxious and embarrassing move, they remained frozen in place as he raised his voice to ask his question. It wasn't a particularly good one, but none of them were able to think clearly under the pressure of the deafening roar of the crowd.

In a soft yet clear voice, he asked "Teacher, which is the greatest commandment in the law?"

Without hesitation, Jesus declared, "You shall love the Lord your God with all your heart, and with all your soul, and with all your mind. This is the great and first commandment."

The old man nodded in agreement, his eyes closed, remembering the words from the book of Deuteronomy.

"And the second is like it," he continued to everyone's surprise. Reaching his arm out to draw a poor, emaciated old man to his feet, he brought the two together.

"You shall love your neighbor as yourself."

The two old men stood facing each other awkwardly, both of them Jews, but from entirely different worlds, both of them taught from birth to despise the other.

"On these two commandments depend all the law and the prophets."

Frustrated that they were getting nowhere, the religious committee gathered together again, but Jesus interrupted their scheming to ask them a question of his own.

"What do you think of the Messiah? Whose son is he?"

Jesus watched with amusement as the sages and scholars, the best and the brightest to be found in all of the land, argued at length with one another, floating possible answers back and forth, feeling the question out for traps, straining to come up with something profound and clever, and finally settling on the obvious answer they had all produced when the question was first asked, an answer that nearly everyone in the surrounding ocean of uneducated non-scholars had long since concluded.

A proud spokesman, a perfect picture of thoughtful scholarship and wisdom, said with all the sincerity he could muster, "He is the son of David."

The crowd enjoyed a good laugh at his expense.

Raising his hand to the crowd so that he could continue, Jesus asked, "How is it then that David, inspired by the Spirit, calls him Lord, saying,

'The Lord said to my Lord, sit at my right hand,
till I put thy enemies under thy feet?'

If David thus calls him Lord, how is he his son?"

The crowd roared once again, the perplexed scholars looked at one another for direction and found none, and finally turned to leave in humiliation. They had had enough.

And Jesus had also had enough. The long season of authority and control for the shepherds, the leaders of the nation of Israel - the men entrusted with the care and protection and guidance of God's chosen people – was coming to a close. They had been given every chance, every opportunity, every warning to change, to listen and to humble themselves before God and lead the nation of Israel in a way pleasing to God, but at every turn they refused, becoming more entrenched in willful and defiant stubbornness with each generation. The prophecies against the shepherds recorded by Ezekiel were finally coming to pass:

> "Ho, shepherds of Israel who have been feeding yourselves! Should not shepherds feed the sheep? You eat the fat, you clothe yourselves with wool, you slaughter the fatlings; but you do not feed the sheep. The weak you have not strengthened, the sick you have not healed, the crippled you have not bound up, the strayed you have not brought back, the lost you have not sought, and with force and harshness you have ruled them."

> "Therefore, you shepherds, hear the word of the Lord: As I live, says the Lord God, because my sheep have become a prey, and my sheep have become food for all the wild beasts, since there is no shepherd;
> "Thus says the Lord God, Behold, I am against the shepherds; and I will require my sheep at their hand, and will put a stop to their feeding the sheep."

> "I myself will be the shepherd of my sheep, and I will make them lie down, says the Lord God. I will seek the lost, and I will bring back the strayed, and I will bind up the crippled, and I will strengthen the weak, and the fat and the

strong I will watch over; I will feed them in justice."

There would be no more debate; there would be no more pretenses at working out common ground or finding a way to avert the coming, inevitable power confrontation, and both sides knew it.

And so, as the angry party of religious leaders attempted to take their leave, Jesus called after them in a loud voice, "The scribes and the Pharisees sit on Moses' seat; so practice and observe whatever they tell you, but not what they do; for they preach, but do not practice."

Eliab the proud Sadducee from Bethlehem stopped in his tracks. He could feel the eyes of the crowd boring into the back of his head, watching him depart as the...he could not bring himself to even think the word rabbi...the rabble-rousing blasphemer insulted him, humiliating him publicly. He was nearly at the doorway that would rescue him from what was without question the absolute worst moment of his life, but somehow he found himself frozen, unable to take another step, and yet unwilling to turn back and face him.

And Jesus was just getting started.

"They bind heavy burdens, hard to bear, and lay them on men's shoulders; but they themselves will not move them with their finger. They do all their deeds to be seen by men; for they make their phylacteries broad and their fringes long, and they love the place of honor at feasts and the best seats in the synagogues, and salutations in the marketplaces, and being called rabbi by men."

Sweating profusely, Eliab glanced to his left and his right and noticed that all of his fellows were similarly frozen. To his horror, he noticed a few of them turning slowly around to face the tirade behind him. He looked at his feet, willed them with all of his might to move, but they would not. And the onslaught continued.

"But woe to you, scribes and Pharisees, hypocrites! because you shut the kingdom of heaven against men; for you neither enter yourselves, nor allow those who would enter to go in. Woe to you, scribes and Pharisees, hypocrites! for you traverse sea and land to make a single proselyte, and when he becomes a proselyte, you make him twice as much a child of hell as yourselves!"

At that very moment, the atmospheric pressure within the courtyard suddenly dropped, and a chilling wind kicked up, blowing stray leaves in circles among the crowd. Lightning flashed all over the sky above them, followed by deep thunder echoing back and forth. Jesus glanced up at the hillside above Jerusalem, just beyond the Fortress Antonia.

His enemy was here.

Unshaken, he continued in the face of the rising storm, raising his voice to match the howling wind.

"Woe to you, scribes and Pharisees, hypocrites! for you tithe mint and dill and cumin, and have neglected the weightier matters of the law: justice and mercy and faith; these you ought to have done, without neglecting the others. You blind guides, straining out a gnat and swallowing a camel!"

Huge raindrops began to fall sporadically on the crowd, and though they were transfixed by this unbelievable display, some began to look for shelter. Jesus stepped toward the huddle of humiliated scribes and Pharisees, whose carefully tailored and decorated garments were beginning to cling limply to their bodies, while the colorful cloaks and headdress gear began to bleed color.

"Woe to you, scribes and Pharisees, hypocrites! for you cleanse the outside of the cup and of the plate, but inside they are filled with extortion and rapacity. You blind Pharisee! first cleanse the inside of the cup and of the plate, that the outside may also be clean."

The rain was now setting in, heavy and cold, and the gusting wind was driving it in sheets, dispersing the crowd, who were running away in every direction for cover. And still the tirade continued, and still the Pharisees, Sadducees, scribes and lawyers remained nailed in place, forced to listen against their will.

"Woe to you, scribes and Pharisees, hypocrites! for you are like whitewashed tombs, which outwardly appear beautiful, but within they are full of dead men's bones and all uncleanness. So you also outwardly appear righteous to men, but within you are full of hypocrisy and iniquity.

"You serpents, you brood of vipers, how are you to escape being sentenced to hell? Therefore, I send you prophets and wise men and scribes, some of whom you will kill and crucify, and some you will scourge in your synagogues and persecute from town to town, that upon you may come all the righteous blood shed on earth, from the blood of innocent Abel to the blood of Zechariah the son of Barachiah, whom you murdered between the sanctuary and the altar. Truly, I say to you, all this will come upon this generation."

The crowd was nearly gone, with only handfuls of shivering followers huddled here and there, determined to hear the Master out until the end. As his voice finally was silent, the drenched leaders of Israel, fully enraged and fully humiliated, finally found the power to move and exited the courtyard without looking back.

Jesus stood there in the slackening rain for another few minutes with his disciples and friends. He seemed to be thinking, to be reflecting. Finally, looking up once more to scan the empty temple courtyard, he spoke once more, softly:

"O Jerusalem, Jerusalem, killing the prophets and stoning those who are sent to you! How often would I have gathered your children together as a hen gathers her brood under her wings, and you would not!"

He turned and looked for a long moment at the golden temple door, brilliant and gleaming even on a cloudy day, and finally finished, saying, "Behold, your house is forsaken and desolate. For I tell you, you will not see me again, until you say 'Blessed is he who comes in the name of the Lord.'"

The evening turned to twilight, the twilight to darkness, and the wet, hungry, miserable band of disciples trudged slowly up yet another pathway through the olive groves toward another non-descript clearing near the brow of the summit overlooking the Kidron Valley, this time a little farther south than the previous evening. When they finally stopped, many of them slumped to the ground without a word, and drifted quickly to sleep. Jesus withdrew, as expected, and James, John and Peter followed him for a short distance to make sure he was safe, and then huddled together against the base of an ancient, gnarled olive tree. John was shivering from his wet garments, so his older brother huddled in a little closer, putting his arm around him. For a few moments, they said nothing, content to sit quietly in the darkness and rest. It had been a long day, with their only meal early in the morning, which now seemed so long ago.

Finally, James asked Peter, "Why can't we go back to Bethany? Did you hear them grumbling along the way? They were right, you know; we could be lying in warm beds right now, after a warm meal."

Peter hesitated.

"I think..." He paused again, and looked around. "I wonder if he is worried that perhaps we are being watched."

"Watched by whom? Of course we are being watched."

"Watched by the Romans, watched by the Jews...I don't know; maybe a spy."

James was incredulous, "A spy?"

"Shhh...not so loudly. Why not a spy? The Jews will stop at nothing to silence him, especially after today."

"Well, that much is true."

"He is not worried," John spoke quietly, for the first time.

"What?" replied both James and Peter at the same time.

"You said that he was worried that we are being watched, but I don't think that is the case. He may be aware that we are being watched, but he is not worried."

James, offended in a typical older brother fashion, replied "And how do you know this?"

"Have you ever seen the Rabbi worried about anything? No. And as far as being watched, if we are wondering if this is a possibility, would the thought not also occur to him? Clearly, we are moving around when we are alone, sleeping in a different spot each night, to thwart those who may be watching us. But even if he is worried, it is not about this."

They were quiet again for a few moments, finally warming up and relaxing.

"So what is he worried about?" Peter asked with a long yawn.

"He is concerned about us, that much is clear; but there is something else..." John let the words trail off.

Peter thought for moments, remembering glimpses of something dark over the past few weeks, remembering the Rabbi's reference to his own death. "I think you are right, there is something."

Again, there was a long pause as the two of them listened to James breathing deeply, snoring softly.

Peter spoke once more in a drowsy voice, "Whatever it is...we will...protect him." And there was nothing more said.

Wednesday

As the enormous army of invisible warriors continued to grow throughout the night, gathering just outside the city, the council of nine met privately one last time with the ruler of this world. He had been briefed by every commander and every spy with any shred of news, and had formulated the strategy based on the information thus gathered:

1) The enemy was within the city, within reach of both the Jews and the Romans
2) He was systematically humiliating the rulers of the Jews
3) His daily rabble-rousing was making the Roman governor very nervous, who, with his eye on the swelling mob, was clearly bracing for trouble
4) There was a potential traitor among the enemy's own followers
5) There had not been a single heavenly warrior spotted in the entire region for weeks
6) The crowd of mere men presented his only identifiable means of protection.

The plan would unfold in three stages, but would work only if in the first stage the crowd could be neutralized. It was a large crowd; they had controlled large crowds before, but never one this large, and never with one hundred percent success. So, in order to ensure the highest success rate possible, the decision had been made to abandon all other activities around the globe and bring together in this one place the entire population of the dominion of darkness, a mobilization so vast, so difficult that it had been attempted only once before, about thirty years ago. Though they had not been successful in that monumental effort, there was a glaring difference this time: there were no angels at hand to defend him.

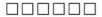

Caiaphas was tempted to gloat over the failure of his old rival form Bethlehem, but the stakes were too high, and now was not the time. He would instead remind himself at a more opportune moment to make use of this new advantage.

At the moment, he was faced with troubling news on nearly every front: the enormous crowd in the temple courtyard, by now numbering over seventy thousand, was growing so large and packed so tightly that men and children were climbing over one another up onto the walls and sitting in the parapets; those unable to get in the gates were spilling out into the streets, creating terrible congestion, which in turn was wreaking havoc with the local merchants. The Zealots were taking advantage of the situation, stirring up trouble with frustrated onlookers, openly stealing from vendors, picking fights, taunting the Romans. Traffic into the city bringing badly needed food and supplies for the coming Passover had nearly ground to a halt; the Roman governor was reportedly bringing in reinforcements from Caesarea; and worst of all, they still had no answer to the question of what to do about the rabbi from Galilee, who showed no sign of letting up, and the Passover would begin tomorrow evening.

Several attempts at arresting the rabbi had been aborted due to the tenacious presence of the sympathetic crowd; twice they had followed him away from the temple in order to seize him away from the mob, but so far they had unable to isolate him sufficiently. Spies were indeed mingling with the crowd, listening, observing, hoping to pick up a clue as to where he was staying at night, but so far, nothing was turning up.

Nerves were wearing thin; the Pharisees were blaming the scribes, for whom most of the spies labored, the scribes were blaming both the Pharisees and the Sadducees, and the Sadducees, who held the majority in the ruling Sanhedrin, obviously blamed everyone else. As their voices rose in anger, Annas sat quietly, observing the pandemonium without participating. Suddenly, Caiaphas had had enough.

"Does my esteemed father-in-law have nothing to add

to our discussion?" he bellowed, perhaps too loudly. His face was hot and red, and his tassels were dancing for all of their might. The noise level suddenly evaporated, and all eyes turned toward Annas in the vacuum that followed.

"Well?"

"I do; I have a question for Manaseh, your eminence."

The old man, who had nearly fallen asleep near the end of the long table, suddenly perked up with the mention of his name. The rest of those gathered looked at each other and groaned: they would be here for hours now, forced to listen to his prattling and worthless gossip.

Caiaphas' face went from red to purple. He gritted his teeth, snorted against his will, and finally blurted out through his clenched jaw, "Father Manaseh – if you would be so good as to come here to answer a question – and none of your foolishness, mind you; I will not tolerate it this morning."

He sprang from his seat with surprising agility, hungry for the attention in spite of the clear disdain exhibited all around him. He stopped in front of Annas, bowing low, and said, "I, your humble servant..."

"Yes, yes, yes, get on with it," interrupted the high priest.

The old man clamped his mouth shut, and looked up at Annas with bright eyes, in a peculiar, canine pose. Those gathered around him snickered, expecting to see his tail wag.

"Did he have a name?" Annas asked.

Manaseh turned his head in thought, still locked in his unusual posture, and then turned back and replied "I'm sure he did, my lord; but to which gentleman do you refer?"

This gem of wit broke the tension in the room, and the old man looked around with a huge smile on his face, nodding vigorously at his peers while they laughed heartily at the absurd turn of events. Annas, however, wasn't amused. When quiet returned, and the old man turned once again to face his questioner, his smile disappeared.

"I seem to remember a story told by you to this very body, not a week ago, about discord within the rabbi's followers; yet I do not recall any *names*. Did the disciple who objected to the wasted ointment have a name?"

"Ah, yes – the ointment. Let me see...he was a man from Kerioth, as I recall..."

"Iscariot? Judas Iscariot?" called someone from down the table.

"Yes! That's it exactly – Judas was his name," cried Manaseh with great excitement at the unexpected validation.

"What do you know of this?" rumbled the high priest, and all eyes instantly diverted down the table.

"Why, this is remarkable your eminence. I have spoken with this very individual on several occasions. We were introduced by one of the temple money-changers about a year ago, and since that time he has sought me out at least twice seeking money for a variety of items he had...acquired along the way."

"Is he a follower of this Galilean?" demanded Annas.

"I believe he is, yes. In fact, I spoke with him just yesterday morning... he was hinting around about money again..." his voice trailed off as he tried to remember the conversation.

"And?" prompted Caiaphas, obviously running out of patience.

"And I am not sure. The meeting was very brief, and he was very nervous. He was clearly worried about being spotted with a Pharisee, and he disappeared before he could finish explaining his proposition."

"Let me make sure that I understand you," Annas said, speaking very deliberately. "A known follower of the Galilean, a man who has been observed in disagreement with the Galilean, a man who is known to love money, approaches you with a proposition, and yet you cannot tell us the nature of that proposition."

"Your eminence, I..."

"I suggest that you find this man, and that you find him today; make every effort to resume your discussion with him, and may I suggest that you make a proposition to him yourself? I suggest that you offer him money - a lot of money; that you tell him to name his price. We need a single piece of information: a location where we can find his rabbi away form the crowd."

"But your eminence, I do not know..."

"Today, my friend; tell him that we mean him no harm, tell him that we wish only to talk to him, tell him whatever it takes, whatever he wants to hear, but talk to him today, without fail. Time is running out."

"Yes, your eminence."

"The plan has been put in motion, your majesty."

"Follow the human. Make sure there is no interference; make sure that the meeting occurs."

"Yes, your majesty."

Peter watched Jesus closely as they made their way once more through the Eastern Gate into the city. The Rabbi had been out by himself in the olive grove very late the previous night, and when he had finally returned to the makeshift campsite, he had been drenched in sweat and breathing with difficulty. Peter had been trying to stay awake, watching for Jesus, so when the Master stumbled into the little clearing, he had wakened instantly. Alarmed at his condition and assuming that Jesus had encountered a wild animal, Peter had raced to his aid.

"Master, what happed? Are you hurt?" he had asked, but there had been no reply. As he gripped him against his shoulder, Jesus had slumped into his embrace, panting, trying to catch his breath. Peter sat him gently down in a bed he had made of leaves and grass hours previously, and then had sat down beside him, at a loss as to how to help him. They had no water, no food. But within a few minutes, his breathing had returned to normal, he had relaxed and the Master was asleep.

Peter didn't sleep the rest of the night, and he was still concerned for Jesus as the disciples had begun to rise just after daybreak; so as soon as they could get ready, he had sent Judas and Andrew ahead into the city to round up something to eat. Peter, Jesus and the rest of the disciples had followed a little later, and they had met at an appointed spot to sit down together for breakfast. Jesus had been hungry, and had demonstrated a healthy appetite, which relieved Peter - at least a little bit.

Now, in the warm morning sunlight, nothing appeared to be wrong. Jesus was focused, warm and in complete control.

Had he imagined the whole episode?

No, he could still feel the weight of the Master's body slumped over his arm, his feet dragging against his leg; he could still feel him shivering uncontrollably; he could still smell his sweat. Peter had never seen Jesus like this before, and though he would never admit it to anyone, it frightened him to his very core. Something was wrong, desperately wrong, and whatever it was, it seemed to be looming over their heads, racing toward them like a violent summer storm.

"Master, there are some Greek men here who wish to speak with you," Andrew whispered into the Rabbi's ear. He had been teaching all morning, it was getting hot, and the crowd was growing lethargic. Philip had come to Andrew with the request, and Andrew thought that perhaps Jesus could use a break. After all, it was just after noon, and there had been no break all morning. But Jesus didn't seem to hear him. Instead of turning aside with Andrew to see the Greeks, Jesus stood up and called out to the crowd with a louder voice and outstretched arms:

"The hour has come for the Son of man to be glorified. Truly, truly I say to you, unless a grain of wheat falls into the earth and dies, it remains alone; but if it dies, it bears much fruit."

Peter leaned over to Andrew and asked him what he had whispered to Jesus. Andrew only shook his head in response, with a perplexed look furrowing his brow.

"Again with the images of death; why do you think he speaks so much about it, Peter?"

Now it was Peter's turn to shrug. But the hair on the

back of his neck began to creep up as Jesus continued: "Now is my soul troubled."

Peter suddenly had a flashing image of a troubled Jesus the night before.

"And what shall I say?" Jesus continued, "'Father, save me from this hour'? No, for this purpose I have come to this hour."

The two brothers looked at each other with alarm, and then looked around at the sleepy crowd, many of them unable to track with what he was saying.

What was he saying?

Jesus lowered his arms, bowed his head and said "Father, glorify thy name."

And then the crowd was suddenly awake.

Turmoil spread around the courtyard in spasms and waves, in response to an unbelievably loud, thunderous noise. Some, indeed, thought that they had heard thunder, but the sky was absolutely cloudless, a clear brilliant blue; others insisted that they had heard or had seen an angel standing on the roof of the temple; but Peter recognized it - for he had heard it twice before – the voice of the God of Israel himself.

And like both of those previous unforgettable moments – the first time at the river Jordan when John had baptized the Rabbi, and the second on the mountain when Jesus had spoken with Moses and Elijah, the very air itself shook in response to the voice.

Jesus raised his hands to calm the panic-stricken crowd, and called out again:

"This voice has come for your sake, not for mine. Now is the judgment of this world, now shall the ruler of this world be cast out; and I, when I am lifted up from the earth, will draw all men to myself."

Few, if any of the crowd heard these words, for while he was speaking a sharp, biting wind stirred the courtyard once, consuming all sound and taking every breath, and then it was gone.

The crowd began to shout questions at him, no longer the drowsy lot they had been but a few moments ago. There was now a subtle edge to their voices, not exactly angry or cross, but no longer entirely sympathetic, either. In the space of less than a quarter of an hour, something had shifted, and Jesus was the only human present who recognized the change.

"The light is with you for a little longer. Walk while you have the light, lest the darkness overtake you; he who walks in the darkness does not know where he goes. While you have the light, believe in the light, that you may become sons of light."

Having said this, Jesus departed from the temple and withdrew from the crowd. Time was running out; he had come among his people looking for fruit and had found none; having known beforehand that he would find none did not make the fact any easier to bear – for he had always known it:

> 'The Lord looks down from heaven upon the children of men, to see if there are any that act wisely, that seek after God. They have all gone astray, they are all alike corrupt; there is none that does good, no, not one.'

Now, after three years of speaking every truth, after thousands of signs and miracles, after all of the teaching and struggling and wooing and correcting, time was running out and he was faced with a choice: he could condemn the world of fallen, faithless, selfish men, a condemnation that all of mankind, from beginning to end richly deserved; he could return to his father, resume his rightful place on the throne, and let them all go to hell.

Or, he could proceed with the unthinkable.

After the crowd was gone, with the sun still high in the hazy late afternoon sky, Jesus emerged from the shadows into the great, empty courtyard. He stood for a long while quietly facing the steps leading up to the inner court, and from there into the Holy of Holies. With him were his twelve disciples and some of the women and a handful of others; these all stood off at a distance except for Peter, James and John, who drew up a few steps behind him, keeping a silent vigil. To their left was the western wall of the temple, with its gate into the city;

behind them was the royal porch, the main entrance into the Court of the Gentiles, with its massive gold-clad gate and colonnades. As they watched in silence, warmed by the sunshine, James quietly pointed out the magnificent architecture of the temple to his friends.

Jesus looked at where James had pointed, at the massive high walls, the immaculate artistry and craftsmanship, the beauty and symmetry that defined the house of God. With a sad voice, he spoke softly, "You see all these, do you not? Truly I say to you, there will not be left here one stone upon another, that will not be thrown down." And taking one last sweeping look around, he finally diverted his misty eyes and walked away, leaving the temple through the eastern gate.

Outside the city, the disciples followed him stoically along the ridge toward the pathway leading to the Mount of Olives, a trail many of them had come to despise. However, this afternoon the Master continued on, past the gardens, and out onto the dusty road leading to Bethany. Looking at one another in astonishment, they quickened their pace to catch up with the Rabbi.

The chatter picked up immediately, and as the good humor spread, Peter, who was walking next to Jesus, noticed a little smile on the Master's face. Peter grinned himself, and as Jesus turned and saw the silly grin, his own little smile warmed into a joyful burst of laughter, at which Peter laughed with gusto and then all of them joined in; days of tension and hardship melted away, and Peter again realized that there was no place on earth he would rather be than walking right here, right now beside the man called Jesus, going wherever he was going.

"How about a nice big meal, my friend?" Jesus asked Peter, still smiling broadly.

"Well, that depends; do we need to bring the rest of these guys too?" Peter responded, and then roared with laughter at his own joke.

The laughter and upbeat small talk continued, and the few miles to Bethany seemed to go by in no time at all. And suddenly, as the sun was just touching the horizon behind them, they found themselves standing at the doorway to the home of Simon, a man whom Jesus had healed of leprosy a year ago. Simon emerged from the house along with a number of people, including many of the men and women who had traveled with the disciples for the last several months. Simon held his arms wide, and greeted Jesus with a kiss on his cheek and a warm embrace.

"Please, come in, come in. We have been expecting you all day. There is plenty to eat for everyone," and catching Peter's eye he winked and added, "even for the Sons of Thunder."

Simon led them through a spacious open air portico, where their feet were washed by an army of household servants, and then ushered them into a domestic area of the house where they could wash and refresh themselves more thoroughly. It had been many days since the disciples had had the luxury of bathing, and they were all grateful. When everyone was finally finished, it was quite dark outside, and a servant led them into a brightly lit, magnificent banquet hall, dominated by two rows of tables piled high with bread and fruit and vegetables and lamb. Their mouths watering with delight, the disciples spread out and sat down, while the servants surrounded them and began pouring wine in large goblets.

Simon, the perfect host, welcomed them with a traditional Jewish toast and invited them to enjoy the meal. The disciples all looked at the Master, who smiled, rose to his feet and spoke a blessing on the house, the host and the food. Plates began to clatter the instant he was finished; for a long time, this and the soft music, provided in the background by a young man playing a harp, were the only sounds to be heard in the room.

Finally, with his mouth filled with food, James leaned over to his younger brother and whispered "I think this must be what the Kingdom of Heaven will be like. The Master is always talking about banquets in the Kingdom; well, here we are, and it is fine with me."

John replied, "I agree, brother, this is wonderful," and here he glanced across the table to Judas, and continued "but I don't think everyone is as happy as you."

James swallowed his food, looked across at the sour expression on Judas' face, and then asked John "What do you suppose is eating him?"

John leaned forward until he caught Judas' eye and then asked "Are you well, friend? You don't seem to be enjoying the meal."

Judas grunted something unintelligible, the scowl still on his face, and turned away. As he did so, he pushed his plate away, nearly untouched. John looked at his brother, and they both shrugged, and both returned to eating the food which never seemed to run out.

Before long, James noticed a woman slowly approaching the head of the table. She was weeping, and carrying in her hand a sealed alabaster urn. He nudged John, who hadn't yet spotted the woman. John looked up, but still didn't spot her since she had come around behind them and was standing directly behind the Master. By now, all other noise had stopped, and her weeping could be clearly heard throughout the banquet hall. John twisted around to see what everyone was staring at as she stepped forward and raised the jar above the Rabbi's head; since he was the closest to her, he tensed and started to rise, but Jesus put a calm hand on his arm to stop him.

The fragrant oil poured down over his head like a stream, matting his hair to his head and his cloak to his chest, and filling the hall with a familiar, haunting perfume. Most of them recognized the smell at once – a smell associated with death, with embalming and burial. John felt a drop of the warm oil spatter on the back of his hand.

Judas had had enough, twice enough.

He jumped to his feet, knocking his plate and cup over, and shaking with rage he shouted across the table, pointing at Jesus:

"Has everyone gone mad? Why was this waste permitted?" he glared around the hall looking for an answer that did not come. "For this ointment might have been sold for a large sum, and given to the poor."

No one breathed while he stood there trembling,

waiting for a response, all of them stunned at this amazing repeat performance, all of them remembering the nearly identical moment just five days ago in the house of Lazarus when Mary had anointed the Master's feet with a similar ointment.

In a voice that was soft yet charged with emotion, Jesus replied:

"Why do you trouble this woman? For she has done a beautiful thing to me."

Judas whirled around, waving off the Master's response as he left the room.

Jesus continued, as the dumbstruck disciples watched Judas retreat down the corridor, "For you always have the poor with you, but you will not always have me. In pouring this ointment on my body she has done it to prepare me for burial. Truly, I say to you, wherever this gospel is preached in the whole world, what she has done will be told in memory of her."

And they heard the distant sound of a door slamming shut.

As he ran along the road back to Jerusalem, Judas was unaware of the hoard of demons accompanying him. All that he was aware of at that moment was rage, bitter rage that filled him completely yet stayed deep inside, refusing to rise to the surface. Alone with his thoughts once again, he rehearsed them over and over again in his mind as he raced along, coming to the same conclusion that he always did. He could reason out no different solution, no different course of action.

No one will understand.

His thoughts were his own, since he believed them, but they were not original.

Greed had long ago infested his heart, shaping his desires and ambitions, and with them his outlook and thought process; through a long season of self-delusion he had grown to see himself as a noble humanitarian charged with the task of righting social wrongs rather than as the common thief that he really was. To him, the rabbi from Galilee was a vehicle in which he could more rapidly advance his social agenda (and his pocketbook), and it was now becoming clear to him that the vehicle was slowing to a mere crawl. Jesus seemed to be reluctant to use his unusual powers to bring about justice or social change, using them instead as platforms for his endless, tiring speeches.

What a waste.

Out of breath, he stopped and found himself on a minor side street in lower Jerusalem, standing in front of a house with a lamp burning in the window. He looked up and down the dark street, but saw no one. In fact, he wasn't exactly sure where he was. He looked up at the house; he did not recognize it, but something within him stirred, and without knowing why he stepped forward to knock at the door. But as he raised his hand, he was startled by a voice behind him.

"Judas, is that you?"

He whirled around in horror, expecting to see one of his fellow disciples, but was instead confronted with a dark silhouette in flowing robes – clearly a Sadducee.

"Why, this is remarkable," continued the man as he emerged from the shadows, "I have been searching for you all day."

Recognition dawned on Judas: this was the very individual he had intended to seek out, the reason he had returned to Jerusalem.

"Simply remarkable; but there is no reason for us to stand out here in the darkness like this: come. Please join me for some light refreshment. We have so much to talk about. Here we are, right through here."

And the two of them entered the house, each assuming that they were alone.

After the best meal that any of them had eaten in months, there were only a few objections when Jesus led them back once more to the lonely Mount of Olives, and these were voiced only because Simon had offered them all a warm, dry bed in which to stay for the night. But none of them had really expected to stay; they were all aware by now that their lives had changed for good since entering Jerusalem with the Master, and sleeping in a different spot each night outside of the city was just a part of that life. Once the Master had chosen the new campsite for the night, they began to settle in quickly, for it was now very late. The unacknowledged and unspoken sub-groups that had silently developed over the past three years were the most evident at these moments, when the disciples spread out to relax. As always, Peter, James and John remained close to the Rabbi, while Philip and Nathaniel moved away a few paces and began recounting all of the events of the evening. Andrew, Peter's brother, was rather gregarious, and roamed from group to group. Thomas, as usual, settled in with Matthew and James (the son of Alphaeus), while Thaddaeus and Simon the Cananaean (the Zealot, some called him) moved away the farthest, again fitting the normal pattern.

Peter looked about, counted heads, and frowned.

But as he turned to make a comment to Jesus that Judas was still missing, he was preempted by James, who had settled in at the Master's feet:

"Rabbi, I have been thinking about what you said earlier today about the temple - about a time when it is to be destroyed. Tell us, when will this be, and what will be the sign of your coming and of the close of the age?"

Peter looked at John and said, "He got all of that out of one comment?"

John simply shook his head, watching Jesus for a response.

"Take heed," replied Jesus, looking off into the distance, "that no one leads you astray. For many will come in my name, saying 'I am the Christ,' and they will lead many astray."

The three disciples looked at one another.

What did this have to do with the destruction of the temple?

"Many false prophets will arise and lead many astray. And because wickedness is multiplied, most men's love will grow cold. But he who endures to the end will be saved. And this gospel of the kingdom will be preached throughout the whole world, as a testimony to all nations; and then the end will come. But before all this they will lay their hands on you..."

"They will do what?" exclaimed Peter.

"They will lay their hands on you and persecute you, delivering you up to the synagogues and prisons..."

"Now, wait a minute," Peter injected, "Why..."

"Peter, sit down and shut up," demanded an irritated James.

Peter crossed his arms in frustration, refusing to sit, but said with a more subdued voice, "I'm sorry Master; please continue."

Andrew approached the four of them, and seeing the serious looks on their faces quietly sat down and joined James and John on the ground.

"You will be brought before kings and governors for my name's sake."

Jesus paused and looked at the four of them while Peter finally sat down, and then he continued softly, "This will be a time for you to bear testimony. Settle it therefore in your minds, not to meditate beforehand how to answer; for I will give you a mouth and wisdom, which none of your adversaries will be able to contradict."

He was silent for a moment, and they sat listening to the chirping locusts all around them. Finally Peter asked, "But *who* will deliver us up?"

He looked Peter directly in the eyes and said, "You will be delivered up even by parents and brothers and kinsmen and...friends." He looked away and continued, "Some of you they will put to death. You will be hated by all for my name's sake. And many will fall away and betray one another."

Jesus stood, brushed the dust from his arm, and looked off into the darkness, toward the now invisible temple.

"But when you see Jerusalem surrounded by armies, then know that its desolation has come near. Then let those who are in Judea flee to the mountains, and let those who are inside the city depart, and let not those who are out in the country enter it; for these are days of vengeance, to fulfill all that is written."

He turned back with a sweeping gaze around the clearing, pausing to look at the weary, slumped disciples sleeping all around him. He sighed deeply.

"Jerusalem will be trodden down by the Gentiles, until the times of the Gentiles are fulfilled."

"What will happen to us after the temple is destroyed?" asked John.

"You will hear of wars and rumors of wars; see that you are not alarmed; for this must take place, but the end is not yet. For nation will rise against nation, and kingdom against kingdom, and there will be famines and earthquakes in various places. All this is but the beginning of the birth pangs."

By now, Philip and Nathaniel, roused from sleep by the discussion, had joined the little circle around Jesus. He went on to tell them about the coming of an evil one who would set up a "desolating sacrilege", as described by the prophet Daniel, in the Holy Place. This, of course, perplexed the disciples, since Jesus had just described the destruction of the temple, which housed the Holy Place. However, without explaining how this could be, he pressed on:

"For then there will be great tribulation, such as has not been from the beginning of the world until now, no, and never will be. And if those days had not been shortened, no human being would be saved; but for the sake of the elect those days will be shortened."

Jesus stood, and becoming more animate he stated, "Immediately after the tribulation of those days the sun will be darkened, and the moon will not give its light, and the stars will fall from heaven, and the powers of the heavens will be shaken," and then with a big voice and gesturing at the black sky, he declared, "Then will appear the sign of the Son of man in heaven, and then all of the tribes of the earth will mourn, and they will see the Son of man coming on the clouds of heaven with power and great glory," and as he finished all eleven disciples were now standing around him with wide eyes, the hair standing up on the back of their necks. "And he will send out his angels with a loud trumpet call, and they will gather his elect from the four winds, from one end of heaven to the other!"

The applause and cheering and noise that followed were clearly a victory celebration; the spontaneous jubilation erased for a few moments all of the aches and discomforts they had experienced through the course of the past four days, the longest four days of any of their lives. Jesus alone was aware that the victory was not yet won, and that it would come at a great personal price; but for the sake of his friends he fought off the dark, flashing images of impending doom and isolation, at least for the rest of the evening. He smiled, participated in the animated chatter, and answered a few more questions.

"Master, how will we know when the end is near?"

Jesus stepped over to one of the ancient olive trees, gnarled and barren, and broke off the end of a small branch. He held it up to his disciples, and said, "From the fig tree learn its lesson..."

The eleven roared with laughter at his apparent mistake, and someone cried, "That's not a fig, Lord, it's an olive!"

Jesus grinned with them, and snapping the dry branch in half, he proceeded:

"As soon as its branch becomes tender and puts forth its leaves..."

"Like the fig tree in full leaf we saw Monday on the road from Bethany!" someone else offered.

Jesus smiled again, nodding, and continued, "When it puts forth its leaves, you know that summer is near. So also, when you see all these things, you know that he is near, at the very gates. Truly, I say to you, this generation will not pass away till all these things take place."

The disciples had all forgotten about sleep, and Jesus, though fatigued beyond human endurance, was unwilling to give up these last few hours shared with his friends. They continued far into the night, sitting comfortably around a little fire someone had built, telling stories, laughing, dreaming about the kingdom to come. Jesus told them a few new parables, focusing on the end of the age and the coming judgment.

As the conversation eventually began to die out, as they

all sat there quietly reflecting, listening to the soft crackling of the fire, John, leaning close to Jesus asked "What will the day of judgment be like?"

As he responded, Jesus took on a distant look in his eyes, as if he were picturing something:

"When the Son of man comes in his glory, and all the angels with him, then he will sit on his glorious throne. Before him will be gathered all the nations, and he will separate them one from another as a shepherd separates the sheep from the goats, and he will place the sheep at his right hand, but the goats at the left."

At this, there was an immediate, though nearly imperceptible movement among the disciples toward his right hand side.

"Then the king will say to those at his right hand, 'Come, O blessed of my father, inherit the kingdom prepared for you from the foundation of the world; for I was hungry and you gave me food, I was thirsty and you gave me drink, I was a stranger and you welcomed me, I was naked and you clothed me, I was sick and you visited me, I was in prison and you came to me."

"How can this be, Lord? When were you ever in prison, or naked?" asked Thomas.

Gesturing to the circle of his disciples, Jesus said, "The King will answer them, 'Truly, I say to you, as you did it to one of the least of these my brethren, you did it to me."

The disciples looked at one another; though no words were exchanged, they all felt the tug of loyalty and kindness and service that each of them had received from the others over the three years of following the Master. Most of them had at one time or another been hungry or thirsty or sick, and the rest had sacrificed to offer food and drink and mercy.

"Then he will say to those at his left hand, 'Depart from me, you cursed, into the eternal fire prepared for the devil and his angels."

They all craned their necks to look at his left, but there was no longer anyone there.

"For I was hungry and you gave me no food, I was thirsty and you gave me no drink, I was a stranger and you did not welcome me, naked and you did not clothe me, sick and in prison and you did not visit me."

The night was far gone by now, dawn was nearly at hand, and the silence around the lopsided circle of disciples was deafening; even the locusts had given up for the night. Looking across the dying fire to the disciple on the far side at the end of the row, who had pulled back ever so slightly from the rest, Jesus finished, "And they will go away into eternal punishment."

"The meeting then concluded, with an agreement reached between the two as planned."

The report, delivered by an invisible spy familiar with the house and its occupants, was brief and to the point, and verified the commanding officer's report with little variation. Under standing protocol, a report of activity or battle delivered by a participating commander was always verified by non-participating spy. Over the millennia, it had become clear that lying and exaggerating could not be prevented in reports when lying and exaggeration was the normal way of life in the dominion of darkness. Truth was a very rare commodity, and was difficult to obtain, assuming that truth was even desired. So in most cases, since reports were expected to be fraudulent, they had to be cross-checked (sometimes repeatedly) if there was any hope to arrive at useful information.

In this particular case, the commander wasn't yet satisfied.

"Tell me their exact words."

"Yes, my Lord. The one in soft robes said, 'Tell me what it is that you want. I assure you that you and I are seeking the same end here; both of us want the rabbi to survive this crisis, both of us want him to step back to a more becoming, a more...fitting position. With all of his provocative and short-sighted speeches, we fear for his safety, you see. It has come to our attention that the Roman Governor has been personally offended, and seems bent on destroying your rabbi. If only we could speak with him privately...,' and then the disciple asked,

'I know where he will be staying tomorrow night. What will you give me if I deliver him to you?' And then the first one said, 'Name your price,' and then the disciple thought for a moment. 'Give me one hundred and twenty denarii,' he said. So the first one reached into his soft, beautiful robe, smiling, and said, 'What an amazing coincidence this is, for I have with me that very sum of money.' And with that, he counted out thirty new silver coins."

At these words, the unseen commander smiled.

Thursday Morning

After the fire had died, and after the last disciple had finally fallen asleep, Jesus spent the early morning hours alone once again in the midst of his beloved creation. This would be his last morning, his last daybreak to enjoy his handiwork before...he tried to put out of his mind the rest of the thought. As the days and now the hours ticked by, it was taking more and more effort to avoid dwelling on...again he had to divert his thoughts. So, he resumed his slow walk along the crest of the hill in the early morning hours on the first day of Passover, praying to his Father in heaven, and at the same time absorbing every detail he encountered. His feet were bare, so as he walked along, praying, he felt the cool comfort of the grass, heavy with morning dew beneath him with every step; the sensation was pleasant, reminding him of long ago childhood adventures on the hillsides above Nazareth. His breath caught as he felt a sudden, familiar emptiness; for memories of Nazareth always brought with them memories of Joseph, his mother's husband.

He had been a good man, a good mentor and father. With tears in his eyes and a wistful smile on his face, Jesus recalled once again the fond memories as he walked along, sensations and images of a happy, healthy childhood under the care and protection of a hard working, decent, godly man. He missed his earthly father; and now he was struggling with the prospect of...

The eastern sky above the brow of the hillside to his right was slowly brightening from deep crimson to a more pastel hue, and looking off to the west he could see sunlight reflecting off of a small flock of birds circling above the valley, looking for a place to rest. In the distance behind them he could just discern the misty outline of the temple, its golden walls reflecting the feeble early morning rays in a soft glow. All around him, the garden was coming to life now, with bird calls and small rustling sounds amidst the tangled brush and olive trees. He stopped beside a tree, plucked a soft bud, and slowly began to pull it gently apart, all the while praying and thinking. He knew what he would find at the center of course; he knew each layer and each subtle change in color and texture, as well as he knew his own hands. Sitting down on a low branch as thick as his leg, he leaned back, enjoying the soft breeze that had just picked up, stirring the hillside ever so gently. He took a deep breath, and smelled the pleasant aroma of a few early blossoms sprouting somewhere within the garden.

He would let his disciples, his dear friends sleep awhile longer this morning; after all it was the last time...he called to his rescue more memories, this time about his cousin, John. Of the two occasions on which they had met face to face, neither of them had been more than a few moments, a few words, and now no more than a few images to remember; but oh, what moments they were! Jesus had always understood and loved everyone he had ever met, but had never experienced that depth of understanding back from someone else as he had in those two brief, poignant moments, gazing deeply into those dark, warm eyes that gazed just as deeply back at him. Words had been spoken, but words had not been what had built the powerful, flashing memories; it had been an understood purpose they had shared, something no one else on earth had held in common with these two. Even in that first meeting, in the Temple in Jerusalem during Passover when they were both twelve years old, they had both known. John had come up with his family from the hill country southwest of Jerusalem, and Jesus had traveled with his family south from Nazareth. There had been no plan for the meeting between the two families, they had simply crossed paths on the last day of the festival, and the boys had been introduced by their mothers, and then left to stare at each other as Mary and Elizabeth spoke briefly, catching up on years of details. The second meeting, of course, was more meaningful, as Jesus stood waist-deep in the slow moving waters of the Jordan River, again looking into his cousin's eyes for just a moment. John's voice had been choked with emotion as he spoke his first words in eighteen years to the cousin he had spent all of that time preparing to reveal: "I need to be baptized by you, and do you come to me?" Jesus could still see the look of humility in his eyes, the look of understanding. And then the moment was gone, and now, so was his cousin. Deep loneliness swept over him once again as he considered...

Jesus stood, shook off the thoughts, and gazed around at the beautiful garden, accented by long, sharp shadows in the bright morning sunshine. He stretched, calling once again on his heavenly Father for strength and endurance for the day ahead, and in spite of everything that the day would hold, he cherished this moment, alone in the garden, for it was a perfect morning.

□□□□□□

The high priest was in rare form. News of the meeting with Judas had spread around the circles of power like a wildfire, and just like that, weeks of chaos and miscalculations and hand-wringing had come to an end. Instead, concrete plans and action could now be taken for the first time with confidence. But speed was essential, since the Passover was to begin that very evening, and tomorrow evening would begin the Sabbath of Passover, a holy day that could not be violated under any circumstance by the troublemaker from Galilee.

A little over twenty-four hours.

Caiaphas shouted for his servant a second time; he was growing impatient, for there were many things that needed to be arranged, and the morning was beginning to slip by. He had performed his toilet, had eaten a quick breakfast, and now it was time to be dressing for his long list of meetings that had been hastily scheduled for the day.

Where was that lazy slave?

"Will someone tell me why I am being ignored in my own home?" he roared at the top of his voice, rattling the plates and utensils lying nearby on the breakfast tray. There was a sudden sound of scurrying in the corridor, and then three or four servants raced into the room with alarmed looks on their faces, questioning what was wrong.

One of the older servants took charge, gathering up the breakfast tray, and called for one of the young men to see to the robes for the high priest, while a third made up the bed and removed the wash basin. The young man hesitated, not sure what he had been asked to do; the older servant huffed at him, slapped him on the back of his head, and sent him out with the tray.

"Will you be in public today, your Highness?"

"Yes, yes, yes – the formal ones. Where is that scoundrel...what's his name?"

"I am sorry, your Excellency, I do not know. Here we are; now please raise your arms – that's it."

By the time the final touches – the jeweled breastplate and headpiece - were at last in place, Caiaphas stormed out of the house, a little more rumpled looking than normal, muttering about his vagrant personal servant as he went. Stepping out into the street, bright sunlight blinded him for a moment, but soon he was smiling, for it was a perfect morning.

☐☐☐☐☐☐

Pontius Pilate, the Roman governor, was agitated, and for a good reason. He had been in Judea now for four years, and he still had no clue as to how he was to control this wild, barbaric people who insisted on serving only one god. From the very beginning of his rule in Judea as procurator for the Emperor, Pilate had run afoul of the Jews, and at every subsequent decision he made, it seemed that friction and resistance only increased. Appeasement did not work; raw display of power did not work. No matter how much he compromised with the religious leaders on the one hand or how many young Jewish men were crucified on the other, nothing seemed to work in this hot, dry backwater of the Roman Empire. And now, on the eve of the hardest week of the year when the city swelled beyond capacity with filthy peasants from all over the world, there were unmistakable signs of unrest and danger, incited by a strange teacher.

Pilate didn't understand the differences between this

man and the religious hierarchy in Jerusalem, but he had heard about the skirmishes, and he was concerned; he was concerned enough, in fact, to move his headquarters, at least for Passover week, from his palace in Caesarea to Jerusalem. Historically, he had stayed far away from the troublesome city during this particular week, but something in the back of his mind told him that real trouble was brewing, and he needed to be here personally. He stationed his own elite soldiers from Caesarea side by side with members from the Jerusalem cohort, placing them conspicuously around the city in an attempt to show his determination to prevent any sort of trouble or uprising. So far, it seemed to be working.

As he leaned over the handrail on his balcony in the Fortress Antonia, basking in the morning sunlight and surveying the crowded streets and temple courtyard, an aide brought him a sealed message.

"Who sent it?" he asked the aide.

"It is from the Jewish high priest, your Excellency."

Pilate broke the seal, unrolled the scroll, and tried to read the message, squinting in the bright sunlight. He stood up, and stepping back into the cool shadows, read the short message requesting a meeting with him at his earliest convenience, on a matter of great urgency.

"What do they want from me?" he said a little too loudly in frustration. "First they send word to Rome that they want a new governor. Then they want no governor at all. Then they want a strong military presence; then they insist that I remove all imperial symbols from the city. There is just no pleasing these Jews. Tell Caiaphas that I have no time for him today."

"Yes, your Excellency," and with an arched eyebrow, the aide gave a curt bow, backing slowly toward the doorway.

"No, wait. Perhaps I should see him. Send word for him to be here in an hour."

"As you wish, your Excellency."

Pilate returned to the balcony overlooking the city; from here he could not only see the bustling streets below, but at this height in the fortress, he could see over the city wall to the east. As he looked in that direction, shielding his eyes against the bright morning sunlight, a lone hawk circling above the Kidron Valley caught his attention. He watched intently for a few moments as the bird caught an updraft and began climbing, his wings spread wide and majestic.

Oh, to have the freedom to soar away like that great bird.

He took a deep breath; the air was fresh and invigorating, and the sky was a clear, deep blue, with just a few puffs here and there of soft white clouds.

What a morning.

He sighed, returned his gaze to the streets below, and saw his aide pushing his way through the crowd with a military escort. He shook his head and stepped back into the shadows of his fortress, back to his confusing responsibilities.

"The High Priest is on his way, my lord."

"Are there any signs of the enemy?"

"None, my lord; none in the entire region."

"Good; see to it that the governor is frightened. He will be crucial to us."

"As you wish, my lord. And what shall we do with the king?"

"Ah, yes, the king; is he in the city yet?"

"He arrived only this morning. He is resting in his palace as we speak."

"Keep him close by and entertained – he will be crucial as well."

"Yes, my lord."

Herod the Great, they called him. What was so great about him?

Herod Antipas' thoughts often turned to his long-dead father when he was in a foul mood, and this morning he was in a particularly foul mood. He had been summoned to Jerusalem by the Roman governor, with no explanation, and to make matters worse, he had no idea when he would find out why. So here he sat waiting in one of the largest and most fabulous homes in Jerusalem, amidst the greatest luxury and opulence money could buy, but feeling no better than a prisoner.

If he had only made me king as he had promised, I couldn't be summoned by a Roman...

"My dear king, why do you sit there and pout so? Come enjoy some wine with me; it is wonderful - imported from Rome, you know," his wife cooed.

"I am not pouting, and I am not interested in your imported *Roman* wine. I have had quite enough of Rome."

"Oh, my dear king, don't say such things; at least don't say them out loud. You can never tell who is listening."

Herod stood up and began pacing across the deep Persian rugs.

"Why did he bring us here? Can you tell me that? And will you quit mocking me that way? There is no need for it here while we are alone."

"But my darling king, whatever do you mean?"

"You know very well what I mean: the title is Tetrarch - I am no more king than that buffoon Archelaus was, or Philip, your foolish..."

"Don't say it; you swore to me you would never say..."

"Very well then, we understand each other."

He sat back down in a soft pile of colorful pillows, with his back to his wife, stiff and brooding. For a moment, she stood looking at his back, trying to decide what tack she should take. He had always been difficult to understand or predict, as long as she had known him. But just within the last year or so, he had become much more sullen and moody, and she was finding it more difficult as the weeks went by to pull him out of it. When they had both been younger, when they had first been introduced, he had captured her attention with his good looks and wit; now, sadly, both were a thing of the past. These days they never talked, they never spent time together, they never...all that she had left was her title and her image.

"Herod the Great: now there is title that makes no sense. They hated the man, you know; everyone hated him –

the Greeks, the Romans, and especially the Jews. Herod the Hated would have been a better name for the outrageous scoundrel," groused Herod, resuming his pacing, clearly warming up for another nasty lecture.

Here we go again, thought his wife.

"He sat on the throne too long – it's that simple. By the time he finally got around to signing that ridiculous will of his dividing up the kingdom, he was a doddering old fool. Had he stepped down a little earlier, while he still had use of his limited mind, Jerusalem would be mine now, not in the hands of a Roman *governor.*"

In a panic that someone would hear his treacherous words, his wife tried to change the subject, blurting out the first thing that crossed her mind, "Did you know that the Galilean rabbi is here?"

Herod whirled around in obvious terror, glaring at her and screaming, "Are you mad? Why do speak of this man again? I tell you, he is the Baptist come back to haunt me, and now he has followed me here to Jerusalem!"

Now in a full retreat, she gushed, "No, no, my king, he is not the Baptist, and he has not followed you. I am sorry; I shouldn't have disturbed you so. Here; let me make it up to you."

She clapped her hands, and from the shadows emerged a dozen swirling, seductive young women, dancing to a rhythm suddenly originating from the next room. Herod's snarling face softened a little. As the young women danced their way closer, he eased back into his perch on the pillows, staring at one of the dancers without blinking, quickly becoming mesmerized. The wife of the king steeled herself, took a deep breath, and then slipped down next to him on the pillows.

"Here, my king. Take a drink; it will calm your nerves."

Without looking at the offered goblet, he pushed it away roughly, so that it spilled on his wife. Gasping in horror, Herodius jumped to her feet, drenched in wine. She stood there dripping, trembling with rage, waiting for him to notice what he had done, but instead he craned his neck in irritation, trying to see the dancers behind her. Herod Antipas, Tetrarch of Galilee was entirely oblivious to his infamous wife as she turned and stalked from the room, humiliated once again.

It was nearly mid-day by the time that the exhausted heap of disciples finally came to life, no longer able to sleep due to the warm sun high overhead. There was a meager breakfast of dried fruit and wine available, compliments of James and John, the Sons of Thunder, who had both risen a little earlier and gone into the city to scrape up what they could. As they were quietly eating, Jesus pulled Peter aside.

"Go into the city and prepare the Passover for us, that we may eat it."

Peter scratched the back of his head, and looked around at the poor, tired lot. A good long meal together in a nice room somewhere sounded enticing; it might just be what they all needed to get them to snap out of the lethargy that seemed to be setting in.

"We'll need some money - I'll check with Judas about that. Where will you have us prepare it?" he asked.

Jesus smiled a quick little smile.

"I know that look," said Peter, sporting a full grin, "I'm going to like this, aren't I? And I'll bet I won't even need any money, will I?"

Jesus put his arm around Peter's shoulder in a warm hug, and gesturing with his other hand, said, "Behold, when you have entered the city, a man carrying a jar of water will meet you; follow him into the house which he enters, and tell the householder, 'The Teacher says to you, Where is the guest room, where I am to eat the Passover with my disciples?' And he will show you a large upper room furnished; there make ready."

Peter chuckled at the prospect, his mouth already watering. "Furnished? As in food and wine enough for this crowd? Consider it done," he said with genuine enthusiasm.

"And Peter..."

"Yes, Rabbi?"

"You had better take John with you. There may be too much food for you to handle alone," he said, still smiling.

"Yes, Rabbi!"

The Fortress Antonia, also known as the Praetorium, had originally been a small fortification built by the returning exiles with Ezra known as the Baris, which had fallen in disrepair over the many decades of warfare and occupation that followed the rebuilding of Jerusalem. When Herod the First was named king of Judea by Octavius Caesar and took his throne in Jerusalem, one of the first things he did was to rebuild the fortress, making it much larger, and he then renamed it in honor of Mark Anthony, who was responsible for securing his appointment as king. From this place he ruled a very difficult domain for nearly forty years before his death. But before he died, he dictated the notorious will, dividing the kingdom between three of his sons. In the aftermath, a bitter dispute arose between two of them, Archelaus and Antipas over who should rule Jerusalem; the argument was eventually taken to Rome, and in the end Octavius, by now declared Emperor Augustus, intervened and Archelaus was banished from the empire, Antipas was left with only Galilee, and the emperor sent his own procurator to rule Judea instead. Now, twenty years later, Pontius Pilate, the fifth Roman procurator, ruled from Herod's sturdy fortress, exercising his broad powers on behalf of the emperor.

However, this morning Pilate was compelled to step outside of the compound, away from the Roman occupied garrison, for his meeting was with the Jewish high priest, and Jews were forbidden by their religious rules to enter the military fortress. Pilate was irritated by this demeaning requirement, and would have refused the meeting had it not been for the uneasy feeling nibbling at the back of his mind that something dangerous was afoot.

Might as well get it over with.

Pilate picked up his breastplate, and his aide helped him strap it on. Whenever he left the fortress, he was supposed to wear his full armor, including his helmet, but he rarely did, and his aide had long since learned to quit fretting over the lack of protection. With no more ceremony, he left the room, descended the steps to the main corridor where he was joined by his personal guards, and strode toward the heavily protected fortress entrance. He could have chosen a less visible location to meet, but had decided that if he had to meet outside, he should at least make the priests squirm a bit.

Stepping outside into the dazzling sunlight, it took a moment for his eyes to adjust. When he spotted the stiff knot of religious leaders off to his left, he had to suppress a smile. Since there was nowhere to sit outside the fortress entrance, for obvious security reasons, the priests had been forced to stand for nearly an hour waiting for him. Surrounded by his guards, Pilate approached them, and spoke first.

"To what do I owe this great privilege, my dear Caiaphas, to see you again so soon?"

Caiaphas was obviously offended for having to wait so long, but could not afford to express his frustration. "The privilege is all mine, your Excellency. I am grateful that you took the time to meet with your humble servants on so short a notice."

"Yes, yes, yes, we are both glad to see each other; now may we dispense with the pleasantries? What is this urgent business that we must discuss?"

By now a crowd of curious onlookers was forming. They all knew better than to crowd around, or even to show obvious interest, but there they were, slowing down as they passed by, or milling about the broad plaza trying to look busy, glancing furtively at the highly irregular sight of the Roman governor speaking with the Jewish high priest.

"Your Excellency, I am sure that you are aware of the presence here in the city of a certain man who has been roaming the countryside…"

"You speak of the teacher who has been filling the temple with huge crowds," Pilate interrupted.

"Yes, your Excellency - the so called 'rabbi' is a dangerous man, as I am sure you are aware, and we fear that he is plotting some sort of trouble during the Passover."

"Trouble? What sort of trouble?"

"We do not know for certain what his plans involve, but

we have information that indicates to us a threat to the peace and security of this very city," Caiaphas said, leaning closer to emphasize the importance of his words.

"Come, come, I have no time for silly rumors. If you have no more specific..."

Another priest stepped forward and said, "My lord, if I may speak?"

"My dear Annas; it is a pleasure to see you again – please, speak," replied the governor.

"My lord, we beg your pardon for this intrusion into your busy schedule. We would have put it off had it not been so urgent, but as the threat involves you, your Excellency..."

Pilate was suddenly alert. "A threat to me? Speak up man; I am in no mood for mysteries."

"Of course, my lord: it has come to our attention that the rabbi of whom we speak has been in secret contact with the tetrarch of Galilee, on several occasions."

"What's this? What has that old fox Herod to do with a street preacher?"

Seeing the exact reaction that he had wanted, Annas continued, "Our question exactly. As you may be aware, King Herod has long been fascinated with popular rabble rousers, meeting frequently in secret with any number of them. He appears to be looking for something, or for someone."

"And?"

"And we have come to the conclusion that he believes he has found what he has been looking for."

"And what, pray tell, has he been looking for?"

Annas paused. They had arrived at the delicate point in his scheme, and he didn't want to overplay it.

"Is my lord aware that King Herod is here in the city as we speak?" he asked with a subtle insinuation.

"It is the Passover. Why is this remarkable?" Pilate responded, with a growing edge of alarm in his voice.

"The king has made it clear on several occasions that he has, shall we say politely, no love for my lord the procurator, or for that matter the imperial throne that he represents. And now he has come to the city suddenly, at the very moment when a popular rabbi, who likewise speaks against Rome, is here."

"What is it that you are implying, Annas?"

"I do not wish to imply anything, my lord. May I ask if the king has informed you of his presence, as I am sure he must normally do?"

"I was not aware that he was in the city until you informed me a moment ago."

"Just as I suspected, my lord," replied Annas. "Let me speak plainly with you about our grave concern: we have come to the conclusion that the king wishes to incite a revolt against my lord, using this street preacher as a tool; if it is successful, he would be on hand to claim rule over Jerusalem as the king of the Jews, a prize that he has long desired. If the revolt fails, as it most certainly will, there is no evidence of his involvement, and he would lose nothing."

"This is madness!" Pilate bellowed, red-faced.

"Madness, unfortunately, is often the reality in Judea, my lord. This would not be the first revolt that a procurator in Jerusalem has faced. We do have a possible solution, however."

"I am listening."

"We have attempted to detain this rabbi on several occasions, using our own temple guards, but have been prevented by the mob that surrounds him, fearing that a public confrontation may incite the very riot we wish to avoid. Yesterday, however, a disciple of the rabbi came to us secretly, willing to cooperate with us in bringing him in for questioning. We now know where he is hiding at night, away from the crowds."

"What do you want me to do?" asked a fully convinced Pilate.

"If you please, provide us with a squad of soldiers to accompany us to collect the rabbi this evening from his place of hiding. We will question him about these affairs, and if need be, we will then send him to you."

Pilate considered for a moment the highly unusual request of putting Roman soldiers at the disposal of local religious leaders. In effect, he would be arming them, in direct violation of Roman law; not even the temple guards were allowed to carry weapons. But under the circumstances, he saw no other option. A tremendous fear had gripped him as Annas had spoken, and he could not shake the feeling.

"Very well then; you will have your soldiers. But mind you, they will be under strict orders to kill anyone who interferes with them, anyone," he concluded, with particular emphasis on that last word as he looked Annas directly in the eyes.

At this point Caiaphas tried to reassert his position, saying, "You have been most gracious, your Excellency, and we are confident that this matter can be resolved in a quiet, timely..." But the governor had already turned to go, and was no longer listening.

"Come, Caiaphas," said Annas in a conciliatory tone, turning to go as well. "We have much to do to prepare for our guest."

Also turning to go was the invisible commander, emerging from the meeting with his massive legion of filthy spirits who had pulled all of the right strings to orchestrate the meeting. Everything had gone according to plan, everything was falling into place remarkably well. It was now time to begin phase two. Scanning the horizon to look for any indication of the presence of the enemy one more time, and seeing the same blank, empty, unprotected view that he had seen now for many days, he nodded to a messenger, sending him on his way with a simple message: "It's a go."

Thursday night, first watch

Peter and John had followed Jesus' instructions, and had found the upstairs room just as he described, furnished with everything they needed to prepare the Passover meal, from tables and oil lamps and tableware and goblets, to wine, bread, herbs and spices, vegetables and fruit, and meats, including a beautiful young lamb. Mary and several of the other women had found the place as well, and had filled the room with a wonderful aroma as they cooked and baked and boiled enough food to feed the disciples for several days. As the afternoon wore on, and the sun drooped low over the western wall of the city, everything was finally ready, and the women said their goodbyes and left for the night. Exhausted and happy, Peter and John sat down against the far wall away from the doorway to wait for the rest to arrive. From this vantage point, they could watch the narrow street below through a low window, looking down over the first floor roof.

After a few quiet moments, John asked, "Do you ever wonder how life would have been without the Master?"

Peter looked over at him, and replied, "What do you mean?"

"Well, just look at where we are. If we hadn't followed Jesus, what would we be doing right now? Three years ago when we left the boats, I never would have dreamed I would be sitting here, in Jerusalem, waiting to celebrate the Passover with...with...Peter, is he really the Christ?"

"Of course he is the Christ. After all we have seen and experienced, how can you even ask that question?"

John sat up straighter, and continued, "I know, I know, you are right; but sometimes I just wonder...why us, Peter? Out of all of the men in Israel, why did he choose us? What does he see in me? I have never been anywhere or done anything; I'm a nobody - just a poor, young Galilean-fisherman-nobody. If Jesus hadn't come along, we would be out there on the lake right now, pulling on our nets; we're just fishermen."

Peter could think of no response, so he just sat there.

"Do you understand what I mean, Peter? I feel...unworthy."

Peter scratched his ear and furrowed his brow, an old habit he displayed unconsciously when he was perplexed; when it was obvious that John was going to wait him out for an answer, he finally said, "Well, yes, I think I understand; I don't feel any more worthy than you do. But what is so bad about being a fisherman?"

Realizing that Peter didn't understand him, John backed off, and said simply, "Nothing is wrong with being a fisherman."

They sat quietly for another few moments, and then John tried again.

"Do you remember what he said to us that first day by the lake, when we had been fishing all night?"

"When he asked me to put the boat back out for a catch?" Peter responded with a frown.

"Yes, but later, after we brought all of the fish ashore."

Ah yes, the fish.

It had been the largest catch Peter had ever seen. The nets had been so full that they were snapping and ripping as the two men had tried to pull the enormous amount of squirming, lively fish aboard. He and Andrew had yelled across the water for their partners to bring help, and James and John had hastily brought the other boat alongside, and then with four men, they still struggled with the swollen nets. By the time they had finally loaded all of the fish aboard, both boats were filled well beyond capacity, sitting low in the water, in danger of swamping with the slightest wave. Even today, three years later, Peter could still feel the exhilaration and fear of that moment.

Peter tugged at his ear again, and then said slowly, "He said 'follow me.'"

"Right - but what did he say after that?"

Peter thought, he scratched first one ear and then the

other, and finally gave up, and looking down at his feet said, "I can't remember."

"He said, 'Follow me, *and I will make you fishers of men.*' Peter, I have thought about that statement nearly every night. I don't really know what he meant by it, but there is something about that phrase that...well, I guess I am trying to say that whatever it is to be a fisher of men, I want to be one. I don't think that I will ever go back to fishing again. Too much has happened, too much has changed. I have changed."

Again they sat silently, and after a moment, Peter said quietly, "I guess you are right; I haven't thought much about it with everything moving so fast, but I guess I have changed too. It is kind of hard thinking about going back to fishing after all that has happened, isn't it?"

"Nothing will ever be the same, Peter. Not since we followed Jesus."

By now, the sky was growing dark; the Passover was beginning.

His pulse quickening with anticipation, John rose and began moving around the room, trimming and lighting all of the lamps except for the one in the middle of the table. He walked around the room, checking once more on all of the details, and within a few minutes, they could hear voices and footsteps in the street below. Peter stood up to look out the window, and could just make out the Master in the deepening gloom, recognizing his gait more than his appearance. The two of them raced down the steps to greet their brethren.

The Passover meal had been celebrated year after year by every generation of Jews, without fail, since the day it had been instituted in the Law, as given to Moses. There had been years of corruption, when Israel had wandered from God, and there had been seasons when the Jews were in foreign captivity, away from the land of promise; but throughout them all, the Passover remained, one of the sacred cornerstones of the Hebrew faith. From earliest childhood, Jewish children have always participated in the celebration, making this meal the most memory-filled, most meaningful day of the year. Times changed, and customs changed, but the Passover meal was observed year after year, a holy, honored tradition woven deeply into the very fabric of what it meant to be a Jew.

Sitting on the floor around the low table, the disciples waited while Jesus made some sort of preparation of his own. Though they were all hungry and ready to begin, they were at the same time somber; the mood was subdued, perhaps because of the ceremonial Passover meal on the table in front of them, perhaps because the Master himself seemed to be more somber than usual. None of them, however, was ready to speak up to ask Jesus what he was doing or what he was waiting for. After a moment, however, Jesus looked up with a tired smile and turning his gaze deliberately around the table, looking directly into the eyes of each man he said, "I have earnestly desired to eat this Passover with you before I suffer; for I tell you I shall not eat it until it is fulfilled in the kingdom of God."

Jesus then leaned forward, and taking a candlestick, lighted the lone lamp on the table, saying, "Blessed are you, O Lord our God, King of the universe, who has sanctified us by your commandments and has commanded us to kindle the festival light."

Sitting back, he continued, "Blessed are you, O Lord our God, King of the universe, who has kept us in life, and has preserved us, and has enabled us to reach this season."

Taking the first of four cups of wine before him, the cup of Sanctification, Jesus raised it and offered the blessing, "Blessed are you, O Eternal, our God, King of the universe, Creator of the fruit of the vine."

The disciples replied, "Amen."

"Take this, and divide it among yourselves; for I tell you that from now on, I shall not drink of the fruit of the vine until the kingdom of God comes." He passed the cup to John, on his right, and each man took a drink from it and passed it on to his right.

When the cup returned to Jesus, John suddenly leaned back to his right, away from the Master, and whispered intently into the ear of Peter, "We forgot the washbasin!"

Peter replied, a little too loudly, "What?"

"The hand washing is next; we forgot the washbasin!"

But it was too late; while the two of them were whispering, Jesus had risen and produced a basin of his own. Kneeling down, he poured water in it from an urn, tied a towel around his waist, and then proceeded to kneel on the floor before each disciple, washing their feet in the basin and then drying them with the towel. The sight was so shocking, that none of them knew how to react at first. This was demeaning; their Master was performing a task usually reserved for the lowest slave in the household. It was not fitting this way...

But Jesus continued, quietly and gently washing and drying every foot, until he worked his way around the table from left to right and came at last to Peter and John. By now, the water was filthy, and so was the towel wrapped around the waist of Jesus. Peter couldn't do it; not because he was reluctant about the dirty water – he just couldn't bring himself to extend his foot and further humiliate his beloved Master.

"Lord, why do you wash my feet?" he asked with a touch of frustration in his voice.

"What I am doing you do not know now, but afterward you will understand."

Still refusing to extend his foot, Peter replied stubbornly, "You shall never wash my feet."

"If I do not wash you, you have no part in me."

Thoroughly confused and afraid he had made an enormous mistake, Peter blurted out, "Then, Lord, not my feet only, but also my hands and my head!"

"He who has bathed does not need to wash, except for his feet, but he is clean all over," and in a soothing tone, meant to reassure Peter, he added, "and you are clean, but..." here he looked across the table, "...not every one of you."

Jesus washed Peter's feet, and then John's, and then setting the basin aside and resuming his place at the table he said:

"Do you know what I have done to you? You call me teacher and Lord; and you are right, for so I am. If I then, your Lord and Teacher, have washed your feet, you also ought to wash one another's feet. For I have given you an example, that you also should do as I have done to you."

Jesus leaned forward and picked up the platter of bitter

greens, and dipping a piece in the saltwater, he resumed the ceremony, "Blessed are you, O Eternal, our God, King of the universe, Creator of the fruits of the earth."

The disciples said the amen, then all leaned forward, dipped a piece of bitter green in the saltwater, and ate it in silence, remembering the bitter bondage and tears of their forefathers as slaves in Egypt.

Jesus leaned forward again, picked up the container called the unity, which held three loaves of unleavened bread in three separate compartments, and removed the middle loaf. He raised the bread, blessed it, and then breaking with tradition, said, "This is my body which is given for you. Do this in remembrance of me." And breaking the loaf in half, he placed half of it back in the unity, according to custom, and passed the other half to his twelve stunned disciples to eat.

This is his body?

Eat it in memory of him?

The solemn meal continued with the eating of the bitter herbs, the drinking of the second cup of wine, and the sharing of the Paschal lamb. Though there was an abundance of food, no one seemed to have much of an appetite, and there was almost no conversation. As they ate without enthusiasm, the atmosphere continued to grow heavier, and John, sitting close by his side, noticed that Jesus was clearly struggling with something, his face and eyes red. In alarm, John leaned close to ask him what was troubling him, but before he could get the words out, Jesus said to them all, "Truly, truly, I say to you, one of you will betray me."

There was a flurry of shocked questions and accusations - a painful, confusing turmoil that gripped them all by the throats. In the midst of the chaotic din, Peter prompted John to ask Jesus whom he was speaking about. John leaned close, asked the question, and Jesus replied, "It is he to whom I shall give this morsel when I have dipped it."

Jesus dipped the piece of bread in the bitter sauce, and handed it across the table to Judas. Suddenly, the clamoring stopped. Judas, aware that every eye in the room was focused on him, took the morsel and ate it, asking smoothly, "Is it I, *master*?"

The atmosphere was suddenly crackling and pulsing with tension, and a deep sense of danger and foreboding drifted around the room like a fog, settling heavily on them all. Those near Judas leaned away from him, as if repulsed by some invisible force.

Without flinching, Jesus leaned forward, and looking Judas straight in the eye he recognized the presence of his ancient enemy; the moment had come, and once again they were face to face. He spoke clearly to Judas and to the one hiding inside of him, "You have said so. What you are going to do, do quickly."

Judas leapt to his feet, convulsing slightly, and with eyes wide and flashing and teeth clenched, he stormed out of the room into the black night, slamming the door behind him. And the oppressive heaviness was sucked out of the room behind him.

They all breathed a collective sigh of relief. The remaining disciples, who except for Peter and John were bewildered by the exchange, had now regained their appetites, and returned to the meal with gusto, chattering and relaxing as they ate. Before long, however, several of them began debating once again who would be the greatest in the coming kingdom. Though he had many things he wanted to say, and time was running out, Jesus took the time once again to patiently address this divisive issue:

"The kings of the gentiles exercise lordship over them; and those in authority over them are called benefactors. But not so with you; rather let the greatest among you become as the youngest, and the leader as one who serves.

"You are those who have continued with me in my trials; and I assign to you, as my father assigned to me, a kingdom, that you may eat and drink at my table in the kingdom, and sit on thrones judging the twelve tribes of Israel."

When everyone had eaten their fill, and the supper was finally through, Jesus raised the third cup, the cup of Redemption, and after blessing it said, "This cup, which is poured out for you is the new covenant in my blood. Drink of it, all of you."

The eleven disciples were again stunned by this departure from tradition.

A new covenant?

This is his blood?

The cup was passed around the table, and each of the eleven drank in silence.

In a voice thick with emotion, Jesus declared, "Now is the Son of man glorified, and in him God is glorified.

"Little children, yet a little while I am with you. You will seek me; and as I said to the Jews so now I say to you, 'Where I am going you cannot come.'"

Jesus was weeping.

"A new commandment I give to you," he said through the tears, "that you love one another; even as I have loved you..." he paused, fighting his emotions, "...that you also love one another. By this all men will know that you are my disciples, if you have love for one another."

Peter, also choked with emotion, tears streaming down his face, asked quietly, "Lord, where are you going?"

"Where I am going..." The vision he had been fighting for days flashed before him, blinding him momentarily, and taking his breath away. John, leaning on his right side, gripped his shoulder to steady him.

"Where I am going you cannot follow me now; but you shall follow afterward."

Peter wasn't going to let it go.

"Lord, why cannot I follow you now?"

"You will all fall away; for it is written, 'I will strike the shepherd, and the sheep will be scattered.' But after I am raised up, I will go before you to Galilee."

Peter was offended. "Even though they all fall away, I will not."

"Simon, Simon, behold, Satan demanded to have you, that he might sift you as wheat, but I have prayed for you that your faith may not fail; and when you have turned again, strengthen your brethren."

Rising to his feet in stubborn pride, Peter declared passionately, "Lord, I am ready to go with you to prison and to death. I will lay down my life for you!"

Jesus, shaking his head in pity, replied, "Will you lay down your life for me? Truly, truly, I say to you, the cock will not crow, till you have denied me three times."

They were all weeping now, openly.

Jesus took a deep breath and smiling softly through tears, he said:

"Let not your hearts be troubled; believe in God, believe also in me. In my Father's house are many rooms; if it were not so, would I have told you that I go to prepare a place for you? And when I go and prepare a place for you, I will come again and will take you to myself, that where I am you may be also. And you know the way where I am going."

Where was he going?

Peter's question still hung in the air, but no one was brave enough to raise it again; well, no one but Thomas, who was either brave or more stubborn even than Peter. He spoke up, asking, "Lord, we do not know where you are going; how can we know the way?"

The rest murmured agreement with this logical conclusion.

"I am the way, and the truth, and the life; no one comes to the Father but by me. If you had known me, you would have known my Father also; henceforth you know him and have seen him."

Philip said to him, "Lord, show us the Father and we shall be satisfied."

Jesus turned to look down the table at Philip and said, "Have I been with you so long, and yet you do not know me Philip? He who has seen me..." and turning to make sure the rest of the disciples were getting it, he repeated, "he who has seen me has seen the Father."

"I will not leave you desolate; I will come to you. Yet a little while and the world will see me no more, but you will see me; because I live, you will live also. In that day you will know that I am in my Father, and you in me, and I in you. He who has my commandments and keeps them, he it is who loves me; and he who loves me will be loved by my Father, and I will love him and manifest myself to him."

"This is my commandment, that you love one another,

as I have loved you. Greater love has no man than this, that a man lay down his life for his friends. You are my friends..." he said tenderly, "if you do what I command you. No longer do I call you servants, for the servant does not know what his master is doing; but I have called you friends.

"If the world hates you, know that it has hated me before it hated you. If you were of this world, the world would love its own; but because you are not of the world, but I chose you out of the world, therefore the world hates you. Remember the word I said to you, 'A servant is not greater than his master.' If they persecuted me, they will persecute you; if they kept my word, they will keep yours also. But all this they will do to you on my account, because they do not know him who sent me. If I had not come and spoken to them, they would not have sin; but now they have no excuse for their sin."

Jesus continued for a long time speaking words of comfort and instruction to his friends, spending the last of his free moments with them. He promised to them help and power, he promised to send a comforter in his place who would teach them everything that they would need to know in a hostile world, and he promised them something else:

"I have said all this to you to keep you from falling away. They will put you out of the synagogues; indeed, the hour is coming when whoever kills you will think he is offering service to God. And they will do this because they have not known the Father, nor me. But I have said these things to you, that when the hour comes you may remember that I told you of them.

"The hour is coming, indeed it has already come, when you will be scattered, every man to his home, and will leave me alone; yet I am not alone for the Father is with me. I have said this to you, that in me you may have peace. In the world you have tribulation; but be of good cheer, I have overcome the world."

Jesus then lifted his voice in a beautiful anthem of praise, and the disciples joined him. It was a sacred moment, and too brief; it was the last time these men would worship together with their Master. As the hymn died out, there were a few moments of silence.

"I will no longer talk much with you, for the ruler of this world is coming. He has no power over me; but I do as the Father has commanded me, so that the world may know that I love the Father. Rise, let us go hence."

Leaving the house, Jesus and his sad, weary band of followers walked along the darkening streets of Jerusalem together, headed once more for the Mount of Olives. As they trudged along, the heaviness and gloominess returned, thicker than the air around them, so that it seemed nearly impossible to breathe. Jerusalem was a dangerous place that night, filled like no other place on earth with every kind of foul and wicked demon, coming and going, clamoring and shrieking, preparing for the long night ahead, and stirring up whatever trouble they could find. Mercifully, the poor, tormented and harassed band of disciples were unaware of the thick clouds of spirits surrounding them on every side; Jesus alone was aware of their mounting presence. By this time there was very little traffic on the streets, and as they left the city, the great wooden doors swung shut for the night, closing them out.

He continued to talk as they made their way along the now familiar road, in order to help his friends keep their courage up; but his words were whisked away by the blustering, buffeting wind that had picked up, which filled the air with wild, unnerving noises. Leaving the road, and beginning the climb up the pathway into the olive grove, their progress slowed considerably, since there was no moonlight and among the dense trees it was very difficult to see where they were going. By the time they finally reached the summit, at a little garden called Gethsemane, they were exhausted and filled with dread. They huddled up close together against the biting wind as someone tried to start a fire, but after several failed attempts with the wind blasting the meager sparks away, the thought of a fire was abandoned, and they simply sat down in the thick, bleak darkness.

Jesus began praying, out loud, the wind whipping both his words and his cloak behind him like a banner.

"Father, the hour has come; glorify your Son that the Son may glorify you, since you have given him power over all flesh, to give eternal life to all whom you have given him. And this is eternal life, that they know you the only true God, and Jesus Christ whom you have sent. I glorified you on earth, having accomplished the work which you gave me to do..."

A tremendous gust of wind hammered the little band of frightened men. And Jesus continued to pray.

"I have manifested your name to the men you gave me out of the world; yours they were, and you gave them to me.

"I am praying for them; I am not praying for the world, but for those whom you have given me, for they are yours;

"Holy Father, keep them in your name, which you have given me, that they may be one, even as we are one. While I was with them, I kept them in your name, which you have given me; I have guarded them, and none of them is lost but the son of perdition, that the scriptures might be fulfilled.

"But now I am coming to you; and these things I speak in the world, that they may have my joy fulfilled in themselves. I have given them your word; and the world has hated them because they are not of the world, even as I am not of the world."

He continued on, praying for not only the disciples themselves, but for those who would come after them as the kingdom of God would blossom and grow upon his departure.

He finally stopped; and sensing the peace that had settled over them while he prayed, Jesus stood, turned, and said, "Sit here while I go yonder and pray."

Thursday night, second watch

Jesus motioned to Peter to follow him, and unable to speak, he simply looked at James and John with wide, pleading eyes, and walked haltingly away. The three of them followed closely; all three wanted to help him, but they were so frightened by his appearance that they had no idea at all what to do. He walked through the dark garden only a number of paces, then stopped and asked the three to wait for him there. Breathing rapidly, his voice came with difficulty:

"My soul is very sorrowful, even to death; remain here and watch with me."

And going a little farther, he collapsed, falling forward on his face, and cried out in agony, "My Father, if it is possible, let this cup pass from me."

He began to shiver uncontrollably, and curled up in a fetal position; his ears were filled with an unearthly howling and shrieking that had been building now for hours, and when his eyes were open, he saw churning clouds of hideous demons diving at him, snarling and cursing and trying to tear at his flesh. The air was thick and suffocating, and Jesus began to perspire.

"Nevertheless, not as I will, but as you will."

He closed his eyes tightly, but that didn't relieve the torment. The jarring, powerful images that had been flashing in his mind with mounting ferocity were now coming into sharp focus, and they left him limp and breathless, as if someone were pounding him mercilessly on his chest.

Even so, Jesus prayed.

Forcing his mind to ignore the invisible demonic tumult roiling on the outside, and to fight back the gruesome, sickening images and thoughts on the inside, he prayed long and hard for strength, for endurance, and for a different ending. The prospect of what he was facing was so unspeakable, so enormous, that it took all of his willpower to overcome the tremendous human urge to call it all off. The raging turmoil was so powerful that after a few moments blood began seeping from his pores and mixing with his perspiration, a product of furious blood pressure and nerves pushed beyond natural limits. He wrestled and fought and prayed until he had no more energy to do so.

Among the narrow streets of Jerusalem, the night was black, with no moon, and filled with strange sounds carried on a stale and clammy breeze. Standing outside the dark house fidgeting and nervous, waiting for the priest, Judas was terrified. Shifting continuously from one foot to the other, perspiring heavily, and snapping his gaze up and down the deserted street, his mind was overloaded and torn with conflicting thoughts: one moment he rehearsed the long string of grievances he had been harboring against the rabbi and his disciples, wounds and perceived insults he had suffered at their hands, building his case to justify what he was about to do; and then the next moment he panicked, wondering how he had come to this. Thus occupied, he was startled when the door behind him suddenly opened and a dark figure emerged.

"Ah, Judas my friend, right on time; shall we begin?" asked the hooded, ominous looking priest.

"I don't know...I was just thinking..."

"Come, come, my friend; I am sure that this is difficult for you, but we both know it must be done. One day soon you will look back and realize how great a service you have rendered to your people, at a very critical juncture. And when the historians record what happens these next few hours, you will certainly be portrayed as the hero you are, and the name of Judas will be immortalized. Come, we must be going."

Lighting a torch, he took the faltering Judas by the arm, and led him through the winding streets to a lonely back alley, the flame of the torch flickering in the gusty breeze and casting ugly, dancing shadows all about them as they went. After several long and disorienting moments of walking briskly through a series of close and oppressive alleyways, they suddenly stopped at a broken looking door, and the priest rapped twice. There was silence for a moment, and then the door flew open, and a number of seedy looking scoundrels were disgorged from the dark opening. They poured out like rats, about twenty of them in all, and Judas noted that among the dirty, smelly and clearly drunken individuals were a handful of robed Pharisees, stiff and weary, who had been obviously given the task of controlling, or at least restraining this filthy mob until this moment. A few more torches were lighted, and the mob came to life, howling and cursing with delight at the prospect of promised action, paid action. They were a gruesome lot, pushing and slapping and threatening one another, and threatening the priest if he tried to double-cross them. Assuring them that they would be richly rewarded for their services, he took Judas by the arm again, smiled, and proceeded toward the fortress.

□□□□□□

The eight disciples that had been left back at the camp were fast asleep, and in spite of the desperate situation facing them, James, John and Peter were fading as well. The heavy, sorrow filled words spoken by their Master at dinner, the demanding schedule they had been keeping up for so long, the black, black night, and now the frightening, wild appearance of Jesus in the garden all conspired together, and proved to be too much for the poor men. Overcome with fear and exhaustion, they had wilted into a slumped stupor.

So when Jesus returned, looking for the only support available to him, he found none. Stumbling in the dark over roots and low hanging branches to where they lay, he knelt down beside the prostrate bodies and gently shook the nearest one by the shoulder.

"Simon, are you asleep?" he whispered hoarsely.

There was no answer. One of them stirred, but no one responded. With a heavy sigh, he sat back awkwardly on his legs and shook his head, filled with sorrow and loneliness.

"Could you not watch one hour?" he quietly asked the sleeping trio.

John sat up, rubbing his face and struggling to wake from the deep haze to which they had all succumbed.

"Watch and pray that you may not enter into temptation," Jesus breathed, his strained voice barely above a whisper. "The spirit indeed is willing, but the flesh...is weak."

John faded again, slipping back into oblivion.

The crowd grew louder as they went, and unsurprisingly, it grew in size as well as they wound their way through the worst, most dismal part of the city, a route that would have appeared a little out of the way if anyone had been aware enough to notice. Eventually, with a crowd now numbering nearly one hundred (including several more Pharisees who had appeared from nowhere), they finally stopped outside a dimly lit entrance to the Fortress Antonia. The gate was closed, and the guards standing watch outside made no sign of surprise at the sudden appearance of an unruly mob in the middle of the night.

The priest stepped forward and spoke briefly with one of the soldiers, who in turn disappeared into the fortress. While he was gone, a few of the shabby, dirty men approached one of the other guards, and began taunting him. They were either too drunk or too stupid to realize it was unwise to provoke an armed Roman soldier, but before they were able to do anything they would regret, the first soldier returned, followed by an officer.

"Greetings, sir; we apologize for the late hour," said the priest, bowing slightly to the rugged, hard looking officer.

The officer waved the statement off, and said merely, "We have been expecting you." He motioned to a guard, who motioned through the doorway, and fueling the twisted glee of the crowd, several dozen armored soldiers emerged, armed with swords, bows, and spears.

"Do you think these are enough?" the priest queried with a little hesitance.

The officer rolled his eyes in disdain, and muttered, "It is enough."

"Perhaps we should provide some weapons for these..."

Cutting him off, the officer replied with a little heat, "Out of the question. Under no circumstances are these..." he paused and sneered in their direction, "*men* to be armed." As an afterthought, he added with heavy sarcasm, "Perhaps they can provide themselves with sticks. I understand we will be pursuing a handful of Galilean fishermen in the woods."

Realizing the futility of continuing the conversation, the priest bowed once again, and motioning to the officer to take charge, he stepped aside as the soldiers formed rank. A few more torches were gathered from within the fortress, and as they were lighted and passed around the crowd, the chattering and jostling returned.

The officer emitted a sharp command, and they were off, with the officer, the priest and a terrified Judas at the lead. They headed for the eastern gate, flames dancing, soldiers marching, crowd howling, and dark shadows following. Judas jerked his head and swatted at something fluttering near his ear. By the time they reached the gate, the mob had swelled to two hundred, as vagrants and villains from all over the city heard the tumult and came racing to see what was happening.

Jesus stood slowly, and returned to his former place of prayer, alone once again to face the invisible flames of torment raging all around him. Again he fell to his face, again he prayed.

"Abba, Father, all things are possible to you; remove this cup from me," he cried in anguish, face down in the dusty grass. He resumed the struggle, faced the enemy within and without, and was quickly drained of all energy. He lay there for a long time, unable to move, barely able to breathe, praying fervently and weeping freely. Finally, he mustered the strength to utter again, "yet not what I will...but what you will."

He pushed himself to his feet once more and with great difficulty shuffled over to where his sleeping friends lay, his head throbbing, his breath irregular, and his eyes puffy and red; he bent over, knelt in the dust and for the last time touched one of his disciples. He loved these men; he loved them desperately, even at this hour of heart rending trial. Through the fog of the demonic onslaught, he saw them as little sheep, helpless in their weariness, about to be violently torn from their shepherd. He prayed for their protection in his absence and for their recovery in the difficult coming days. Though his mind kept pounding him with visions of the horror to come, he forced them aside long enough to recall a few sweet, poignant memories of walks with these men along the Galilean seashore and long chats by the fireside among the lush Judean hillsides. Those days were now gone.

Calling to the guards atop the wall, the officer bellowed out, "In the name of the governor, his Excellency Pontius Pilate, servant of the divine emperor, open the gate, that we may perform his service!"

Recognizing the voice and the password, the guards scurried to comply, and shortly the huge, heavy doors to the city began to swing open. Cheering wildly, the crazed mob squeezed through the gate and burst out of the city amidst fiendish, dancing, sputtering shadows, while the orderly ranks of impassive soldiers followed behind them without hurry.

Jesus rose after only a minute or two beside his slumbering friends, and went to pray one last time, deeply distressed in his spirit and near the breaking point physically. It would be soon now. He lay prostrate, face down in the grass, the soft grass he himself had created. He called on the name of his Father, asking once more to take away from him the frothing, dangerous, overflowing cup, to provide some other way. He prayed with all of his might. But as men all around the land of promise slumbered that night, creation, at least that part of creation within the garden, watched silently and with sorrow as the creator surrendered - willing his heart to quiet and his body to obey, and uttered one last time, "Your will be done."

Progress slowed considerably when the mob reached the slender pathway into the olive grove; they were forced to proceed single file, or at least no more than two at a time, and as they went, many of them took the officer's earlier recommendation about arming themselves literally, and began wrenching limbs and branches from the overhanging boughs to wield as clubs. This notion, though popular at first, enflamed those in the rear of the line with rage, since they were forced to halt altogether and wait for those in front to move on. Pushing and shoving commenced, forcing a few of the soldiers to pull out their whips and perform a little physical discipline in order to regain control. Within moments, they began moving ahead steadily, though not altogether agreeably, forming a long, slithering string of huffing, cursing, belligerent, sweaty and yet eager accomplices, accented here and there with blazing torches and flashing armor. And as they slowly snaked their way up the hillside, stumbling and crashing through the orchard, a foul, invisible tide began to rise with them.

Seeing the pinpoints of light flickering through the trees off to the north, Jesus walked calmly back to where his three closest friends lay, and he knelt down, nudging them all gently, and said, "Are you still sleeping and taking your rest?"

The groggy, embarrassed men sat up, trying to shake the lethargy. Peter asked with a sleepy yawn, "What...hour is it?"

Jesus replied quietly, "Behold, the hour is at hand, and the Son of man is betrayed into the hands of sinners. Rise, let us be going," and pointing to the approaching stream of torches behind them, he finished, "see, my betrayer is at hand."

The three jumped to their feet.

John and James were instantly frozen in shock by the sight of the long line of sputtering flames stretching far off into the distance, and by the awful, mounting sound of a huge mob crashing through the garden. Peter, however, swung into action. He raced down the hill, toward the rest of the disciples, and toward the approaching danger. He began crying out the names of his sleeping comrades, imploring them to wake up. By the time he reached them, the eight remaining disciples were fully awake and fully terrified, surrounded by chaos on all sides. Peter rummaged around in the flickering darkness, looking for something.

"Hold them off!" he ordered, pushing the nearest, panic-stricken disciples toward the oncoming mob.

"Where are they?" demanded the priest, no longer able to display his patient façade. "We don't have all night," he growled through clenched teeth, shaking Judas with surprising force by the arm.

"This is where they were last night," he whimpered. "They have to be nearby...somewhere...I'm...not sure," he added, squinting into the blackness around him, again swatting his hand at something fluttering around his head.

"Over here!" someone cried.

Judas raced toward the voice, and sure enough, he could just make out by the torchlight a little cluster of men hiding among the trees.

"Give us some light!" shouted a soldier, as they advanced on the cowering, panic stricken men. The mob raced forward with clubs and torches raised in the air, shouting and growling like animals, pushing their way through the thick grove of olive trees. Just as they reached the little clearing and began surrounding the disciples, a lone figure leaped from the shadows, brandishing a sword above his head.

"Aaaaaaaaagh!" screamed Peter, charging the mob; he ran straight toward the closest man and with a great whooshing sound, brought the sword straight down with all of his might, glancing the blow off the side of his head, severing his ear and knocking him to the ground in a horrible bloody mess.

"Grab him! Get that sword!" commanded the officer, the first to recover from the sudden, unexpected attack. As they charged toward him, a new voice from just behind them startled them again:

"Put your sword back into its place; for all who take the sword will perish by the sword."

Jesus stepped into the brightly lit circle, and walking up to Peter said softly to him, "Do you think that I cannot appeal to my Father, and he will at once send me more than twelve legions of angels?"

He then looked around at the astonished mob, packed in all around them.

"But how then should the scriptures be fulfilled that it must be so?"

Jesus then stooped down beside the wounded, whimpering man who was holding his hand tightly against the side of his face, trying to stem the dark, thick blood that was streaming freely down the side of his disfigured head. He who made ears to hear picked up the mangled, dirty flesh from the ground, and to everyone's amazement, pulled the man's hand gently away, and placed the ear against his head. He gave him his hand to help him up, and the man stood, his cloak drenched in blood, but his ear whole and intact.

Turning now to the officer, Jesus asked simply, "Whom do you seek?"

The officer was still dumbfounded, staring at the healed man, whom he knew, ironically, to be a slave of the high priest, sent as a secret witness.

One of the priests behind him impatiently blurted out, "We seek Jesus of Nazareth."

"I AM he."

Suddenly, the entire crowd, including the Roman soldiers, fell backward into a struggling heap, as a sudden invisible flurry burst out all around them at these words, and the earth seemed to pitch back and forth for a moment.

Angry at his humiliation and rising quickly to his feet, the priest hissed in the ear of Judas, "Well? Is it he? We have a bargain, as you will recall."

Judas stumbled back to his feet as well, and stepping forward, gripped Jesus by both shoulders and leaned in to kiss him on the cheek, while all around him soldiers and vagrants shook themselves off and climbed back to their feet.

Cheek to cheek, Jesus asked quietly, "Judas, would you betray the Son of man with a kiss?"

Judas pecked him quickly on his left cheek, and withdrew hastily, his hands trembling violently.

At this, the priests tried to rally and press forward, but the officer stood there transfixed, frozen to one spot, thoroughly rattled for the first time in his long career, unable to speak. The crowd, however, had regained their voices. The shouting and snarling resumed with a new ferocity, and at the urging of the priests and Pharisees in their midst, they began to press in on the Rabbi and his friends menacingly.

"Have you come out as against a robber, with swords and clubs?" Jesus asked in a loud voice, penetrating the officer's stupor. "When I was with you day after day in the temple, you did not lay hands on me," and looking directly at the priest who was clearly in charge, he said, "But this is your hour, and the power of darkness."

The officer finally nodded, and the soldiers immediately took charge, seizing Jesus and all of the disciples by the arms in order to bind them with ropes. The crowd shouted and cheered with delight.

"I told you that I AM he," Jesus called loudly, above the roar, and again there was a mad fluttering in the air and again the ground shuddered, though no one fell this time; "So if you seek me, let these men go."

Again the wide-eyed officer nodded, and the soldiers released the disciples. Within minutes they were all gone, crashing headlong with all of their might into the darkness, while the soldiers, followed by the rowdy howling mob, began dragging the freshly bound son of man the other way, and the shroud of deep black darkness rose higher.

Peter stopped to catch his breath, after he was sure that no one was following him. His hands and face were bleeding from repeated falls and from collisions with bushes and trees he encountered in his mad retreat. Breathing heavily, he leaned forward, resting his hands on his knees, afraid that he was going to vomit. Between gasps, he looked up and scanned the black horizon, seeing nothing but the bouncing dots of light off in the distance, fading and winking out.

He was alone, but he didn't feel alone. The air was filled with ominous sounds and smells, and though he couldn't see much of anything, it seemed as if the trees themselves were alive, writhing and moaning their accusations against his cowardice.

A twig snapped behind him, and Peter whirled around, drawing his sword once again.

"Peter, is that you?"

John emerged from behind a tree, and in relief, Peter dropped his sword, trembling so hard he couldn't hold it up. He slumped to the ground, suddenly cold and exhausted. After a moment of silence, he asked in a pitiful voice, "What are we going to do, John?"

"I don't know about you, but I am getting out of this forest; it makes my skin crawl. And if I can catch up with them, I want to follow, to see where they are taking him."

"Are you out of your mind? What if they catch you following them?" Peter asked in horror.

"They don't want me; you saw how easily they let us go – they only wanted the Master. I wish I hadn't run away like a frightened little boy."

John stood there looking at Peter for another minute or so, and when there was no more said, he shrugged and began walking in the direction where the mob had gone.

"John, wait." Peter pushed himself up off of the ground, and gingerly stepped forward to join his friend. "You aren't going to leave me here in this awful place; besides, I don't want you running off getting into trouble, at least not without me."

They walked in silence for a while, picking their way carefully through the dark grove until they at last found the path. Peter grunted as he stubbed his toe on a root, and then asked, "Do you have any idea where they were going?"

"I have been thinking about that. Since they came in the middle of the night, they must have been worried about the crowds during the day. So wherever they are taking him, it is probably a secret, someplace out of the way. I don't think that they would have taken him to the temple, or to meet with the Sanhedrin, for that matter. I suppose that where they take him depends on why they arrested him and what they intend to do with him."

Peter had wondered about that too.

Why had they arrested him? What had he done? Were the Jews angry at him for making them look bad in public? Were they going to forbid him to ever enter the temple again? But that didn't make any sense; they had brought Roman soldiers with them. What did that mean?

"Actually, they might be heading to the Praetorium to hold him for the night. Otherwise, why would they have brought the soldiers?" John pondered out loud.

Peter didn't have an answer. By this time they were descending rapidly along the dark path, accompanied only by the loud chirruping of the locusts all around them.

"Where do you suppose the rest of them went?" Peter asked.

"Who, the rest of the twelve?" John responded.

"Yes; I was wondering where they might go; none of them live in Jerusalem, you know. I don't know anyone in the city, and outside of Judas..." and his face darkened with rage, remembering for the first time what had happened. A nasty growl came involuntarily, and then he said bitterly, "I can't wait until I get my hands on that one. What could have gotten into him?" Feeling the weight of the sword in his cloak, he added, "I will do a more thorough job on him if I get a chance. I'll take that smirk right off..."

John cut him off, saying, "You'll do nothing of the sort. This isn't about him; we need to find the Master, and you have just given me an idea: I know someone in Jerusalem, someone who will probably know where they are taking him."

"Who?"

"The high priest."

Peter suddenly stopped. "The high priest? You mean Caiaphas?"

John stopped as well, and said simply, "Yes."

"You know the high priest?" He asked again, shocked, and not certain he believed him. "I have known you for thirteen years, since you were just a little boy skipping rocks on the lake; since when do you hang around with powerful religious men in Jerusalem?"

"You don't know everything about me, Peter. Come on. Let's go. I know one of the maid's at his house and..."

"Oh, now I get it..." Peter began with a smile.

"Shut up, Peter. Follow me."

They emerged from the deep darkness of the olive grove, and though there was still no moonlight, they could see just a little better walking along the road leading to the city gate.

The city gate; How were they going to get in?

They stood there looking up at the massive wood doors, topped by the imposing stone archway and tower of the Eastern, or Beautiful Gate. At this time of night, there was no getting through the gate, for the guards opened it for no one unless they were on official Roman business and had proper authority.

Peter began to panic, worried that they would have to wait for dawn; however, John gripped his forearm, and motioned him to be silent. He was looking down the road, away from the city, listening.

"What is it?" whispered Peter.

"Shh."

After another moment of silence, Peter heard it too, the low rumble of approaching hoof beat. They stepped back, away from the gate and ducking into a low clump of bushes, they waited as the rumble grew more distinct, and eventually they could here the unmistakable sounds of a Roman legion on the march.

John leaned close to Peter, and whispered, "If we time it right, we might be able to slip in after them before the doors close."

"I was afraid that you were going to say that. We could be arrested, you know."

"Do you have a better idea?"

They fell silent again as the commander and a few officers came into view on horseback, at a very slow pace. Lagging behind them a long stream of foot soldiers in full battle gear trudged their way along, carrying shields and spears, obviously weary after a long march. The commander called out to the guards atop the tower; and presently, the doors swung open.

Peter and John watched with apprehension, looking for their opportunity, as hundreds of drooping soldiers marched by them into the city with heads down, forcing one foot in front of the other by sheer force of training. Near the end of the procession came the slaves, hauling provisions and supplies on several rickety wooden wagons. Suddenly one of these wagons tipped, throwing its contents out onto the road, and there followed a flurry of activity as the slaves scurried to retrieve the scattered containers and baskets, followed by roman task masters brandishing whips to encourage them.

"This is our chance!" John whispered as he darted from their cover. Peter hesitated, eying the roman whips, but then followed, and the two of them joined in the cleanup process. Within minutes the excitement was over, and the slaves resumed their difficult work of moving the wagons; dragging the huge, ungainly vehicles into the city by hand, no one seemed to be aware that the load was now a little lighter with four new hands pulling along with them. The doors closed, and Peter and John were inside the city.

"Wait here, officer," the priest said airily, now back in his element and assuming command. He climbed a short set of stairs into a small garden, and disappeared into the shadows under a low portico. The officer motioned, and his soldiers fanned out around the prisoner in a defensive posture, ready to fend off any attempt to free him. Curious, he walked slowly over to the prisoner and stood looking at him, face to face.

"What have you done to make these Jews so angry?" he asked casually.

There was no response. The only sounds were the flickering of torches and the fluttering of cloaks in the rising wind.

"I see. Well, it makes no difference to me; I am simply following orders. I don't need to know why."

A junior officer stepped up beside him and spoke in his ear.

"Really? This is him?" He stepped back for a better view. He walked slowly around Jesus in a circle, examining him from head to foot. Working his way back around to face him again, he said, "Have you ever been to Capernaum?"

Again, there was no answer. "But of course you have, I can tell that you are Galilean."

He thought for a minute, and then addressed him again: "A very good friend of mine, a centurion of the Caesarean cohort tells me about a rabbi, a wise man from Galilee that healed his servant." Resuming his pacing around the prisoner, he stroked the side of his face thoughtfully, and added, "The odd part of the story was that the slave was at home in bed when the healing occurred, while the rabbi was standing in the street among a large crowd, on the other side of town."

He stopped again, face to face with Jesus.

"He healed him with a word, I am told. He never met the slave, never touched him. Can you explain this to me?"

Jesus returned the steady gaze, eye to eye, but still did not answer.

"If such a man existed, if such a power of miracles existed, he would be a very dangerous man." He paused for a moment, and then just before he stepped away, he added softly, "And if such a man existed, I would follow him."

The priest returned, and with him came a handful of similarly clad men, all of them high ranking Sadducees. The officer motioned again, and the prisoner was brought before them, where the torch light was a little better.

"So, you are the famous rabbi from Galilee. We have long desired to meet you face to face and discuss our...differences," said Annas. "You have spoken some rather unkind words about us and about our God-ordained leadership. Do you have anything to say to us now?"

Jesus remained silent.

Annas nodded at the officer, who hesitated, looking at Jesus intently, and then he reluctantly nodded at a nearby soldier.

Crack!

The whip came from nowhere, and struck Jesus across the back with a thunderous blow, knocking him to his knees.

Gasping for breath, Jesus struggled back to his feet, and resumed his silence.

"Very well; we shall see how long he will hold his tongue. Come this way, if you please." And turning toward the street, he descended the steps into the thick, deepening darkness, along with his peers bearing torches, followed by the officer and his peers bearing arms, and dragging the lone prisoner with them.

Thursday night, third watch

Having slipped away from the Roman slave service at a conveniently dark turn in the roadway, Peter and John ran for their lives, certain that they would here cries of "escape!" behind them. However, hearing nothing, they ran on, plunging down street after street, changing direction often and paying no attention to where they were going. When they finally had to stop to catch their breath, panting furiously and leaning forward with their hands on their knees, John looked up and down the dark alleyway in which they found themselves, trying to get his bearing.

He mopped his brow with his sleeve, and said between breaths, "I'm not sure... I know where...we are. Do you?"

Peter didn't even look up. He simply waved his hand once in the air and shook his head.

John left Peter where he was, and sweating profusely, with steam rising from his soaked tunic, he walked to the end of the next block and looked both ways. Still seeing nothing familiar, he turned left and walked out of sight.

After another moment, Peter stood up straight, a little light-headed, but able to move again. He followed John's direction to the corner, and as he was turning to go left, he collided with someone, and they both fell to the ground.

"Would you watch where you are going?" John complained as he pulled himself back to his feet. "You nearly scared me to death."

Peter stood up beside him and asked, "Did you find out where we are? I thought that you knew all about Jerusalem."

"I never said that, but yes, I think I know where we are. Follow me."

John turned around and instead of heading left the way he had gone first, he walked briskly to the right, this time setting a little more reasonable pace. The new direction took them down another dirty, narrow alleyway that smelled of something rotten.

"Ugh, what is that terrible smell?" Peter complained.

"Shh, not so loud; you probably wouldn't really want to know, anyway."

After several tentative twist and turns, they broke out into a wider street, something of a thoroughfare. Here John turned back to the left, this time more sure of himself.

"Here we go. The high priest's house is just a little further..."

And he stopped suddenly, causing Peter to run into his back.

"Hey! Why did you..."

"Shhh! Look!"

Peter followed John's pointing finger with his eyes, and just up the road, disappearing into yet another dark side street, he saw the shadowy forms of Roman foot soldiers.

"Do you think that they are looking for us?" Peter asked in near panic.

"I don't think so; we are too far away from the Praetorium for that. Come on – let's see where they are going."

Keeping to the deep shadows along the walls, they hurried forward, glancing around to make sure that there were no soldiers straggling behind the ones that they had seen, or indeed, following the two of them. Carefully peering around the corner where the Romans had disappeared, they saw what might be the tail end of some sort of troop movement, for this time there were plainly more soldiers in view, some of them bearing torches; and then they disappeared again around another bend.

"It might be them!" exclaimed Peter, obviously referring to the Romans who had arrested Jesus.

They hurried forward to catch up, darting from cover to cover, and soon they were slowing down not far behind them, trying to stay at a safe distance.

"Look! There's the Master!" cried Peter so loudly that John had to cover his mouth and pull him down into the shadows, for fear that they might be spotted.

"Would you please keep it down?" requested John, carefully looking up over a low lying bush they were hidden behind. He noticed that the troops were slowing down, and suddenly he realized where they were.

"See that big house over there - the one on the right? That's the high priest's house. I think that they are going to take him in."

And sure enough, the soldiers stopped at the doorway, holding the prisoner with them, while several others stepped through and disappeared into the house. John motioned for Peter to be silent and follow him. Creeping forward a little at a time, they navigated their way quietly to a spot just outside of the light cast by the flickering torches. Here they could listen to what was being said among the armed guards.

"No sir, he don't seem to be the kind that is used to keeping company with our type, now do he?" said one of the soldiers who were standing around in a little circle facing the Master. He laughed at his own statement, and a few others joined him.

"No sir, he is too good for us, you know what I mean? Why, look at his hands; he ain't worked a day in his life, I tell you. He's one of those rabbi types that goes around telling others what they do wrong. Isn't that so?" he demanded, suddenly standing face to face with Jesus, both of his hands on his hips, and his legs spread wide. He began toying with his whip which he held loosely with his right hand, the tip fluttering slightly in the breeze. When it was clear that there would be no response, he stepped closer, his right hand now flexing and gripping the handle more tightly. He was a big man, with huge muscles rippling in his tense arms.

"I said, isn't that so?" he said very distinctly, grinding the words out one at a time. Suddenly, without warning, he slapped him across the face with the back of his left hand so hard that blood and spittle flew from his nose and mouth. Jesus gasped at the searing pain in his jaw, but still said nothing.

"Haw, did you see that? I fooled him; he thought that I was going to use the whip. He never saw it coming!" He laughed heartily, and again a few of the others joined him, though not as enthusiastically. He gripped the end of his whip and pulled back in a threatening gesture, but one of the other guards squatting near the wall spoke up.

"Would you knock it off? It's going to be a long night, and we don't need your foolishness."

The first soldier threatened with the whip again, waving it back and forth high above his shoulder.

"I said enough!" growled the second one, rising to his feet. He was a massive man, even larger and more menacing than the first. His armor, though well fitted, was pitted and scarred, suggesting regular battle experience, something which most of the Jerusalem cohort could not boast.

"Aw, I was just having a little fun," said the first, lowering the whip and walking away sulking.

Peter and John were horrified and speechless. Peter's first instinct had been to lunge at the belligerent guard, but that notion wilted quickly in the face of the raw display of power before them.

With wide, pleading eyes, he turned to John and whispered hoarsely, "What do we do?"

John shook his head, and appeared to be in feverish thought. He rose slightly to peer once again over the shrub at the dark doorway, and then sat back down. As if on cue, they heard muffled voices floating on the gusting wind. Both Peter and John rose carefully and saw two figures emerging from the doorway.

"Captain, would you be so kind as to bring our guest this way?" called a muffled but familiar voice. The second soldier nodded in his direction, and then spoke to his troops: "You and you remain here and keep lookout; and stay out of trouble (he said this with a particular eye on the first soldier); the rest of you come with me." And taking Jesus by the arm, blood still tricking down his cheek, he escorted him into the building, and climbing the few steps, they again disappeared.

John again motioned for Peter to follow him quietly. Hunched over, they retreated around a nearby corner, and making sure that no one was within earshot, John then spoke in a hushed voice: "I think I can get inside to see what is happening. I will have to go around to the servant's entrance, and it may take a little while. You go back and wait where you were until you see me come out of that doorway."

"But what if you don't get in? What if they figure out who you are and arrest you too?"

"Leave that to me; you are going to have to trust me. Can you do this Peter?"

He hesitated just a second, and then blurted out, "Of course, of course. What do we do once we get in?"

"We'll figure that out when we get there." John grinned, patted his friend on the shoulder, and then slinked away in the other direction, away from the two soldiers who had now taken up posts by the door.

Peter sat back down in the dark, wondering what hour it was. He judged it to be approaching midnight, but he wasn't sure. If so, he would soon hear the call of the watchman from the fortress tower for the third watch of the night. He settled in, assuming that it would be awhile before John could work his way through the delicate situation inside the house and signal him. He leaned his head back...

Peter awoke with a jerk.

How long had he been asleep?

He shook his head a few times, trying to overcome the grogginess that had overcome him, and then turned around and peered up over the shrub, looking for John. And there he was – waving discreetly in his direction, but trying not to attract attention from the soldiers, who looked bored and were standing with their backs to the door.

Off in the distance, Peter heard the faint, mournful cry of the tower watchman calling out the third watch.

Perhaps he had been asleep for only a few minutes.

Peter stood slowly, revealing himself, wondering if he was about to walk into a trap. He took a deep breath, and stepped forward nervously, trying to decide what to say when the guards spotted him and came forward to challenge him. He made it to the door without incident; a woman, presumably the maid of whom John had spoken, came down the steps to meet him there. Ushering him in with a silent motion not to speak, she escorted him past the sleepy looking guards without drawing any attention at all. They mounted the steps, and finally Peter and John were back together, standing at the entrance to a huge courtyard.

"How long were you waiting for me?" asked Peter as he looked around the brightly lit courtyard, noting the abundant signs of great wealth.

"Not long; I saw you looking for me almost as soon as I came out. It took a little longer than I had expected to rouse someone at the servant's door, however. Now Peter, I think I can get inside the house to try finding out what is going on, but I am afraid you will have to wait out here. There is a fire, so you should be warm."

"I'll be fine. You go on in. We need to find out what they want, what they are planning to do with the Master. Go."

"I'll let you know as soon as I find something out," John said as he turned and headed for a covered portico to his left, presumably the entrance to the main house.

Peter was nervous; he had never been in the home of someone so powerful, and certainly never under distressing circumstances like these. He took a deep breath to calm his nerves, and then proceeded to look around, studying his new environment. The house was very large, with two stories, and built in a rectangle around the central courtyard. The secluded and carefully maintained court and garden was nearly a paradise, filled with rich and exotic plant life. Scattered throughout, to Peter's surprise, were a number of fine marble statues, *Roman* statues. The far wall away from the main entrance to the house framed a series of terraces, with mounds of dense green plants draping down from one to the next. And in the center of it all, there stood a magnificent cascading fountain, rising in flowing tiers to well above eye-level, which was flanked all around by a circle of flaming pots hanging from tall posts. Near the fountain stood the open fireplace, with a warm fire glowing and crackling inside; Peter was growing cold, so he eased over to the fire, hoping to avoid notice by the men and women, including soldiers, who were huddled around it.

Inside the house, a select, hand-picked group of Jewish leaders were assembled. Annas was there of course, along with Caiaphas, the host, Eliab from Bethlehem, and four or five others, all members of the Jewish high council, or Sanhedrin, and all of them close supporters of the high priest. The gathering hall was brightly lit, and the walls were lined with a strange mixture of unarmed temple guards and armed Roman soldiers. A table had been set up, behind which sat the cluster of priests and Sadducees, looking very much like judges at a tribunal. Before them stood the prisoner, bound at his wrists with rope, and flanked on both sides by armed soldiers.

"Bring in the witnesses," bellowed the high priest, who was clearly energized by this rare opportunity to flex his muscles.

A door at the far side of the room opened, and several ragged looking men were ushered in, escorted by more temple guards. The first witness was singled out and brought forward, and stood quaking in fear before the table, side by side with the prisoner. Caiaphas studied the dirty individual for a moment, and then began his questioning.

"Have you ever seen this man before?"

The witness was startled by the question, and looked around nervously to make sure that it was indeed he who was being addressed.

"Do you mean me?"

"Of course I mean you! Tell us what you know about this man!"

"Why...what would you like to know?" he asked, with a look of profound confusion spreading across his face.

"Where have you seen this man before?" Caiaphas demanded, already out of patience and roaring at his very first witness.

Terrified, and now afraid of making a mistake on his golden opportunity to make some money, the man scratched his chin and looked sideways out of the corner of his eye at the prisoner. He leaned forward toward the high priest and whispered, "Is this the man you wanted me to...?"

"Next! Get this worthless individual out of here."

The man was swept from the room and hastily replaced by another ill-clad citizen. This one was a stooped old man with thin white hair, who upon entering the room tripped twice, and when he was left standing before the table, he faced a little to his right.

Caiaphas looked in the direction of the man's gaze, and seeing nothing he cleared his throat and asked, "Could you look this way, if you please?"

The man shifted his face toward the voice.

"Now then; tell me – have you ever seen this man before?"

Without looking at the prisoner and without hesitation, he replied, "Yes sir, I have seen him many times."

Caiaphas relaxed, and smiled over at his father-in-law, who rolled his eyes in return.

"And where have you seen the prisoner?"

"I have seen him on numerous occasions at the temple."

At this revelation, Caiaphas shot a nervous glance down the table.

"At the temple - here in Jerusalem?"

The old man grinned and nodded, looking off again to his right.

"Didn't you say that you had seen him at least once in Caesarea...?" Caiaphas offered, trying to lead him to the testimony he wanted.

"Well, yes, now that you mention it, I saw him there once also."

"And he was meeting with someone...?"

"He was meeting with the king," the man answered triumphantly.

"Well now; this is very interesting. You saw this man in Caesarea, meeting with King Herod. Can you tell us for what purpose they met?" Caiaphas was back in a good mood.

"Before he answers that question, I would like to ask a few of my own, if I may."

Everyone in the room turned around to look behind them, startled by the interruption of a new voice. Annas was the first to recover from the shock, and spoke up smoothly:

"My dear Nicodemus; we are delighted that you have joined us. Come, we have only begun just moments ago."

Nicodemus stepped around the table, and ignoring Annas, addressed Caiaphas instead: "My lord high priest, I am alarmed to find that a man of our own race, a child of Israel has been taken captive and brought by night to be examined privately, without the benefit of a public inquiry, as required by law. I was under the impression that in Israel we still give men a fair hearing."

The face of Caiaphas turned crimson with anger at the charge, but before he could choke out a response, Annas spoke again: "My dear friend, we all desire fair and open justice. I must say that we were all dismayed when so many of our brethren failed to show up this evening. We waited as long as we could, but when the hour began to grow late, we reluctantly proceeded with the representation you see here."

"Do you suggest," Nicodemus said hotly, still addressing the high priest, "that the entire Sanhedrin was informed about this cozy little meeting in the middle of the night, and I might add, on the eve of a holy day?"

"The high priest suggests nothing," said Annas, still smooth and under control. "You by your very presence testify that you were aware of the hearing. Now if you would please take your seat..."

"I was informed of this secret meeting only within the last hour."

Caiaphas could hold it in no longer.

"And who, pray tell, did this informing?" he spit out, the words barely intelligible.

Nicodemus scrutinized the high priest, as if seeing him for the first time.

"The name of the individual is of no concern here, but mark my words, you and I will take that particular issue up at a later time. Let us simply say that the frightened old man who came to me possessed delicate information, and he was concerned that a terrible injustice was underway..."

"May we please proceed?" Annas interrupted with a bored tone. "You are welcome to stay if you wish, but mark my words, we shall continue with or without you."

The two men stared at one another for a moment, and then Nicodemus looked away and sat down heavily in the seat offered without saying anything more.

"Thank you. Now we were about to hear from the witness his thoughts about the meeting he observed between..."

"Excuse me," interrupted Nicodemus again, "But could you have the witness describe the prisoner?"

"My dear sir, if we could only..."

"Please; just humor me."

Annas looked at Caiaphas, who was studying his hands, refusing to return the look.

"Very well, would the witness describe the prisoner?"

The witness, who had been fascinated by the previous exchange was startled by the sudden shift of attention back to him, and humbly asked for the question to be repeated, still gazing off to his right.

"The prisoner to your left: please describe him for us."

The witness wobbled his head in a series of circles, opened his mouth and said, "Ahhh..." and then stood gazing off to his right as before.

"Blind witnesses, my lord Caiaphas?" goaded Nicodemus with a smirk. "Perhaps you were wise to hold a secret hearing in the middle of the night, after all."

At the back of the room, standing among a number of curious observers, John smiled for the first time that night.

Maybe there is still hope; thank you God for Nicodemus.

"The witness is excused," snarled the high priest through clenched teeth.

Peter had been standing by the fire for only a few moments when he heard someone breathing close by. He looked slowly to his right, and flinched at the face staring at him from only inches away. His heart pounding wildly, he backed away until he recognized who it was: John's friend, the maid who had escorted him in.

Peter breathed a sigh of relief, and tried to relax. "You gave me quite a scare, my dear..."

"The one on the inside – the one called John: he is a friend of the prisoner," she whispered fiercely.

Peter shivered, wondering if John had been arrested, and said nothing. The woman closed in on him, again thrusting her face only inches away from Peter's. Her breath reeked of something foul, and Peter had to suppress the urge to gag.

"You also were with Jesus the Galilean."

In panic, Peter looked around and noticed that several people were watching the exchange.

Was this a setup? Was she trying to get him arrested?

Peter stammered, and said in a voice loud enough for the eavesdroppers to hear, "I...I...I...do not know what you m...mean."

He turned his back on the woman and staggered away from the fire, sweating profusely in spite of the cold night air, plunging into the unusually thick darkness surrounding him.

□□□□□

The next witness was a woman who at least looked respectable, in contrast to the previous two. She was clean, of medium age, and wore a pleasant, though nervous look on her round face.

Caiaphas began in a low voice, "Would you please tell us where you are from?"

"I am a humble resident of this very city, my lord."

"And have you ever had an encounter with this prisoner?"

She glanced at Jesus nervously, and responded, "Not directly, my lord. I have never met him, but he healed my son about a year..."

"What was that you said? You claim that this man, this impostor..."

Annas cleared his throat; Caiaphas turned and saw the frown on his face and remembered that Nicodemus was listening to every word.

"I beg your pardon; you were saying?"

Bewildered and more than a little intimidated, the woman changed her approach, not wishing to offend the high priest. "Sir, about a year ago, this man...met with my son, and claimed to have healed him of blindness."

"I see," Caiaphas said carefully, "was your son in fact blind?"

"He was born blind, and remained blind for nearly thirty years."

"And you contend that he is no longer blind."

"That he is no longer blind, my lord, is irrefutable."

Caiaphas was stymied; he couldn't recall why he felt this woman would be of help, and as a result he wasn't sure how to proceed.

Annas, sensing the trouble, asked, "My lord, if I may ask a question or two?"

Caiaphas exhaled in relief, and said, "By all means."

"Dear lady, did you speak with the authorities about this case?"

"We did, my lord; when it was clear that he could now see, we waited until the next day and took him before the Pharisees."

"The next day; why was it that you waited until the next day?"

"Why, my lord, I thought this was why I was summoned: my son was healed on the Sabbath."

A flurry of whispering ensued along the table, and the countenance of the high priest brightened perceptibly.

"Just to make sure we are clear," Caiaphas said, resuming control, "your son was healed on a Sabbath day, and this man next to you claimed credit."

"That is correct, my lord."

"One more question, if you please," interjected Annas. "When you took your son to the proper authorities, to whom did they give the credit for his healing?"

"They said to 'Give God the praise.'"

All along the table, heads nodded to one another, tassels and headpieces fluttering.

Nicodemus, on the other hand, was growing agitated by

the line of questioning, and spoke up again: "Are we to conclude that a man should be taken prisoner for healing someone born blind? Just what is it we are trying to demonstrate here tonight, if I may ask?"

Caiaphas snapped back, retorting, "If you will be patient, my friend, and try to hold your tongue, you will presently see where this all leads. Next witness, please."

☐☐☐☐☐☐

The entire neighborhood surrounding the house of Caiaphas was so packed, so overwhelmed with lethal spirits that the very air in the streets seemed stained and thick; a heavy fog lay across the entire city, but was clearly the heaviest and most suffocating at that very house. Everything there seemed to be alive and moving of its own volition: the wind-buffeted trees and shrubs taunting and striking one another within the courtyard; the churning, angry water frothing within the fountain; the thick, roiling clouds in the ominous black sky; and the creeping, swirling, sinister fog all seemed to conspire together in frightening, unnatural behavior.

Wickedness was on the prowl that night; with no angelic presence, with the Lord of creation himself bound with ropes, there was no restraining it. All over the city men and women awakened to the screams of terrified children, or to sudden, unusual sounds within their homes. Dogs everywhere were barking and howling. Horses tied up or bedded down for the night whinnied and pranced nervously. Trouble began sparking all around the city, spreading quickly as the darkest and lowest impulses of men were easily ignited by thousands upon thousands of invisible spirits testing and flexing their muscles. Tentative, petty theft led to overt plundering, plundering led to assault, assault led to violent confrontations, which before long led to a number of deaths and murder. The lid had finally come off of the long restrained cauldron of evil, and the hellish contents were rapidly spilling out.

Soldiers who had been sleeping soundly within the fortress were called to arms and mobilized all over the city to quell a wide variety of skirmishes and domestic battles and looting, and to confront bands of roaming, marauding villains. When the tide of crime continued to rise, reinforcements were added. Before the night was over, every soldier within the city was involved, and brutality was the only recourse. The jails filled up; the maimed and wounded were hauled away for what treatment could be found, and the streets were stained with the blood of the dying as wickedness was exalted that night among the sons of men. And the real trouble was just beginning as the black tide rose still higher.

Peter had avoided the fire and the clump of people huddled about it for as long as he could by wandering slowly around the courtyard, examining details, trying to keep his mind away from the fear of what could be going on inside the house, as well as the terror of what might happen to him out here. But now he was cold. He rubbed his hands together, stomped his feet, and pulled his cloak tighter, but to no avail; he was shivering and he longed for the warmth of the cozy looking blaze. He took a step toward the fire pit, but catching one of the men looking at him, he turned away again. Instead, he took another slow circuit around the perimeter, and when he drew near to the fire again, he took a deep breath, stepped up into a gap in the crowd, and reached his hands out to the comforting warmth, closing his eyes and luxuriating in the relief.

When he opened his eyes again a few minutes later, he was horrified to see that nearly everyone present was casting furtive looks his way, a couple of them whispering and nodding to one another. He backed away, and as he turned around to leave, he stumbled into a short, balding man.

"I think you are right," the grinning, curious little fellow said to someone in the crowd as he studied Peter. "I think he was with them."

Peter tried to turn in the other direction, but was confronted by someone else, also grinning fiendishly.

"What?" Peter asked in a high, thin voice, trembling with fear. "What do you want from me?"

"You also are one of them."

"Man, I am not; I don't know what you are talking about." And he squeezed his way through the crowd and disappeared into the gloomy shadows in the darkest corner of the courtyard.

Thursday night, fourth watch

By the time of the fourth watch of the night, with dawn just a few hours away, Caiaphas was beginning to grow nervous, and it showed in everything he said and in every gesture he made. His peers were watching him, expecting him to make the case against the Nazarene, but it wasn't coming together as easily as he had expected. As a result, he was becoming more peevish with each failed or confused or contradictory witness. And the presence of Nicodemus was making matters worse; he had not expected to face opposition in his own home. And so, as the hours had worn away to no avail, Caiaphas had vowed to himself repeatedly that he would find out who had tipped Nicodemus off about the hearing and he would personally strangle that individual; no one was supposed to know about it outside of those present and members of his own household.

So there he sat, frustrated, rubbing the back of his neck, and contemplating what to do next. There had been a total of nine witnesses interviewed so far, and he was no closer to making a clear case than when he had begun. He had, in fact, within the last hour been forced to slow down his pace in order to give his subordinates time to scurry around the city and awaken fresh households in an attempt to recruit and coach more witnesses. His list was growing thin.

And, of course, Jesus had been standing silently before them now for several hours.

"May I make an observation?" asked Nicodemus in a tired voice.

"No; no you may not. I have had enough of your interruptions and comments, and I find your attitude most alarming. We are engaged in serious business here, very serious, and you have done nothing but look for ways to stand in the way."

"But my lord, Caiaphas..."

"I said enough!" he screamed, rising to his feet, trembling with rage. "I will have you removed from the house if you say another word; nay, I will have you removed from the council and barred from the temple!"

"I suggest that we all take a deep breath..." began Annas, attempting to defuse the suddenly volatile atmosphere, but Caiaphas would have none of it.

"Have I made myself clear?" he roared, leaning on the table in front of him, staring defiantly at Nicodemus, his face mottled and fiery, and his eyes bulging.

He seemed to have struck a nerve; Nicodemus looked down at his feet and after a moment nodded almost imperceptibly.

"Very well then," Caiaphas muttered, resuming his seat, pleased with himself. "Bring in the next witness."

The man was small and lean, with a dark, weathered face. He wore the simple clothes of a poor peasant; by his coloring and look it was clear that he was a Galilean farmer. He stood beside the prisoner and bowed to the men at the table.

"Could you tell us what you know about this man, if you please?"

"My lords, I am but a humble man of the earth; I raise my wheat as God provides, I pay my taxes, and when there is enough, I feed my children. I do not ask for much. But this man and his filthy friends..." here he stopped and looked at Jesus, who returned his gaze without malice. "This man and his friends stole food from my very table."

Shocked whispers spread around the table, followed by a wave of relief that someone had finally come up with something.

"Could you be more specific? Did they enter your house?" asked Annas, hoping for juicy details.

"Well, not exactly; but it was the same thing as if he entered my house. They stole the food away from my children, that's what they did."

Caiaphas decided to slow down. A familiar, sinking feeling was spreading in his stomach, and he was afraid this story would unravel too.

"Tell us how they stole your food," he said.

"About six months ago, I was sitting in the shade near my house, when I heard someone talking and laughing out in my wheat field. It was in the middle of my field, mind you, and no one should have been out there except me. I stood up and listened, but couldn't make out who it was or what they were saying. So I decided to find out what was going on. I followed the voices, and when I came up behind them, I caught them stealing my wheat."

No one said anything in response for a moment; all of the men present were painfully familiar with the Law of Moses which allowed poor Jews to glean grain from their neighbor's fields. If this was what the Nazarene and his disciples had been doing, there was no crime here.

Annas cleared his throat and spoke up: "How were they gathering the wheat, my friend? This is an important detail. What tools were they using?"

"Well, now, they weren't using any tools; no sir, it was the Sabbath: they were plucking the heads of wheat by hand, and eating it right there in the field. They were taking the food right out of the mouths of my children, they were."

"The Sabbath, you say? Are you certain?" asked Caiaphas, with a glimmer of hope returning to his eyes.

"As sure as I am standing here; he stole from me on the Sabbath."

"Do you have anything to say for yourself?" Caiaphas asked the prisoner. When there was no response, he continued, "He seems to be a very busy man when it comes to the Sabbath. He exhibits no regard whatsoever for the laws and traditions handed down from Moses to our forefathers."

"Am I going to get paid for my stolen food?" asked the farmer.

"We shall speak with you later about your losses," assured the high priest. "Thank you for your assistance."

And with no more to say, he was ushered from the room.

All around the dark city, wicked spirits continued to wreak havoc as the enormous black enclosure continued to rise and spread. They ignited dark passions; they prompted disputes, frightened children, aroused anger, caused destruction, tormented the guilty, fanned jealousy, incited drunkenness, and invaded dreams. And among those homes affected was the governor's residence, where the governor's wife spent a fitful night, troubled with a recurring dream of an innocent man butchered and put to death at the hands of her own husband. She cried out in her sleep, horrified again and again by the bloody images replaying continually before her, but her cry was in vain, for she was unable to wake and escape the vivid details of the gruesome nightmare.

Judas paced in the same spot that he had occupied earlier that night, outside the Pharisee's house, waiting for word about the Rabbi. Earlier, he had fled from the garden like the other disciples when Jesus had been arrested. Now he was carefully avoiding them; he couldn't face any of the disciples, or Jesus for that matter, until this was all over and the Rabbi had come to terms and made peace with the Jewish leaders.

Surely he would come to some kind of terms with them.

He must, if he wishes to survive.

He won't survive, and neither will you.

His conflicting thoughts were beginning to frighten him, his heart was pounding, and he was finding it difficult to breathe in the heavy fog churning all around him.

I did what I could; it's up to him now.

Remember the way he treated you; he deserves whatever they do to him.

No, no, he is a good man.

Whatever happens to him, it's your fault.

Something dark flew just above him, brushing his head. He jerked his head down and looked around in terror, but saw nothing.

You should have asked for more money.

It wasn't the money; it wasn't about money.

His entire body began trembling with uncontrollable convulsions; he tried to think of something else, anything else, but it was no use.

What if he refuses to cooperate?

They are going to kill him.

What if he defies the entire Sanhedrin?

They are going to nail him to a cross, and he will blame you.

Would they? Could they?

Whimpering in panic, Judas again rapped loudly on the door, aware of the futility of the gesture, but so agitated that he had to do something.

What was taking so long?

Perhaps you should go to the high priest's house and see for yourself.

While he was waiting for additional witnesses, Caiaphas decided to question the prisoner directly. Annas had strongly cautioned him against doing so, but the idea was just so tempting. He leaned forward, tilting his huge head to one side to get a better vantage (which just happened to allow the tassels to flutter just so), and carefully studied the man from Nazareth.

What did they see in him? What was the great attraction?

There was a quiet yawn somewhere down the table to his left, but Caiaphas ignored it. True, they had been up all night long, but he couldn't even think of resting, not yet. Before they left this hearing they had to identify and formalize the charges they would bring against the Nazarene when they convened the full Sanhedrin in the morning, and after that they would have to charge him before the governor himself. This hearing was supposed to have been a simple formality, an uncomplicated job of putting down in writing all the man's offenses they had long grieved about; it was turning out to be nothing of the sort. If they didn't come up with something more substantial very soon, the plan they had already set in motion would unravel, and the coming Sabbath would stand in the way of finishing the job on schedule.

"I have a question or two that I would like to ask the prisoner," he began.

There were a few puzzled looks and frowns along the table, since they had all assumed that Caiaphas would heed the advice of his father-in-law. Annas said nothing, indicated nothing. Without looking directly at him, Caiaphas noted that he made no visible sign of objection, so he plunged ahead.

"There have come to my attention many reports of shall we say...inappropriate remarks...made by the prisoner and his followers concerning those who sit at this table and our esteemed brothers who are not present. I would like to invite the prisoner to explain himself, if he wishes."

There followed a long pause in which the two stared at each other.

"Does the prisoner have nothing to say? Perhaps he would like to take this opportunity to share his views on violating the laws of Moses." The high priest smirked at Jesus, waiting for a response, obviously amused at his own wit.

"Nothing? I am disappointed; I was sure that the prisoner would have something wise to teach us," he said, chuckling and leering around the table, looking for support.

When the response came, it startled him, as if he hadn't really expected Jesus to speak:

"I have spoken openly to the world; I have always taught in the synagogues and in the temple, where all the Jews come together; I have said nothing secretly. Why do you ask me? Ask those who have heard me, what I said to them." He looked to his right, nodding at a couple of the temple guards against the wall, "They know what I said."

An officer of the temple guard standing near lunged at Jesus, slapping him viciously across the mouth, again drawing blood. Raising the back of his hand to strike again, his face contorted and flushed, he asked in a loud, challenging voice, "Is that how you answer the high priest?"

Jesus responded without fear or malice, though now with a slight slur, "If I have spoken wrongly, bear witness to the wrong; but if I have spoken rightly, why do you strike me?"

And before he could strike again, a rather young looking Pharisee burst into the room, announcing the arrival of some very important, key witnesses. The officer reluctantly stepped back to allow him room to pass, and the excited newcomer huddled close to the high priest, the two of them whispering in urgent tones for several moments. Caiaphas motioned for Annas to join them, and the whispering continued. At last, Annas resumed his seat with no change of expression, and the young man left the room in a flurry. Caiaphas, however, now wore a look of great relief as he called for everyone's attention.

"We have two more witnesses. I believe that what they have to say will confirm all of the damaging reports we have heard tonight, and will leave no room for doubt as to the danger this man represents to this nation. Bring them in."

Of all of the dubious looking witnesses dragged before the table that night, these two were undoubtedly the worst. They both had the sly look of common thieves, with body language and mannerisms that shouted depravity and falsehood. One was short and very fat, with a nasty scar running the length of his bloated cheek, and down his bare neck, disappearing into his cloak. The other was tall, very thin, and shrouded in a deep, dark cloak, clearly hiding his face from scrutiny.

Caiaphas ignored their appearances, and asked rather politely, as if speaking to a couple of revered old friends, "Could you gentlemen please tell us what you told the young man a little earlier this evening regarding the prisoner?"

The short one attempted to bow, grunting with the difficult effort, doing his best to grovel and fawn before the high priest and his associates, while the other one made no move at all, though his cloak seemed to flutter ever so slightly in response to his friend's efforts.

"If you please, your majesty, may I speak freely?" asked the winded fat one.

"Of course, of course; please – speak freely."

"Well, your worship, do you recall the time when this man," he said, jerking his thumb at Jesus, "when this man was storming around the temple, blasting the money changers and rooting out all of the animals, and breaking up the tables and..."

"We remember a detail or two of that incident," intervened Annas dryly.

"Well, sir, we was there, the two of us. We witnessed the whole thing."

"And?" prompted Caiaphas.

"And, your honor, this man blasphemed the holy temple, he did."

A faint buzz stirred among the tired old men at the table, all of whom were desperately trying to stay awake, none of them used to these late hours.

"And what did he say?" asked Caiaphas, a little louder, trying to rouse his friends, afraid that they would miss the point.

"He said, 'I am able to destroy the temple of God, and to build it in three days,'" came the reply - not from the fat one - but from the mysterious cloaked one, speaking in a low raspy voice that sent a chill down the high priest's back.

"Is this so?" squeaked the high priest as he looked away from the tall man, straining to control himself, shuddering slightly in response to the sound of the his ominous voice.

"This is so, exactly, your magnificence; those were his very words," replied short man.

"Well." It was all the high priest could say at the moment, he was so overcome with a strange mixture of repulsion from the dark witness and at the same time relief that they had finally secured testimony from two witnesses, corroborating testimony that put the prisoner in very bad light. This was good progress, but they were not quite there yet. Turning to look at Annas for help, he cleared his throat, and again said, "Well."

Fat man looked at his partner, clearly pleased with the effect their testimony had made on the powerful men behind the table, and began mentally counting the silver coins that they had been promised for a good showing.

□□□□□□

Peter's head snapped forward. He was shivering, alone

in the deep shadow of the house, and though he kept falling asleep, his senses were on high alert since he expected at any moment a Roman soldier to appear and accuse him of deserting, or even worse, to accuse him of conspiring with their prisoner. Glancing around, he pulled his tunic tighter around his shoulders. He was freezing. He rubbed his arms and hands furiously, but the chilly, foggy air seemed to cling to and penetrate his clothing, canceling out any effort he made to warm himself. He stood and quietly walked a few steps to peer around the landscaping at the fire. It was still blazing, and there was still a crowd standing around it, basking in the warmth. He was sorely tempted to join them, his frigid, aching body crying out for relief; but his fear of further confrontation trumped his desire for comfort, and he returned to his lonely hiding place.

"My lord, these are certainly damaging reports, very damaging," commented Annas. "Perhaps you could give the prisoner an opportunity to answer the charges," he coached.

"Very well; does the prisoner have anything to say in response to these grave charges?"

No answer.

And Caiaphas had finally run out of patience.

Jumping to his feet, he roared "Have you no answer to make? What is it that these men testify against you?"

But Jesus remained silent, looking down at his feet.

Bristling with rage, his eyes bulging and his bloated face turning purple, words suddenly came to him, and he shouted them at the top of his voice, "I adjure you by the living God, tell us if you are the Christ, the Son of God!"

His huge voice reverberated down the corridors of the house, waking servants and family from fitful slumber. And all around the room eyes watched and ears listened closely; from the corners, from the rafters, in the hallways and closets, among the soldiers and witnesses, hovering in the air all around the prisoner, filling the room and the house and the courtyard and the neighborhood to overflowing, silent, invisible warriors held their breath, waiting for a response from the prisoner, their enemy, the son of the living God.

Slowly, Jesus raised his head to look directly at the high priest.

"I AM."

There was a sudden blast of shock from those present, and a tremendous crash as Caiaphas tumbled backward over his seat.

"And you will see the Son of man seated at the right hand of Power, and coming with the clouds of heaven."

The high priest was clawing and panting, struggling to regain his feet and composure, snarling like a wild animal. By the time he finally stood up, the rest of his associates had risen to their feet as well, and had withdrawn a few paces, fearing residual damage when the prisoner would be struck down by lightning, or some other form of the wrath of God.

Breathing heavily, Caiaphas gasped out through a constricted throat, "Why do we still...still need witnesses? You have heard..." and grasping the neck of his pure white, ornamental tunic, with great drama he ripped it apart and finished, "his blasphemy!"

Peter found himself surrounded by a growing crowd, all whispering to each other and nodding at him. He had finally succumbed, finding the warm glow of the fire irresistible, and had cautiously ventured near it, keeping his eyes to himself, and holding his numb fingers out toward the wonderful blaze. Now, with rising panic as his route of exit closed behind him, he wished he had never been so foolish.

Caiaphas was back in control, in full glory standing in their midst, his celebrated priestly robe properly torn in symbolic response to blasphemy. Looking around the room at his brethren, he could see the horror in their eyes, and he knew exactly what to do.

"You have heard his blasphemy," he repeated calmly; "What is your decision?"

The impassioned answer came swiftly and loudly: "He deserves death!" Only Nicodemus refrained, deflated completely by the dramatic turn of events, and too stunned to speak. Much later that day, and far too late to be of any use, he would realize that it had never occurred to any of them that the rabbi's claim to the Messianic title might in fact be genuine; they were not looking for a messiah and in reality they didn't want one.

With a satisfied nod of his head toward the officer, Caiaphas invited his friends to retire with him for some refreshment while they waited for sunrise, and the prisoner was rounded up by the bored soldiers and dragged in the opposite direction toward the door. The crowd of onlookers, including the pale, terrified John, was pushed out in front of them.

"This man was with the Nazarene."

Peter turned away, struggling to free himself from the hands that were reaching for him.

"He was," said a filthy, bent old woman. "I saw him come in with...with that one over there!" she shrieked, catching his arm in one hand and pointing at John with the other, who was racing down the steps into the courtyard.

In full panic, Peter jerked his arm away from her cold grasp, breathing far too rapidly and on the verge of passing out. Turning to his right, he tried desperately to escape, but a soldier stepped in his way, and said loudly, "Certainly you are one of them, for you are a Galilean."

"It's him!" cried yet another. "He's the one who struck my brother with a sword!"

Peter snapped.

With surprising strength, he pushed his accusers away, including the soldier, cursing, and shouting in their faces, "I do not know the man!"

Lurching back to his left, he froze: his eyes locked with

those of his betrayed Master, who was standing between two soldiers at the foot of the steps, behind a stunned John. And behind him the first glimmer of sunrise tinged the horizon as the cock crowed heartily, announcing the new day.

Friday Morning, First Hour

"The Jews have pronounced the sentence, your majesty."

"I see that you are pleased with yourself, but we haven't attained our goal just yet; there is still much to do and much that could go wrong. Make sure that nothing does, or I will hold you personally responsible."

"Yes, my lord," replied the high ranking spirit, fully comprehending the implied deadly consequence. He bowed low, and left in haste. A short while later, standing atop a barren hillside just outside the city in the dim early morning twilight, he met with his commanders to finalize the details for the day. It was a brief meeting, and though they had gained confidence throughout the last twenty-four hours, they were still operating blindly, more from wishful thinking than from an actual battle plan. There was still widespread doubt about whether they could actually pull it off.

"There can be no mistakes; make sure that nothing goes wrong, or I will hold each of you personally responsible."

The assembly of commanders bowed and murmured together, "Yes, my lord," and then each of them sped off in their various directions to spread the threat as widely as possible.

While the soldiers waited in the frosty courtyard for orders to march the prisoner over to the Sanhedrin, they found it necessary to provide themselves with amusement to stay awake. There was the usual taunting and bravado common among soldiers, as well as harmless storytelling and gambling. But eventually, the amusement focused on the prisoner, and after another round of taunting and bravado at his expense, and after exhausting their normal methods of bullying and torment, their activity turned brutal as they began improvising in order to keep it interesting. Someone found a dirty bit of cloth lying near the fountain, and making a blindfold he tied it around the prisoner's head. They spun him in circles until he vomited, they shoved him from man to man - sometimes catching him, sometimes letting him fall; they beat him with their fists and the flats of their swords. Finally they asked him to prophesy who among them was striking him; thankfully, the fire had died out, or hot coals and heated weapons would have been used in the sport.

By the time the sun was finally clearing the skyline, Jesus was slumped in a heap against the wall, no longer able to keep his feet. He was bruised and bloody, with a swollen lip and several ugly marks on his face. The soldiers, moving about the courtyard yawning and stretching, had lost interest and were growing impatient to be moving. Eventually there came a dull thud from the direction of the house, and the commanding officer descended the steps, strapping on his helmet. He started to say something, but stopped when he noticed the condition of the prisoner. He glanced around quickly at his soldiers, but no one would return his look.

"I thought that I made it clear I wanted no foolishness."

His men continued to look at their feet or off into the distance; no one looked at the officer and no one said a word.

"Get him to his feet. The priests will be out momentarily."

And sure enough, the door burst open again, and a large number of men clad in pure white descended the steps, with the high priest leading the way wearing his torn ceremonial garment like a badge of honor. They were chattering and animated as they walked briskly toward the street, pointedly ignoring the soldiers and their dirty, disheveled prisoner. They were on a mission this morning, and there was much to do.

Deep in the bowels of the Praetorium, several levels below the street where daylight is never seen, the worst offenders of Roman law were kept under heavy guard in small, rodent infested cells carved right into the bedrock beneath the city. In most cases, the men and occasional women who find their way into these hellish pits never come out again until the day of their execution. They were ill-treated and ill-fed, and were allowed no visitors. Since there was nowhere in the region more closely guarded, there were also no escapes.

On the day that Jesus was arrested, however, most of the cells were empty; two weeks previous to that day all of the residents had been destroyed together in a fire, since one of them had been discovered with early signs of leprosy and the jailers were afraid it would spread. Among the three or four men, placed in this pit of horror since that time, was a particularly brutal individual who had been evading arrest for many years. He had been roving the countryside with a band of zealot rogues, disrupting the Romans where possible, stealing from the Jews when they needed it, and brutally murdering anyone - Jew or Greek - whom they suspected to be sympathizers with the Romans.

The growing band of zealots had eventually become legendary, famous in some circles as heroes who stood up to the Roman oppression, and infamous in other circles, condemned for killing and stealing from their own brothers. To the Romans, they were more of a nuisance, since without real weapons they were not very effective in direct combat or confrontation; but the Romans did not tolerate murderers, even if the victims were just Jews. So the hunt had been engaged for months to find the man without a name, the leader of the zealots who referred to himself simply as 'son of my father', or Bar Abbas. When he was finally trapped and captured in the Judean highlands and brought to Jerusalem on the Monday before Passover, the moment went largely unnoticed, due to the overshadowing presence of the rabbi teaching in the temple. But by Thursday, he had been in his dark, oppressive cell long enough, and had begun to make noise. Bar Abbas wasn't used to staying in one place, and he wasn't used to rats.

"Hold it down in there! If you keep up that racket, I'll send someone in there to cut your tongue out!" said a muffled voice from the corridor outside his cell.

"Get me out of here! How long am I going to rot in this place? When will I be brought out for trial?"

The voice laughed for a moment on the other side of the low door and said something to someone, and then both of them laughed together.

"Oh. You'll be brought out all right, and soon enough. They'll either roast you over a fire like a pig or nail you to a cross; probably will give you your pick." The two laughed together again, and the sound of their laughter faded away. Bar Abbas slumped back against the cold stone, shivering in the darkness, cursing the Romans and feeling very alone. But, of course, he wasn't alone at all.

Outside the city, several hawks were already circling high overhead in the first hint of rising air currents, watching and looking; and as the first flash of brilliant sunlight peeked above the barren wilderness to the east, a mild breeze picked up with it. Before long, trailing behind the rising sun, a dense black haze slowly rose above the horizon, distorting and smudging the early morning sunlight ever so slightly. On the hillsides all around Judea cattle and sheep paused in their grazing; deer and wolves in the forests, goats and gazelles in the wilderness and God's creatures everywhere stopped and took notice of the subtle yet ominous change in the sky.

Out of breath and so disheveled and unkempt that he looked as if he were out of his mind, Judas rapped loudly at the door through which Jesus and his captors had just left. When no one responded, he knocked louder, and began shouting and cursing and kicking the door. For those inside, it had been a long night, and none of them had slept, so this new disturbance was not welcome. The servants who were still conscious did their best to ignore the racket, hoping that whoever it was would tire and go away. But after it became clear that he was not going to relent, the sleepy maid forced herself to rise, to clothe herself properly, to cross the length of the house, and finally shuffled down the steps into the courtyard, around the fountain and over to the outer door which opened to the street. The noise and pounding outside was by now intolerable. She opened the peep hole and vehemently scolded the stranger she saw standing there with his hand raised to pound again. She rebuked him in very colorful language for creating so ugly a scene at this early hour.

"God bless you, young woman; I am sorry to disturb you. I am looking for the high priest and the man whom they took into custody last night. Are they here?"

"Lucky for you that his worship the high priest is not here, or else he would have you whipped for your bad manners; they have just left, not a quarter hour ago."

"Please; you must tell me where they were headed. Were they going to see the governor?"

"The high priest does not consult with me about his plans," she said, closing the little window, and ending the interview.

"Please don't go," he called in a panic. "You must have some idea; perhaps you heard one of them say something?"

Turning away from the door and heading toward the comfort of her bed, she called over her shoulder, "Nor am I in the habit of eavesdropping on the high priest. Now go away, or I'll send for the Romans and have you arrested."

Peter ran, unheeding where his feet were taking him. He had never been so frightened, so angry, so humiliated, and so ashamed.

News had spread about the arrest in the middle of the night, and by the time the entourage from the high priest's house arrived at the meeting hall in the temple, adjacent to the Court of the Gentiles, the room had been packed for over an hour. All of the rulers of Israel were there, all seventy-one of them. It was a rare meeting of the Sanhedrin when more than two-thirds were present, but this morning the turnout was quite spectacular. According to the long standing custom, the high priest and his relatives took the center of the table, and the president of the Sanhedrin, or the 'prince' sat next to the high priest's right, while the vice-president, the several secretaries and the constables all crowded around these on both sides. The rest of the huge, raised table was filled in descending order of importance, with the youngest and the newest members stationed at both ends, far from the elite and powerful who sat near the leaders at the center.

When the high priest had finished making his rounds and sharing his greetings, all the while flaunting his torn robe, he at last stepped to the seat of honor and invited his brethren to sit down. Immediately he took on a grave expression, and proceeded to explain the reason for the meeting on so sort a notice.

"As many of you are aware, we have been concerned for many months about a young rabbi from Galilee who has been touring the nation, stirring up unrest and promoting a philosophy that encourages the breaking of both Jewish and Roman laws."

A number of heads nodded in agreement, and an undercurrent of buzzing disapproval swept the table. Encouraged by this response, Caiaphas continued:

"On several occasions, we have sought to discuss our concerns with the young man, but he has proved to be obstinate and unwilling to speak with us in a civilized manner. As a result, we were forced to seek him out and bring him in for such a discussion. Our intent was never to harm him, but merely to open a dialogue. Even so, when we sent for him, he refused to come, and we were compelled to take him into custody against his will."

"My lord, High Priest, if I may..." began Nicodemus, but Annas had expected the interruption, and quickly cut him off.

"My friend, you will have an opportunity to speak your mind freely in a few moments, but I suggest that until then you keep your peace and let the high priest explains this very delicate situation to us."

"But my lord, I object..." he tried again, rising to his feet, but Annas was not to be outdone. He also stood, and calling for the temple guards, he raised his voice, declaring:

"My friend, you are out of order; if you will not be still, I will ask the guards to remove you from your place and we will proceed without you."

Everyone present knew that he could and he would use force to silence his opponents, but most of them were taken by surprise at this sudden confrontation. There followed a terrible moment of crushing tension as the two locked eyes, Annas ready to pounce, Nicodemus smoking with anger and resentment. Someone down toward the end of the table, a safe distance away, called out for Nicodemus to back down and wait his turn, and several others seconded his sentiments.

Shaken by the threat and by the inexplicable hostility rising up all around him, Nicodemus nevertheless opened his mouth once more to plead for caution, but before his words could be heard, he was drowned out by many of his colleagues, who with red faces and angry gestures raised a din of boos and hisses and calls for him to sit down, a shocking spectacle that was unprecedented in the history of that esteemed body. Bewildered, angry, and now humiliated, Nicodemus finally gave up, turned and walked out of the room, followed by a round of cheering and applause.

Annas smiled at Caiaphas, who nodded his approval and called for order. Once the room quieted enough for him to be heard, he resumed his speech.

"Now then; I was explaining how we were compelled to take the rabbi into custody in order to speak with him about our concerns. When he arrived, we invited him to share his views with us and to explain himself, but the rabbi, as I said earlier, was obstinate and refused to discuss any of our serious concerns. He was given ample opportunity to clarify his ideas and philosophy with us, but instead he was rude and mocking, repeating many of the degrading things he has spoken about this humble body of servants in his public speeches."

The level of grumbling and buzzing around the table began to rise, as the leaders of Israel were collectively offended by the arrogance of this young upstart.

"The meeting was difficult, my friends, and we did all we could do to diffuse the hostility, but the rabbi would not relent, and in the end made a declaration that I must sadly bring to your attention. His words were so shocking, so offensive, that you would not believe me if I repeated them to you, which of course I could never do."

By now the mood in the room had grown sufficiently hostile, so Caiaphas nodded to the officer near the door, who stepped outside.

"My friends and esteemed brethren, I warn you to brace yourself for what you are about to hear. I deeply regret the need to subject you to this outrage, but in order to remove all doubt about our desire for truth and justice, it is unavoidable. Bring him in."

Jesus, still bound with ropes but cleaned up and dressed with a fresh tunic was ushered in under a heavy silence. Men all along the table craned their necks and shifted their positions to see the offensive and belligerent teacher from Galilee; for many of them this was the first time that they had ever seen him. He stood quietly before the highest court of justice in the land of Israel, looking down at his feet.

"Young man, a few hours ago, we tried to reason with you, to discuss with you the concerns we have about your teachings and activity, but you refused to answer. At the close of the interview, I asked you a question; I will now ask the same question: will you tell us – are you the Christ?"

The silence was disturbed by a collective, noisy drawing in of breath, so shocked were the leaders of Israel at the question itself. They all leaned forward with wide eyes, holding their breath, the hair standing on the backs of their necks, waiting for his response.

Jesus looked up with sad eyes, and scanned the entire length of the table before he spoke. After what seemed an eternity of waiting, he finally said, "If I tell you, you will not believe; and if I ask you, you will not answer."

The anticipation jumped a level at this response, and the buzzing returned.

Raising his voice to match them, he continued, "But

from now on the Son of man shall be seated at the right hand of the power of God."

The room exploded in a torrent of questions and accusations as many of them leaped to their feet:

"Answer the question!"

"He is speaking blasphemy!"

"Who is this Son of man?"

"Make him speak plainly!"

And finally, one question rang out, and was taken up by several, almost in a chant:

"Are you the Son of God, then?"

"Are you the Son of God, then?"

Caiaphas, who had been watching the prisoner, saw that he was about to speak, and raising both of his arms called for silence. When a relative calm was restored, he repeated the question once more:

"Are you the Son of God, then?"

"You say that I am."

Bedlam burst forth, this time with a wild, incredible furor. Caiaphas let the outrage grow to boiling before he called for the response that he knew he would get:

"What further testimony do we need? We have heard it ourselves from his own lips. What is your judgment?"

"He has blasphemed the Holy One!"

"He is a blasphemer!"

"He deserves death!"

"Death!"

That one word sentiment was urgent, violent, and unanimous. None of them had ever heard such a shocking claim, and none of them would ever forget this unbelievable moment. Thoroughly aroused with indignation, the whole company arose, and following the high priest, they set out to drag the unforgivable blasphemer before Pontius Pilate.

"How is this possible?" Judas whined. "You promised that he would be put in his place and then sent on his way. How is this possible?"

They were standing just outside the Temple in the clear morning light. The huge crowd from the hearing had just left, and Judas had missed them again.

"Come, my friend, let us be straight with each other: you and I both knew where this would lead; you can pout and pretend and protest your noble intentions, but in the end, you have what you wanted and we have what we wanted."

Judas suddenly thrust the bag of coins into the Pharisee's inflated chest.

"This is not what I wanted," he growled. "The deal is off; I want Jesus back."

"You want what?" he replied, nearly choking with laughter.

"I want him back!" Judas repeated. Offended by the mocking laughter he lunged for the man's throat; but a couple of temple guards had slipped in behind them while this heated exchange had been developing, and were prepared for just such a move. They were on him in an instant, slamming him to the ground and twisting his arms around behind him. Judas howled in pain as the guards twisted his arms to an unnatural angle.

"Take care, my friend; if you persist in this childish behavior, you may find yourself standing with your master before the governor. Now I suggest that you take your well-deserved money, spend some of it on good food and wine and enjoy yourself tonight. We will forget all about this little incident, and mark it down to overwrought emotions."

Judas was by now completely subdued, his entire body heaving with uncontrollable sobs. The guards released him, and he curled up in a tight ball, smashing his fists into his head as he continued to wail. The Pharisee was repulsed by the weak display, and stepping away, he muttered under his breath, "Pathetic, simply pathetic."

Judas suddenly lunged to his feet again, screaming incoherently, pulling great handfuls of hair from his head, his teeth grinding and his mouth frothing. He attacked again, this time much quicker, and seizing the startled Pharisee by the neck he began squeezing with unbelievable strength, and looking him straight in his bulging eyes he said with a strange, gurgling voice, "He won't survive, and neither will you!"

The Pharisee was suffocating in spite of the valiant effort of half a dozen guards trying desperately to pull the crazed man away. His attacker's fingers were clenched in a death grip, threatening to crush his windpipe. Just as he began to lose consciousness, Judas was finally ripped away, and the Pharisee fell back, gasping for air while a growing number of guards piled on top of his assailant. He tried to call for more help, but his voice was gone, at least temporarily. And then to his horror, the struggling pile of guards began to slowly rise and was suddenly thrown off like so many discarded wineskins flinging in every direction, and Judas was again standing before him, wild and menacing.

And then just as suddenly he slumped to the street as if someone had crushed him, and began sobbing again.

"I have sinned!" he wailed in a more familiar voice. "I have betrayed innocent blood!"

The Pharisee, wheezing fearfully and struggling to breathe, didn't know what to do, and the temple guards, unused to dealing with such fierce resistance, were likewise frozen and useless.

Judas pushed himself up onto his hands and knees. He slowly reached out and picked up the bag of money lying in the dirt in front of him, and sitting back on his heels, he opened it up. As he squatted there like an animal in the street, alternating between heart-rending weeping and an eerie babbling, his hands trembled so violently that the coins within jingled furiously and began spilling out. And then with one last sudden change, he leapt once again to his feet, his face contorted and his eyes dilated, howling like a wounded dog, and flung the open bag toward the terrified Pharisee, causing the remaining coins to spray out in a flashing arc and tinkle to the ground all around him. He then ran away, ripping once again at his hair with both hands and screaming incoherently.

The Pharisee remained motionless long after the bone-chilling shrieks had died away, but when he noticed the guards eying the silver coins scattered in the dust, he summoned his strength and croaked out a command to gather all thirty pieces and bring them to him. Though it was blood money and could not be returned to the temple treasury, it was still money after all, and could not be left in the street. They would find some use for it.

Friday, Second Hour

Pontius Pilate, Procurator of Judea stepped out onto the balcony to see what the commotion was all about, and was surprised to see a rather large early-morning-crowd gathered at the entrance to the Praetorium. In the soft glow reflected from the high Temple and fortress walls, he could identify among the crowd a number of Pharisees and leading scribes, as well as a mixture of poorly trained temple guards with some of his own veteran soldiers. In the midst of the soldiers, he could just make out a lone man who appeared to be bound with ropes.

That must be him.

A rap at the inner door brought his attention back, and he called out, "Enter."

Stepping through the door, an officer bowed slightly and said, "The high priest, your majesty."

"Ah yes, I was expecting him. Send him in."

The officer coughed.

Pilate looked at him and then cursed, momentarily losing his temper as he faced once again the arrogant Jewish aversion to all things Roman, particularly Roman floor space in Jerusalem.

"They want my help, they want my support, but they won't come into my fortress," he fumed. "Very well; I will go out to them, once again. But there will come a day, perhaps sooner than they think when these fine, pure priests will regret this shabby treatment."

And strapping on his armor, he descended the long stairway to the rear gate.

It had been a long, agonizing night for the disciples; since there had been no contingency plan to fall back upon if something were to go wrong, none of them had any idea what to do or where to go. It had been nearly three years since any of them had been home, wherever home was, and right now the safety of home was an appealing consideration. However, as the long night wore on and they had discreetly found one another roaming around in the dark orchard and had begun to regroup, two common sentiments emerged: they were all mortified by their collective cowardice the previous evening, and they were all determined to rectify it somehow. With the sun now rising high in the morning sky and clearing away the shadows and doubts, James counted heads once again, even though they all knew that Peter and John were still missing, along with the traitor.

"What should we do?" Nathaniel asked James, who was now clearly their leader in the absence of Jesus, Peter and John.

"I don't know. They have probably taken him inside the city, either to the Sanhedrin or to the Romans."

"We can't fight the Romans," whined Thomas, "We will all be killed."

"Then go home, Thomas," shouted someone. "Jesus has been taken prisoner by the Romans, and we are either with him or we are not. I'm not going to run away again, even if it means fighting the Romans."

They were walking along the now familiar pathway that led down the slope from the Mount of Olives, heading slowly toward Jerusalem. They continued to argue about what to do as they walked, oblivious to the rising noise ahead of them until they reached the road from Bethany. Stepping out into the open road, they were immediately awash in an ocean of people, babbling and animated, all moving in one direction: into the city. There seemed to be an urgency to the crowd; there seemed to be an atmosphere of expectation that reminded the disciples of the many occasions when huge crowds formed around them in Galilee, coming from all directions to see Jesus.

"What do you think is going on?" one of the disciples called out to James above the din. James shook his head in response, and then stepping out a little farther into the stream of humanity, he tried to get the attention of a pair of women passing nearby.

"Pardon me, woman; could you tell me why all of these people are rushing into the city?"

"You are entering Jerusalem as well, and you don't know?"

"I don't; could you tell me what is happening?"

"Why, it's the rabbi."

"What about the Rabbi?" James replied sharply, his eyes wide with surprise. The two women stopped and looked at him, and then at each other.

"He has been arrested and will stand before the Roman governor today. They say he will be sentenced to death."

The women found themselves suddenly surrounded by the panicked disciples, who were raising their voices and asking questions all at once:

"Death? Why would he be put to death?"

"Where did you hear this rumor?"

"Are you certain it was the rabbi from Nazareth?"

"When will the trial take place?"

"How can this be?"

"He has done nothing wrong!"

A crowd was now forming around the animated disciples from the foot traffic flowing into the city, stopping out of curiosity about the disturbance. Within minutes, bystanders were now asking the questions:

"Are you friends with the rabbi?"

"Were any of you with him when they arrested him?"

"These men know the rabbi!"

"Will you try to defend him before the Romans?"

"Are the Jewish leaders looking for you also?"

"Why did the rabbi go with them?"

"Why didn't he strike them down?"

"Is the rabbi the Messiah?"

The disciples were quickly becoming overwhelmed and frightened by the growing attention, so James began forcing his way through the mob, shoving his friends ahead, toward the city, and away from the questions.

"We need to get out of here," he cried to Andrew,

looking over his shoulder at the people pressing behind them. "And we need to find out what is going on. Where should go?"

"To the Praetorium," replied Andrew. "If he is indeed to be tried today, they will be holding him at the fortress."

The Jews, arrayed in their finest robes and jewelry and wearing their gravest faces, entered with great pomp and ceremony the infamous walled courtyard that was part of the Fortress Antonia, but technically not within it. The Pavement, as it was called, was a location worked out as a compromise between the previous Roman governor and the stubborn Jews who refused to enter the Roman garrison and become ritually unclean. So when there was a matter of state that required the presence of both the Jewish leaders and the Roman governor, they met here at this place. The visitors were kept waiting in an outside antechamber until the governor was ready, who was always seated upon a marble throne six steps above the sandstone pavement when the Jews were finally ushered in.

On this particular morning, there was an unusually high level of security, as evidenced by the large presence of temple guards accompanying the Jews and their lone prisoner, as well as the hundreds of Roman foot soldiers around the perimeter of the massive empty courtyard and at least a dozen personal bodyguards flanked around the governor. An officer led the High Priest to the front of the crowd, where he was to address the governor. As Caiaphas bowed low before the throne and poised to speak, he was struck by the stern, inscrutable expression on governor's face.

Surely he is prepared to cooperate. He must cooperate.

"Your majesty, I present to you the so-called 'rabbi', the trouble-maker of which we have spoken."

Without acknowledging the High Priest's words or his lofty position, Pilate asked rather abruptly, "What accusation do you bring against this man?"

Caiaphas was instantly flustered. He had expected clear sailing at this point, and was not prepared to present charges. He was under the impression that a deal had been worked out, and that Pilate would simply accept their word that a death sentence was warranted.

"He..." Caiaphas began and then stopped. "The prisoner..."

What could he say?

"If this man were not an evildoer, we would not have handed him over."

Caiaphas began to sweat in the silence that followed, while the governor shifted his weight on the throne, clearly dissatisfied with the answer.

Pilate looked at the prisoner, who was standing quietly and looking down at his feet, and then back at the High Priest. After a long moment, he stood and said, "Take him yourselves, and judge him by your own law," and then turned to leave.

"Nay," Caiaphas bellowed out, trying to step forward, but was stopped by a drawn sword. He stepped back, duly intimidated, but nevertheless called after the governor, "It is not lawful for us to put any man to death!"

At the mention of this word, Pilate flinched, and hesitated.

Caiaphas saw his chance and pressed on, speaking to the governor's back, fearful that if he missed this opportunity, he wouldn't have another.

"He must be put to death; he has said...he said..." Caiaphas struggled to come up with something quickly, but he was drawing a blank. "We found this man perverting our nation and..." another blank, "...and forbidding us to give tribute to Caesar, and..." and then with his face lighting up he finally blurted out "...and saying that he himself is Christ...a king!"

Pilate's shoulders slumped. He had known this moment was coming, but had hoped to somehow avoid it, for a variety of reasons. But here it was: the charge of treason against the enigmatic young teacher, in public, in front of potential witnesses both friendly and hostile. Somehow, and he would never know how, word would surely get back to Rome if he were to try to dodge this issue. Reluctantly, against every fiber of his already strained judgment, he turned back and slowly walked to the front of the raised platform to face the prisoner.

"Are you the king of the Jews?" he asked with very little energy, anticipating the affirmative answer that would condemn him from his own mouth, and feeling the invisible scrutiny boring into him from all around.

Jesus raised his head and replied, "You have said so."

Pilate brightened just a little.

Perhaps all is not lost.

Stepping back and regaining his composure, he stood erect and addressed the High Priest and the gaggle of robed finery behind him, saying, "I find no crime in this man."

Suddenly another man stepped forward, another priest or scribe who looked vaguely familiar to Pilate, and declared rather vehemently, "He stirs up the people, teaching throughout all Judea, from Galilee even to this place."

And Pilate brightened quite a lot at that statement.

Of course: this is why Herod has been so interested in him!

"Am I to understand that this man is from Galilee?" he queried, trying to keep the glimmer of hope out of his voice.

Annas knew instantly that he had made a mistake. He knew better; he had warned them all ahead of time that there should be no mention that the man was from Galilee, but somehow the word had just slipped out. Now that the governor had picked up on it, however, there was no point in dodging the question, for Pilate would find out easily enough from where the man had come.

"Yes, your highness, the man is a Nazarene."

"A Galilean;" Pilate actually smiled. "Well, then; this changes things, doesn't it? Let us send the man to my dear friend King Herod, Tetrarch of Galilee," he said pleasantly, and then turning to look directly at Caiaphas he added, "Whom I understand just so happens to be here in the city, as you yourself have recently pointed out to me."

Feeling suddenly exposed, Caiaphas and Annas both winced.

"Yes, send him to Herod; let the king decide the fate of his own subject."

And with that, he turned and strode away before anyone could ask any more questions.

The commander was furious, and was in no mood for excuses.

"What happened? How is it that the governor, your governor, failed to convict him?"

The report had just come to him from spies hidden all around the Roman garrison, spies that did not answer to the spirit before him now, the failed and now humiliated prince of Jerusalem.

"There must have been tampering, my lord," was the sullen reply. "I swear that he had been prepared adequately and could not possibly have overcome the influence he was under without outside help."

"And yet here he is, walking away and leaving us to pick up the pieces."

"He must have been tampered with," the sullen, stubborn spirit maintained.

"Did you, or did anyone in your command see any evidence of enemy forces? Did you or anyone in your command see anything at all - even one single heavenly warrior?"

When there was no immediate response, the commander gave some hidden signal and the spirit under exam was instantly seized and dragged away screaming by a swarming, vicious pack of former peers.

With the sound of wild, panicked terror slowly fading off in the distance somewhere, the commander turned to those remaining before him and said, "I will not tolerate incompetence. You – over there – you are now the prince of this city and you will find a way to kill the man before the day is over."

"Yes, my lord; I will not fail."

Outside the city, a lone body hung limply from a lone tree, surrounded by a cloud of homeless demons that could no longer terrorize the betrayer. And off in the distance, the dense, black haze along the horizon spread.

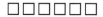

"You have guests, your majesty," said a soft looking, round-headed servant, his voice as soft as his looks.

Herod was still in his bed when the servant made his announcement, and he wasn't ready to rise yet. He growled, waved for the attendant to leave, and rolled over.

"I am very sorry, your majesty, but they are quite insistent. Something about a prisoner sent to you from the governor."

Herod rolled onto his back, growled again, and lay motionless for a few moments. The servant, used to this routine, waited patiently at the doorway without saying any more.

"Who did you say wants to see me?" Herod asked, still laying flat on his back trying to get his eyes to focus. It had been another long, sleepless night, accented with an occasional plunge into terror through a recurring nightmare.

"I believe that it is the High Priest, your majesty, along with quite a number of others, both official and military." By the euphemism 'official,' he meant high ranking Jewish leadership, a word that Herod used frequently to avoid drawing the distinction between himself as an Idumean (a non-Jew) and the Jews over which he ruled as Tetrarch.

The king slowly sat up, trying to avoid another nasty hangover.

"Yes, but you said something about the governor. Is he here as well?" he asked, a trace of apprehension showing on his face.

The round face turned away momentarily to hide the fact that he was smiling, amused at the image of both the High Priest and Governor Pilate showing up at the same time at the doorstep of Herod.

What arrogance this man possesses. And fear: he is clearly afraid of Pilate.

"No, your majesty; the procurator is not here. I meant

to say that the High Priest is here regarding someone that the governor has sent to you."

The fog in his head began to lift, and he replied, "You said a prisoner."

"Indeed; it seems that the High Priest is accompanied by a prisoner."

Herod jumped to his feet and nearly collapsed from the sudden movement.

"It is the Baptist!" His hand trembled as he pointed toward the door as if a ghost were making an appearance there. "Why is he following me? What does he want with me?" he screamed.

"Your majesty, I..."

"My darling, what is it?" cried Herodius as she raced into the bedroom.

The servant quietly stepped out, wisely avoiding entanglement with the wife of the king.

"Did I call for you?" he growled in response, angry that she had heard him lose control again.

"Don't do this, darling; don't shut me out. I know that something is wrong, and I just want to help you..."

"Help me? Help me? It is your fault that the Baptist still haunts me, still follows me wherever I go. If you want to help me, then get out of here!"

"But darling, the Baptist is dead..."

"Is he? Then why do they bring him here this very morning?"

"No, my lord, you must mean the rabbi, the Man from Nazareth. Don't you remember? We have spoken about him often, and you have remarked several times that you wish you could see him perform his miracles with your own eyes."

"The rabbi?" he said in a small voice, as if he were a child.

"Yes, my love, the Galilean. I have been hearing rumors all morning that the Jews have taken him prisoner."

Herod pondered this possibility, his forehead wrinkled with thought.

"But why would the Roman governor..."

"Let them in, my darling, and we shall see. Perhaps you

shall have an opportunity to see a few miracles at last."

"That would be entertaining, wouldn't it?"

Herodius called for the servants, and was instantly surrounded by at least a dozen men and women with wide, curious eyes. She instructed them to wait for a quarter of an hour to give the king time to freshen up, and then to announce the king's guests.

"As you wish, my queen," murmured the round head as he backed away, herding the others out with him.

Friday, Third Hour

"His majesty, Herod Antipas, Royal Tetrarch of Galilee and Perea; I present to you my lord Caiaphas, High Priest of the Holy One of Israel, and his noble brethren."

The scribes and priests, who had been waiting now for well beyond the appointed quarter hour, all swallowed their frustration and bowed low before the king sitting upon his gaudy throne, and the king in turn nodded benignly at them and motioned for them to proceed. The room, though large and lavishly decorated, was uncomfortably crowded with so many robed leaders and soldiers and servants and friends of the court, and Caiaphas had a hard time making his way to the front where he could be heard. Struggling to the center where he made a fuss to create a little breathing space, Caiaphas at length took a deep breath and began his case:

"Your majesty, we are pleased that you have taken the time on such short notice to receive us, and since we are aware that your time is valuable, we would like to get quickly to the point. We approached the governor to request a death sentence for this man, since it is not lawful for us Jews to do so."

That is a curious phrase, 'us Jews,' thought Herod.

He wasn't sure if Caiaphas was taunting his non-Jew heritage or trying to somehow include him as an honorary Jew, a notion that had never quite worked for his father when he had been king over all the land of Israel. He decided to let it pass.

"Not so quickly, my friend. I have long been curious about this man, yet have never had the opportunity to meet him face to face. I have a few questions of my own for your prisoner."

The Jews exchanged nervous glances, but said nothing, helpless as they were to steer the king in their direction.

"First of all, I would like to ascertain his identity."

"His identity, your majesty? Do you mean his parentage?" asked Caiaphas.

"I mean – who is he? This is not a difficult concept."

"He is the so-called rabbi who has been traveling the countryside, teaching all of Israel to beak our holy laws and to rebel against the Romans," he answered, not sure where the king was going with the question.

"WHO IS HE?" Herod asked once more, in a loud and very distinct voice.

Caiaphas, entirely lost, hesitated.

"He is Jesus of Nazareth, the son of Joseph, a carpenter," answered Annas.

"Are you sure?"

"We are absolutely sure, your majesty."

"There is no possibility that he is actually someone else, say...the Baptist?"

And the Jews, aware of the king's rumored paranoia about the dead prophet, suddenly understood.

"The king is wise to suspect trickery in this man," said Annas, taking the lead, "but alas, he is not the Baptist. He is nothing like him at all, as you can see for yourself. Whereas the Baptist was frugal and observed our custom of fasting, this man is a glutton; he has made a regular practice of eating and drinking with the worst of sinners, and does not wash or keep any of our customs. This man is not the Baptist, your majesty, he is a dangerous fraud."

Herod clearly relaxed at this point, settling back more comfortably on his throne.

"And yet, if this is indeed the rabbi, it is rumored that he performs miracles."

"There have been many rumors about this man, but we have not been able to verify any of them regarding supposed miracles, your majesty."

Herod stood. He walked over closer to the prisoner and looked at him deeply for the first time.

"You are right, I see: this is not the Baptist," he said, speaking sideways to the Jews while still examining Jesus. Then raising his eyes to meet the prisoner's, he asked, "Are the rumors true? Can you perform miracles?"

No response.

"I have been hearing stories about you, about healing men with the most hideous of leprosy, and giving sight to the blind, and even raising a friend or two from the dead. Are these stories true?

Again, no response.

"We have found him to be most uncooperative, your eminence," observed Caiaphas. "The only thing that we have been able to confirm from his own mouth is his persistent and blasphemous claim to be the Christ of God."

"Really? Did he say this himself?" asked the surprised king.

"We have all heard him say these things ourselves, your majesty."

Herod looked at the prisoner, and tried again.

"Are you the long awaited Christ? Is it not the Christ who will overthrow the Romans and restore the splendor of Solomon to Israel? Is this your intent?"

No response.

"Come now, I am asking politely: I would like some proof that you are the Christ. Show us one of your miracles, even a small one. You don't have to raise the dead for me; you can fly around the room or something of that nature. Just once - show us that you are the Christ."

"Your majesty, if we could just..."

"I command you to perform a miracle! Do you defy your king?"

"Your majesty..."

"Quiet! I will have a miracle!"

The cluster of Jews hastily stepped back, packing together in a tight knot to one side, leaving some space around the now isolated prisoner. The king was fuming, pacing around him in a circle, offended by the lack of respect that he was receiving from this strange preacher.

"Your majesty," said Annas carefully after a brief silence, "This man is not only defying you, he defies Rome as well. He is dangerous, and must be condemned to death."

"I wonder..." Herod murmured as he continued to pace around the prisoner.

"I remember a story that my father, Herod 'the great' once told about a young Jewish maiden who gave birth to a son. This son was visited by a strange group of travelers from the east, who declared him to be king of the Jews."

Herod stopped and looked around to see if anyone was following him.

"The Christ, you see, the king of the Jews."

He resumed his pacing and continued his story. "My father also said that he had the little baby king put to death, along with all of his little Jewish friends, in order to ensure that some day one of his own sons would sit on his throne."

He stopped again.

"That would be me, you see."

There was no sound in the room, scarcely even a breath.

Standing face to face with Jesus, eye to eye, Herod asked, "Did the king of the Jews survive that night?"

No answer.

"Your majesty, the governor sent this man to you..." began Caiaphas, clearly agitated by this strange diversion and lack of progress.

"Ah, yes; the governor: I don't believe that you have told me yet why our esteemed...procurator could not find it in his heart to condemn this man himself," he said with a sly grin as he resumed his seat on the throne. "Why is that?"

Caiaphas actually sighed, as if dealing with a child or a half-wit.

"Governor Pilate did not wish to infringe on your jurisdiction, your majesty," Annas interjected before his son-in-law said something that they all might regret. "He sent this man to you as a gesture of good-will, since he is a Galilean. Nevertheless, my lord, the governor was entirely convinced that the prisoner is a menace and should be condemned to death immediately."

There arose a low rumbling among the Jews in agreement, urging the king to take action against the Galilean. The king sat there for a moment, smiling, listening to the growing clamor as if he were entertained by their religious hysteria. But when the myriad of angry voices became loud enough to become irritating, the king raised his hand for silence, the smile gone from his face.

"I have had quite enough for the day, thank you. Since the prisoner refuses to entertain us, I grow weary and must ask you all to leave."

"But your majesty..."

"I will hear no more of your nonsense on the matter. Now if you will be so good..." he said in a bored tone, making a shooing motion with one hand and nodding toward the grand hallway.

The face of the high priest was once again crimson red, in brilliant contrast to his flowing white robe, and he looked as if his head might explode from his shoulders. Annas took him by the arm, bowed to the distracted king, and began making his way toward the door, with the prisoner following in tow behind.

"No, wait; I might have been a bit hasty," called Herod, rising again from his throne. "Bring him back."

The entourage of priests and soldiers did a sudden and rather awkward reverse in the tight space, and the prisoner was presented before the king once again while the Jews looked on hopefully.

"He claims to be the Christ, the king of the Jews, does he not?"

"Yes, your majesty, indeed he does," replied Caiaphas in great relief.

"Then where are our manners? If he is a king we cannot let him go out in public looking this way, can we?"

The Jews looked at one another in bewilderment.

"Wait here," Herod cried with glee as he raced from the room.

"What do you suppose he is up to now?" hissed Caiaphas at his father-in-law, who simply shook his head in response.

Herod returned dragging a beautiful flowing robe behind him, with his wife pulling at the other end in the opposite direction.

"No, my king!" she wailed, trying to slow his progress, without much success. But when she looked up to see the astonished circle of faces in the throne room, she screamed and ran back the way she had come.

"There," he said as he flung the robe at one of the guards standing nearby. "A present for the king of the Jews from my dear wife; She has kept that thing around far too long, a memento from a former husband. Put it on him."

The guard did as he was told, wrapping the obviously very expensive robe about the prisoner, raising a few snickers from the crowd.

"Now then, that is more like it! He is ready to meet his subjects. Now get him out of here; take him back to Pilate with my best regards. I have no use for him."

Standing before the imposing wall of the fortress, the band of nine disciples weren't sure what to do. The entryway was closely guarded by a very large crowd of soldiers, armed to the teeth, and the huge crowd milling about waiting for news was growing larger by the minute. Simon wanted to mingle and ask a few questions, but James and Andrew vetoed the idea in light of their experience on the road outside the city.

"I say we wait with the crowd to see what happens," whispered James to Andrew.

"But how do they even know if he is here? What if he has been taken somewhere else?" Andrew replied, scanning the area around them to make sure that no one was listening.

"Why would they do that?"

"I have no idea, but..." Andrew stopped when he heard a low rumbling noise echoing down one of the streets to his left.

"What is it?" asked James.

"Shh... listen...soldiers on the march."

And sure enough, within minutes, the rumbling sound had grown more distinct and many in the crowd raced away in the direction of the noise to see what they could. Almost immediately, however, they were forced into reverse, scrambling and shoving one another to get out of the way as the first of the military escort appeared around the corner, marching indifferently, oblivious to the civilians packing around them. They came on in waves, dozens of well-trained Roman soldiers, who spread out as they entered the broad plaza in front of the fortress and set up a protective perimeter, followed by the less well trained temple guards. These were followed by the contingent of flowing robes and official frowns, who were followed by more Roman soldiers. In the midst of the last group of soldiers walked the prisoner, still wearing the imperial robe of Philip.

The disciples didn't know whether to laugh or cry at the sight; they were relieved and filled with joy to see their Master, but at the same time they were overwhelmed with shame and fear as the crowd shouted their epitaphs at the prisoner or the Romans, it was hard to tell which.

And then he was gone, sucked through the doorway into the fortress compound along with all of the priests and Pharisees, soldiers and guards. Having now seen the prisoner with their own eyes, the crowd was growing more animated and hostile, and the disciples were again intimidated. James let out an involuntary yelp as he felt someone grab him by the arm. Whirling around to face his assailant, he was relieved to be looking into the eyes of his tired, dirty brother.

"John...," was all he could choke out as they embraced, weeping openly.

The rest of the disciples gathered around, receiving their lost friend back with great feeling, and their total was back up to ten.

"Where have you been?" asked Philip, voicing the concern that they had all been sharing for hours.

John turned and looked in the direction where Jesus had just disappeared, and then turned back with gloomy eyes and said, "I have been following him. It has been an awful night." And beginning at his encounter with Peter in the garden and their subsequent adventure of getting into the city, John brought them up to date on everything that had happened throughout the night.

"But wait," said James, "What happened to Peter when you left the house of the High Priest?"

John shook his head sadly. "I don't know. He just stared at the Master with a terrible look on his face and then ran off into the darkness; it was very strange."

About that time, Matthew noticed movement toward the entrance to the fortress, and a buzzing among the crowd.

"What is it now?" he said wearily.

"I'll go and see," said Simon, disappearing into the mob. Within moments he had returned with the news that the Romans were going to open the gates to let the crowd in to the Pavement.

"What does this mean?" asked Matthew, who was quite sure that it couldn't mean anything good.

"It means that there is going to be a public trial," answered a quiet John.

"Can you tell me why I must again see these...these arrogant, irrational Jews and listen to their hysterical religious charges against this nobody? Can you tell me that?" Pilate was fuming at the news that they were once again at his doorstep, returned from King Herod without any verdict or action taken.

"They say only that the King would not pass judgment, and therefore they must look to you as the voice of Rome to settle the issue."

"Since when are they interested in the voice of Rome?"

Pilate gazed out the window at the rising bank of storm clouds on the horizon, and shivered. It looked as if they were in for some very bad weather. He turned his back to the menacing sight, and tried to think of a way to stay out of the quarrel.

Something is just not right here.

"Can we put them off?" he asked his aide without much conviction.

"My lord, I am afraid that under the circumstances, this might neither be possible or advisable. Caiaphas seems determined to use whatever means necessary to bring this to a conclusion today. Prolonging it will only make matters worse; there is already a large crowd waiting outside, in anticipation of a public trial."

Pilate shook his head slowly.

Why is this one man so troubling?

"Well then; if I must see them again today, let us get it over with. Prepare for a trial within the hour, and open the gates. I want these troublesome Jews to see what their fine leaders are up to."

Their instructions were not hard to follow: spread among the crowd and pass out handfuls of money, as much as necessary, to ensure that there would be no sympathy for the prisoner at his trial. They had finally gotten their forum, and the shepherds of Israel would leave nothing to chance. So with great dispatch, a large number of young scribes and disciples of the Pharisees, all of them normally reserved and distant, raced into the swelling mob with huge sacks of silver coins they had unloaded from the temple treasury. They were eager to speak intimately with as many dirty, smelly merchants and slaves and shepherds and farmers as they could, just as quickly as they could. The race for public opinion was on.

Friday, Fourth Hour

The Roman occupation of Judea had not come by way of an accident. Long before their highly disciplined legions marched for the first time into Jerusalem, Rome had once been nothing more than a minor hamlet with minor power, quietly escaping notice outside of the reach of previous empires. But obscurity was not Rome's destiny, for among the silent, invisible forces battling behind the scenes and helping to shape human history, a powerful force of dark warriors settled in and made this region home.

And so, quiet little Rome slowly muscled its way into local notoriety, developing a reputation for cold, brutal strength. A member of the loose confederation of city-states called the Latin League, organized with the common purpose of fending off outside invaders, Rome rose to prominence and began flexing its muscles. Soon, it outgrew the need for an alliance; swallowing their former partners, Rome emerged from the shallow waters of local feuding as the Roman Republic, which over a period of several centuries of grinding, relentless military expansion evolved into the Roman Empire. By the time Octavius Caesar was crowned Augustus, the first divine emperor, the Roman juggernaut was gobbling up powerful nations and entire regions in a methodical, organized sweep of the known world.

Which led them to Israel.

To the Roman Emperor, this little nation was nothing more than an irritation on the dry, eastern frontier of the empire; but to the wicked spirit ruling behind the throne, it was the dangerous land of the enemy, the place where He chose to dwell, a natural and inevitable target.

Sadly, the children of Israel were oblivious to the unseen warfare as it swept once more into their land. To the Jews, the Romans were just the latest thugs, the most recent invaders to trample and abuse and humiliate them in their own land, in front of their own children. They had suffered a long, long history of abuse, from the Assyrians to the Babylonians, to the Persians, the Medes and finally the Greeks. All of these enemies had been drawn to the same target and had enslaved and impoverished the children of Israel, until the day when the Jews could finally take no more humiliation and had revolted under the Maccabees and finally driven the remnants of the splintered Greek Empire out of Israel. The subsequent freedom had been short-lived, however, for the sound of Roman foot soldiers were already ringing in the background, consuming everything as they came.

On the day that the son of God stood before a Roman governor, the Romans had been ruling in Jerusalem for many decades. And along with their strong military presence and in spite of the occupying demonic spirits had come the Pax Romana, or Roman Peace, one of the very few positive by-products of Roman occupation. By this time the borders of the empire had been stable for nearly half a century, as outward expansion had declined in favor of increased security. Nothing - other than the uninterrupted collection of tax money - was more important to an occupying Roman official than keeping the peace: Roman Peace; the Jewish leaders who were about to stand before Pontius Pilate knew the priority of this objective very well.

As He began to climb the steep stone stairway, prodded from behind with the butt end of a spear and closely surrounded by grunting, sweaty soldiers, He looked up in dismay: there were at least twenty steps before Him. He had been awake now and on His feet for more hours than He could remember, and was beginning to grow lightheaded, His vision swimming a little. He had endured another beating while in the depths of the Praetorium, just for the sport of it, and had nearly fainted in the thick and stifling air. Now, however, back outdoors, the air was refreshing and filled with a confusing jumble of sounds. He took the first step, wincing in pain, but was unable to linger as the spear was jammed rudely into His tender, throbbing side, so He took the second and then the third steps. As He ascended the stairwell, moving from deep shadow into the bright sunlight, the sounds around Him became more distinct, and He could identify them: the call of birds, the clanging of armor, and the steady hum of many voices.

With five steps left to go His head cleared the wall, and His senses were struck all at once: the sound of the powerful roar erupting from the crowd as they caught sight of Him; the panoramic view of the huge walled plaza before Him filled with hundreds of soldiers and the largest crowd He had ever seen; the chill of the stiff unhindered breeze; the jangling nerves and raw emotions running rampant all around Him. Pausing for just a moment, He took these all in without a word, and was again prodded rather immodestly from behind. He stepped forward on tender bare feet, having lost His sandals somewhere in the night, moving where He was directed, until He stopped at the base of yet another set of stairs. All around Him the roaring and tumult of the crowd continued unabated as they all waited for a signal from the throne. Several minutes passed, and finally the lone figure, clad in regal splendor at the top of the stairwell rose and majestically raised both hands to the crowd. The incredible roar increased even more for a moment before deflating and then steadily diminished in a long decrescendo, until there was finally no other sound to be heard but the voice of the birds overhead.

Looking up into the sunlight from the bottom of the Pavement, He could see wings flapping, the air heavy with creatures both visible and invisible chasing around in jagged loops and twists. He could also see off in the distance the wall of darkness steadily raising higher, an unnatural, ugly smear across the entire sky, from one horizon to the other.

The soldiers around Him withdrew a few paces.

The richly clothed figure descended the steps, and turning aside into a low doorway, motioned for Him to follow. The room was small and bare and dark, with nowhere to sit, so the two of them stood, gazing at one another in the gloom.

"I have no desire to destroy you; however, I am under

great pressure from Rome regarding public disturbance and threats to the peace. And as you are no doubt aware, the Jews take full advantage of the situation. If I am to find a way to spare you, you must help me: consider carefully the question I am about to ask you before you respond."

He said nothing, and the two continued to gaze at one another for a long moment.

"Consider carefully now – I have asked you this question once before, and you did not answer me: are you the King of the Jews?"

"Do you say this of your own accord, or did others say it to you about me?"

This was clearly not the correct response.

"Am I a Jew?" was the hot response. "Your own nation (this was said with a savage gesture toward the crowd outside) and the chief priests have handed you over to me," and stepping closer yet, the face leaned in close and asked, "What have you done?"

"My kingship is not of this world; if my kingship were of this world, my servants would fight, that I might not be handed over to the Jews; but my kingship is not from the world."

The face backed away, and with a look of astonishment said, "So you are a king!"

"You say that I am a king. For this I was born, and for this I have come into the world..." He paused, and sensing the atmosphere around Him charging with the presence of many invisible listeners, He declared "...to bear witness to the truth. Everyone who is of the truth hears my voice."

Frustrated arms flew upward in the air, and sarcasm entered the voice; "Truth? What is truth?" and the disappointed figure turned away and strode back out through the doorway into the bright morning sunlight.

Standing once again at the bottom of the steps before the now impatient and murmuring crowd, He searched in vain for familiar faces, and sensing that the trial was about to commence, He lowered His eyes to His feet.

The accusers were recognized, the same inflammatory charges were made with great vehemence, and the crowd began to clamor once again. Added to this, His ears also heard the background commotion of fluttering wings and despicable, shameless taunting from His swarming, invisible enemies.

"Do you not hear how many things they testify against you?" hissed the voice from the top of the steps, as the clamoring increase in intensity.

Again, He did not respond.

The hands were raised again, and again the roar reluctantly diminished.

"You brought me this man as one who was perverting the people; and after examining him before you, behold, I did not find this man guilty of any of your charges against him..."

The crowd expressed their offense at this statement with a loud burst of ugly roaring, to which the outstretched hands tried in vain once more to subdue. When the deafening sound finally lost a little of its edge, there was now a querulous tone to it as the voice resumed: "...no - neither did Herod! - For he sent him back to us. Behold, nothing deserving death has been done by him; I will therefore chastise him and release him."

Something snapped, and the tumult turned ugly at this point. Angry voices and grasping hands sparking violence all over the broad courtyard as men and women and even children were suddenly caught up in a deadly, irrational frenzy. Soldiers sprang into action, systematically crushing force with greater force, obviously prepared for such an event, and sparing no one in the effort. Within a few bloody moments, the uprising was subdued, and there were dozens of limp bodies lying on the floor of the Pavement.

"Listen to me; you have a custom in this city that upon the feast of Passover the governor releases any prisoner whom he chooses. Whom do you want me to release for you, Bar Abbas, or Jesus who is called Christ?"

There was a stunned silence for just a breath, followed by a multitude of voices crying out in near desperation for the murderer. The name quickly became a chant, "Bar Abbas! Bar Abbas! Bar Abbas! Bar Abbas!"

"Why? Why would you not have me release this man?"

"Bar Abbas! Bar Abbas! Bar Abbas! Bar Abbas!"

"The man is a murderer and should be crucified!"

"Bar Abbas! Bar Abbas! Bar Abbas! Bar Abbas!"

"Then what shall I do with Jesus who is called Christ?"

"Let *him* be crucified!"

"Bar Abbas! Bar Abbas! Bar Abbas! Bar Abbas!"

"Why? What evil has he done?"

"Away with this man! Let him be crucified!"

"Bar Abbas! Bar Abbas! Bar Abbas! Bar Abbas!"

"I have found in him no crime deserving death; I will therefore chastise him and release him."

The chanting continued, even as the soldiers led Him away to be scourged, the rhythmic sound ringing in the corridors behind Him as they descended into the depths of the Praetorium.

He was roughly stripped to the waist, thrust upon a stone pillar that bent Him over double to expose his back, and His hands were shackled to the ground.

He could still hear the faint call of the chanting right up until He felt the first blow. Suddenly, as if He were struck by lightning, His back was on fire and the wind in his breast was slammed from his body. He tried to suck in a ragged breath, but before he could recover, there came the second and third blows. His mind couldn't process the barrage of pain it was so severe; each new blow scorched his nerves and shattered his ability to think at all. By the tenth blow, His vision was gone. His heart rate was rising and pounding, his lungs were heaving, and his body soon slipped into shock as the irregularly spaced blows continued to rain down on his back. He went limp as the scourging continued, blow after blow.

He sucked in a deep breath, abruptly reviving at the shock of cold water splashed across His back. The beating had stopped, and He was now soaking wet, shivering already from the trauma He had just suffered. A strong hand released Him from the shackles, allowing Him to slump to the floor next to the concrete pillar. Lying there in a motionless crumple, unable to move in the midst of His own blood and gore, His vision slowly returned, though He was unable to focus His eyes on anything.

A foot kicked His side, bringing His nerves back into play, and His whole body trembled at the shooting pain.

"Get up, you."

He tried to push himself up with his arms, but there was still no strength in them and He slumped back to the wet stone pavement, His face crunching as it struck the floor. The same set of strong hands yanked him up and twisted him into a sitting position against the pillar, causing Him to cry out in agony at the contact with His back.

"No, no, no...Get him on his feet," cried another voice.

Gripped by both arms, He was dragged to his feet where he would have collapsed, had the two sets of hands not kept him from falling. He heard someone behind Him snort a little chuckle, and then He cried out in fresh agony as something very sharp was jammed down on His head, bringing a trickle of blood down his face and into his eyes. His wet, pulverized shoulders and back were then covered with something heavy, and after the searing pain from this fresh contact subsided, He recognized the smell of the royal robe he had been forced to wear earlier in the morning before King Herod.

"There – now that's more like it. Now he looks like the king of the stinking Jews."

He took a weary, painful look around at the dozens of soldiers standing around, gawking at Him. One of them stepped forward and knelt before Him in mock worship, while the rest laughed and called out for more, and someone to His right bellowed, "Hail, King of the Jews!"

There followed a round of hearty laughter just before He was again shackled around the wrists and led stumbling down the long dark corridor, back toward the noise.

Stumbling at last into the blinding sunlight, his weak, trembling body was shaken to the core at the blast of enthusiastic roaring when He stepped into public view. The hands still tightly gripped both of His arms, keeping Him on His feet as the crowd roared on and on. He tried to open His eyes to see them, but the daylight was just too powerful for His blurry, stinging eyes.

"See, I am bringing him out to you, that you may know that I find no crime in him."

The mammoth roar in response was savage.

"Behold the man!"

A familiar voice nearby shouted, "Crucify him, crucify him!"

The response was swift and surprisingly angry: "Take him yourselves and crucify him, for I find no crime in him."

Another voice nearby shouted above the din of the crowd, "We have a law, and by that law he ought to die, because he has made himself the son of God."

There was a sudden commotion around Him, and He was dragged away again, out of the sunlight into a cool place of deep shadow, but not far from the noisy, rabid mob. Opening His eyes and looking back over his shoulder, he caught a glimpse of the darkening horizon above the crowd, the black wall of enemy forces now high in the sky.

"Where are you from?" He was asked, the voice strained and clearly shaken.

He made no response.

"Will you not speak to me?"

"Do you not know that I have the power to release you, and the power to crucify you?"

He opened His eyes and saw the man standing before Him, a distraught and pained look on his blurry face. He finally spoke, His voice raspy and dry, "You would have no power over me unless it was given you from above; therefore he who has delivered me to you has the greater sin."

As He watched, the man stood before him a long moment, struggling with his emotions. The sad face shook slowly, the shoulders sagged, and again the man turned reluctantly and disappeared through the low doorway, dragging with him at least a dozen demonic spirits clinging and clawing at his back. The hands tugged at His arms once again, and He was led back out to the Pavement.

He turned His face toward the sky with His eyes closed, listening. He could hear the unrelenting, overpowering din of the mob, He could hear the ugly flapping of thousands of demonic wings and the tromping of many feet and the rattling of swords and spears and armor, but He was having difficulty finding the happy sounds of chirping birds or rustling leaves. He longed for one last hour alone with his creation, but He knew that this would not happen; instead the moment was nearly upon Him when He would have to say goodbye.

"I have examined this man you have brought before me as one who perverts the law, and I have found in him no crime against Rome."

The angry roar around Him drowned out the words, and He could hear the nervous rustling of robes and chinking of armor and fluttering of invisible wings as the enemy repositioned and re-attacked.

"In the name of Caesar, then, I will now release him."

He opened his burning eyes once more, and straining to keep them open, witnessed the seething mob descend into maniacal chaos, shouting and cursing and pushing one another, pressing forward with the apparent intent to seize Him or to die trying. Though His vision was still somewhat blurry and distorted, He could see hundreds of soldiers spring once again into action and race forward, brutally beating those at the front of the mob to the ground, and trampling over them, begin beating back those behind them. It took several minutes, but in the end, the exhausted crowd backed away, but not very far.

And then the chanting returned.

"We want Bar Abbas! We want Bar Abbas!"

"Crucify this man!"

"We want Bar Abbas!"

As the intensity began to build once again like a relentless tide on the ocean, He heard the voice of the High priest boldly call out above the rest, "If you release this man, you are not Caesar's friend! Every one who makes himself a king sets himself against Caesar!"

"Behold your king!" shrieked the panicked voice of the governor in return, barely discernable above the froth of the crowd.

"Away with him! Crucify him!"

"We want Bar Abbas! We want Bar Abbas!"

"Shall I crucify your king?" the voice rang out in a sudden, unnatural still, as if all other sound was momentarily sucked away.

"We have no king but Caesar," was the ominous response from someone near the throne, and the debate was finally over. A bowl of water was brought before the governor, who declared while washing his trembling hands, "I am innocent of this man's blood; see to it yourselves."

And the deafening blast of approval sent shock waves around the city, ringing in the empty streets, resounding on the cold walls, and soaring into an atmosphere thick with invisible celebration.

Friday, Fifth Hour

He was again stripped of the magnificent borrowed robe and prepared for the long march through the city to his death. He was surrounded by an ocean of faces, some angry and insistent, shouting obscenities and insults, others smug and satisfied, and still others aloof and businesslike. Hands were laid on Him, pushing and prodding, tugging and holding, as He was strapped to a heavy burden, the tight cords around His forearms cutting into His flesh and causing the blood to surge in His throbbing hands. When the hands released Him, He collapsed to the pavement under the sudden, enormous weight on his back. Hands again gripped Him, and feet kicked at Him as He was forced back to His feet.

And then the march began.

His tortured back, which had finally grown numb while standing before the governor, was again on fire, shocked anew by the burden on His shoulders and by the frequent application of a whip or prod when He didn't make sufficient progress in his stumbling. He took one painful step at a time, His breathing labored and His vision blurred by something dripping from His forehead. He wanted to keep His head up, to gaze at the precious, misguided faces around Him one last time, but it took all of His effort and concentration just to put one foot in front of the other and keep going.

The thin line between the physical, bodily torture he was enduring and the invisible demonic torment began to blur, as he saw twisted, angry faces, both human and non-human floating all around him, screaming and shrieking in a surreal background to His breathtaking agony. He stumbled and fell, crashing His face to the street with no way to stop His fall. His vision blacked out momentarily from the incredible pain to his face. Hands gripped at Him again from behind, pulling Him back to His feet, and a whip across his back brought fresh pain throughout His body and fresh air into His lungs, reviving

Him enough to get His feet shuffling once again. But before long, He stumbled again, for He was simply running out of strength and muscle control. They had moved no more than fifty yards at this point in the long grueling procession that lay before them.

Under the influence of the prodding and whipping, the screaming and cursing, He pushed himself to his feet again, and moved three more steps before He fell one last time, and was able to rise no more; the burden on His wounded body was just too great. He floundered for a few moments in a stupor under the weight on his shoulders, absorbing yet another wave of savage kicking in both of His sides, and whipping on his back and legs, and urgent, abusive screaming in his ears. But it was all to no avail; He could no longer find the strength to rise and put a stop to it, so He laid there in agony, gasping for breath in the deepening blackness, His traumatized senses slowly shutting down.

And then the pounding suddenly stopped, and somewhere way off in the distance He felt the binding around His arms relax. And then His hands started pounding in time with his heartbeat. And then the weight was removed from His back, and several hands dragged Him back to His feet. He was still delirious from the recent abuse, and could not yet stand unassisted; so when the hands began to release Him, He slumped forward onto His hands and knees, sweaty, grimy and bloody, breathing rapidly and on the verge of nausea. Raising His face, He was able to focus his troubled vision for a moment, and saw before Him a handful of weeping faces, all women, trying desperately to reach out to Him but restrained by others.

Somehow, He was able to summon enough strength to speak; He lifted His head just a little, and fixing his dilated and bloodshot eyes on them said in broken gasps, "Daughters of Jerusalem...do not weep for me...but weep for yourselves...and for your children..." He gagged for a moment, spit out some blood, and then continued, "For behold...the days are coming...when they will say... 'Blessed are the barren...and the wombs that never bore...and the breasts that never gave suck'...Then they will say to the mountains... 'Fall on us'...and to the hills... 'Cover us'...for if they do this," and here He slowly looked around before finishing, "when the wood is green...what will happen...when it is dry?"

And then He was yanked to His feet and the procession began again. Without the weight of the burden on His back, He was able to keep to His feet for the most part, winding His way carefully through a dizzying labyrinth of swaying, shifting bodies, all the while peppered by dust and small rubble and spittle from the rude, jeering mob and by diving, clawing, flapping spirits.

He felt the wind pick up on His cheeks, and looking up He could see in the distance the tops of a few trees rising above the city wall. They were beginning to bend and sway, and beyond them was the thick black shroud on the horizon, still rising higher, slowly filling the late morning sky. He tripped on an uneven stone in the pavement and remembered to concentrate on the road ahead to keep from falling; His balance was shaky at best, and with His stinging and bleary eyes, His labored breathing, and His tender, throbbing back, He was aware that His body couldn't take many more tumbles. His body hurt everywhere, and with each painful step, He prayed to his father for strength to endure the next one. Time seemed to stretch on slowly, agonizingly, as He made His way toward the Damascus Gate. He knew where they were taking Him: out of the city to the place of death, a favorite Roman spot for killing Jews called Golgotha, or 'place of the skull.' He had seen the blighted place twice before, littered with bones and decay and frequented by huge flapping vultures. He had known all along that someday He would end His life at that horrible place.

He stumbled and fell once more, just before they reached the gate, again at the point of exhaustion. And again He felt the savage blows to His back and legs, and though He tried, He was unable to muster the energy to rise to His feet and put an end to it. Finally, after what seemed an eternity, the beating stopped and His stunned, trembling body felt hands gripping him from both sides; this time, however, the hands did not release Him, but slipped roughly under His arms and across His tortured back, taking His breath away. Closing His eyes and bracing Himself against the jarring pain, He was unceremoniously dragged forward without His help and without the use of His feet. After a long and excruciating journey at the hands of others, He sensed a change in direction, and mustering a little energy, he raised His head, looked up, and saw that He was now outside the city, and rapidly descending. He could still hear the shouting and jeering of the crowd mingling with the unearthly clamoring of the wicked spirits all around Him, but there was now a clear change in intensity.

And suddenly the motion forward stopped. He lifted His head again, opened His eyes, and saw a handful of soldiers making some kind of preparation, and beyond them He saw that they had already crucified two other men, with an obvious gap left between the two. And then His legs were knocked out from beneath Him, and he fell backward into the grasp of hands that stretched his arms wide.

The long-dreaded moment had finally come.

All around that region activity among God's creation ceased: the previously gathering wind quietly wilted and died; the bending, rustling trees grew still and clapped no more; the birds in the sky withdrew and fled; the sheep and cattle on the surrounding hills, the deer and fox and lion in the nearby forest, the goat and gazelle on the distant mountains, and every other living thing with breath stopped where they were and looked away, as their faithful, guiltless, loving benefactor was raised from the earth, nailed to a tree.

The hush was profound; all sound came to an end as if the very air itself refused to cooperate with the poor, foolish humans caught up in their own madness, laughing and gesturing, cursing and spitting at the lover of their soul. The Author of life had not given his beloved animals and plants the ability to weep, or a voice to express sorrow; the earth with its oceans and cliffs and deep valleys had not been designed with an ability to say '*No, this must not happen.*' So when man proceeded with his greatest of follies, his most egregious offense of all time, he proceeded alone, surrounded by mute silence.

The hush spread from that lonely place of death to other valleys and other regions. The mild rolling waves on the Sea of Galilee died out to a listless slick; the soft golden fields of swaying grain grew still; the deep steady flow in the Jordan River dried up to a trickle; the foaming and churning breakers on the mighty oceans tossed about no more; and everywhere on God's green earth, all creatures, from the reptiles of the desert, to the wild zebras of the savannah and the mighty elephants in their herds all stopped in their activities, bowed their heads to the earth, and silently mourned for their Creator.

□□□□□□

In their mad rush to get the prisoner to Golgotha and up on a cross before the coming Sabbath, neither the soldiers nor the Jews had paid attention to their rapidly changing, unusual surroundings. Even now, with the deed done and the condemned in terrible agony, they were still preoccupied with details: who should get his cloak, what epithet should be displayed above his cross, what to do with his body once he was dead. Even the remaining crowd, which had dwindled significantly once the action was over, seemed to be oblivious to the deepening gloom. John was there, along with Mary and a few of the other women, but he too was distracted with concern over his friend and that friend's mother. The only person present that day who observed the ominous changes taking place all around them was the Roman officer who had accompanied the prisoner throughout his ordeal. After performing his grizzly tasks and putting aside his tools, he had stood off to one side, away from the mob, wearily wiping the blood and grime from his arms and face, and had observed that the noise around him died out.

Completely.

There was no longer any sound at all, even the normal background hum of insects or chirping of birds. He dropped his soiled towel and shifted his weight uneasily, looked around at the stark horizon and shuddered slightly when he spotted the towering wall of black clouds rising all around them, blotting out the sunlight.

What was happening?

Everything about this day had bothered him, from his first contact with that smooth, dangerous Pharisee, to the mockery of justice he had witnessed, to the outrageous and shameful treatment of the Galilean, which had been overly sadistic even by Roman standards. And now nature itself seemed to be ripping at the seams.

What did all of this mean?

The man didn't deserve it; of this he was certain, and he was equally certain that his cowardly governor had known it as well. But...he was a Roman soldier and he had a job that he was expected to do.

So when those still lingering in the crowd could no longer ignore the deadly black sky, boiling and seething and closing in all around them finally ran for cover, the officer stood his ground. But he too was shaken; in all of his years of training and mortal combat, nothing had prepared him for this moment; however, he would not allow himself to give in to the cold, rising fear slipping in closely all around him like a nest of snakes. Shaking himself to steady his nerves, and taking up his post beneath the crosses, he forced himself to survey his bleak surroundings from horizon to horizon. Everywhere he looked, all he could see was angry streaks of lightning, flashing and spreading in the deep gloom. Only two or three sturdy witnesses had remained, huddled in a little cluster a few yards away braving the fearsome display. But there was no one else left on the God-forsaken hillside but the officer and the three crucified men. Even the Jews had long since fled.

Come what may, he vowed to himself, *the rabbi would not die alone.*

And then the flashing of lightning slowly died out, and there was nothing left but deep, silent blackness.

Friday, Sixth Hour

Everything around Him seemed to be writhing and bending, even though He could see nothing. His hands and feet were burning, burning, and the smell of foul decay filled His nostrils. Intense pain rippled in waves up and down His body, scorching every nerve and every member, causing Him to shudder uncontrollably, and taking away His ability to breathe. Something slapped at His face.

Where was He?

He wasn't dead, but He was no longer among the living either.

There was no light. There was no sound. There was no one else, no one at all. His arms were still stretched wide and fastened through the wrists with nails, and blood was still oozing from the wounds, though He couldn't see any of it.

Where was He and why was He so alone?

He gasped for air and opened His eyes widely, but still could see nothing but blackness. Something slapped at Him again.

He tried to shake His head to clear the cobwebs, but found that He couldn't manage that simple motion; His traumatized and ruined muscles were not responding.

Where was everybody?

He tried to block out the terrible pain from His mind so that He could think; He tried to recall the last thing that had happened, but everything, including His memory was fuzzy and blurred together.

They had already offered Him the poison; He remembered that much. Or had they? Was He recalling a memory, or was this something that was yet to happen?

He was shivering violently from head to toe, although He felt as if He were on fire. He could tell that there was very little energy left in His failing body, and what was left was being spent on involuntary spasms. Soon His organs would begin to shut down, and then His mind. He tried to remember something, anything that would help clear His confusing, disorienting thoughts.

Why was He here? There was some purpose to this...

Something slapped His face again, this time much harder, followed by another.

Was it a hand?

No, for some reason it didn't feel like a hand, at least not a human hand.

That was it! He was a human.

Memories began to return. He could picture faces of dear friends. He could remember the feeling of a cool breeze gently touching His cheek on a warm evening. He could remember His mother. And with these memories came a flurry of flapping and slapping all around Him, as if in protest. He was suddenly jarred with a blinding, searing flash, a now too-familiar explosion of emotions and sensations, interrupting His thoughts and memories with memories and thoughts that were not His own.

He tried to make Himself focus, and ignore the interruption; He was nearly gone physically, but He knew that He wasn't finished yet. There was something more that He had to do.

What was it? What was the reason that He was in this lonely place?

There was something about fruit...or was it about bread? He could recall sketchy images of a crowd of some sort, clamoring for food, clawing at Him, demanding something from Him, slapping at Him...but no, He was confusing the past with this strange, surreal present. Something was slapping at Him now, trying to get His attention, or perhaps trying to keep His attention from something else. Something else...

He remembered the beating. These images were fresh and painful, and took His breath away again as He felt the sharp blows anew and the horrible burning throughout His body as the lashes pounded on and on...

He recalled a trial, a series of trials perhaps, or what should have been a trial. He could see the faces of angry men leering at Him, clutching at Him, slapping and clawing...

You are doomed.

That was not His voice. It was familiar and ugly, but it was not His.

He remembered eating with His friends, and He remembered that they had all wept together for some reason. He remembered a crowd in an open square, all sitting around Him, listening to Him, and then they suddenly all rushed forward, reaching for Him grasping, swatting, slapping...

There is no way out of this place. You are doomed.

With fierce determination, He ignored the voice and probed deeper, intent on finishing whatever it was that He had started. He recalled riding on an animal of some sort, entering the city. This seemed to be important. With this memory, a dim...something came near the surface of His thoughts, casting a troubling shadow. He remembered walking along roadsides, foraging through fields, sleeping out in the open under starry skies...and going somewhere in a boat. He felt a fierce slap against the side of His head.

It won't work – you will never escape. You have been forgotten.

He remembered stepping into the river. That seemed so long ago now, but even then there had been some great purpose, something looming over the memory, just out of reach. Before that...well, there didn't seem to be anything before that.

How could that be?

He must have missed something.

Though His physical strength was fading, somehow He was able to continue this cerebral quest, actually gaining mental strength, as if the two...natures...were operating in different worlds. He raised Himself up on his crushed and bloody feet in order to gulp in a fresh breath, sending a fresh wave of incredible pain and nausea throughout his frame. But the breath helped: His mind cleared just a bit more.

What had He missed?

It had something to do with...a garden...

Ugly, perverted images suddenly burst upon His senses like a bolt of lightning, stunning Him at a deeper level than He had ever experienced. Voices began clamoring all around Him, mixed with wild, hysterical laughter. His body was buffeted by an incredible barrage of slapping and punching. He closed His eyes, but He couldn't make the obscene and violent images go away, and His body, stretched out wide was defenseless to the invisible onslaught.

You are a fool, you are lost, you are doomed...

He fought to remember, in spite of the horrendous pain within and without. The garden...

Don't go there...you will be sorry!

What happened in the garden?

It won't help – stay away!

In the garden...He had laid down His rights.

The air around Him exploded in a violent fury of shrieking voices and flashes of memories and images and disgusting smells and flapping, and slapping, and pounding, clawing, ripping, and tearing abuse beyond all imagination. But He remembered.

Though the enemy, *His* enemy poured out upon Him unrestrained wrath, He remembered, and now that He was no longer disoriented by His nearly dead flesh, He was able to ignore it.

Welcome to hell.

He knew where He was; but unlike His ancient foe, He also knew why He was here. All of His years on the earth, all of His human experiences had been preparation for this one terrible moment; and in the garden, He had been given one last opportunity to avoid it. But in the garden He had instead surrendered and given Himself up to be slaughtered. However, knowing where He was and why He was here did not make the deadly loneliness of the moment or the terrifying path that lay ahead any easier to bear, for the worst – *by far* - was yet to come.

All around Him the blackness trembled. Summoning His remaining strength, He pushed Himself up for one more jagged breath. His mind was now clear, in spite of excruciating, throbbing, crippling pain. He remembered: He was human, but He was also God.

And He was ready.

Looking up, He saw out in the darkness a tiny point of light moving swiftly toward Him. As it drew closer, it slowly expanded into a flame, then into a blinding fiery ball, and finally as it came to a stop above Him, He could see that it was a monstrous, seething, boiling cauldron of fire, frothing and overflowing with horrific and grisly contents. A more shocking and frightening object could not be imagined; and as He watched, the immense container began to tip and pour out its filthy, nightmarish ingredients, one drip at a time, toward His face.

And the pure, undefiled Lamb of God opened His mouth.

He was suddenly in agony, His throat filled with boiling, blistering liquid, and His mind filled and defiled with scorching visions and accusations.

You killed my father.

And He had. He had robbed and beaten the poor man, and then dragged him away to a dark lonely spot where He stabbed him repeatedly until he was dead, and then moved on in search of other victims. He was a serial murderer.

You abandoned me.

He had slapped His own daughter, looked into her eyes and cursed the day she was born, and then had walked away in a drunken rage without turning back, leaving her to care for herself at the age of twelve. He was an abusive, selfish coward.

You ignored me.

He had been absorbed in His own pursuits, and had neglected His wife, the love of His life, and had driven her into the arms of another man.

You cheated on me.

He had been the lonely wife.

And He had been the lover.

You took away my dignity.

You led me astray.

You offended me in front of all of my friends.

You ruined my life.

The scalding flow increased, and He drank it. And as He drank, He found Himself sinking, weighed down by the awful burden bearing down upon Him. He was falling into some kind of yawning chasm, yet still poised beneath the filthy boiling cauldron with His arms spread wide.

You laughed at me, just like all of the others.

The young man had been tormented repeatedly by a gang of bullies, and He had failed to defend the pitiful fellow, instead joining in the mistreatment in order to avoid trouble Himself. The young man had eventually taken his own life to escape the torment.

You turned me away.
You wouldn't help me.
You let me starve to death.
You tortured my family and made me watch.

In His terrible agony, He looked up with tear-filled eyes at the smoldering urn above Him; it was still full, and it was pouring out toward Him in a flaming torrent.

You lied to me.
You broke your promise.
You conspired against me.
You didn't love me.
You turned my boyfriend against me.
You burned my house to the ground.

The accusations and vivid memories were all true. He was the arsonist; He was the arson. He was the woman caught in adultery; He was the adultery itself. He was the selfish rich man hoarding His wealth; He was the envious poor man who pilfered from the rich man's hoard.

You slandered my name.
You violated my trust.
You caused me to stumble.
You taught my son to use filthy language.

He looked down, His eyes wide with dread. There seemed to be no bottom to the loathsome pit into which He was rapidly descending, a place of ever deepening misery and despair. His heart began to burst with loneliness. What had happened to God?

> *You refused to forgive me.*
> *You defrauded me in court with false claims.*
> *You didn't care.*
> *You forgot about me, and left me without hope.*
> *You killed my baby.*
> *You destroyed my village.*

He was a rapist; He was the act of rape; He cheated, He robbed, He lied, and He was the lie itself. He beat without mercy; He ruined without conscience; He plundered, tortured, gossiped, demanded, took no pity, took no prisoners, took no second thought.

And still the massive flaming cup was full and pouring out like a river.

He was selfish, He was rude; He thought only of Himself, served only Himself, defended only Himself, and enriched only Himself.

> *You kept me from everything dear to me.*
> *You infected me with a fatal disease and never told me.*
> *You betrayed me.*
> *You hated me.*
> *You used me.*

As His crimes and wickedness continued to mount and parade before Him, He realized to His horror that He had descended so deeply and was so isolated that He could no longer sense His father's presence at all. He was utterly alone.

> *You took everything I owned.*
> *You destroyed my faith.*
> *You watched my despair and did nothing.*
> *You said that you were my friend.*

You tempted me.

He was jealous, He was abusive; He inflicted hardship and sorrow, He spared no one. He was petty and vindictive and quarrelsome, a starter of fights, a challenger of character. He valued nothing, ruined everything, and blamed everyone else. He started wars; He burned bridges; He incited riots. He butchered, He maimed and He destroyed. He inflamed wicked and perverted passions in others and indulged Himself in them. He hated for every reason and for no reason.

His enemy was not the guilty one in all of this, He was.

He had sinned in every way imaginable, He had broken every commandment; Precept upon precept, line upon line, every warning, every rule, every law, and every restriction: He had violated them all. Big, glaring, ugly transgressions and small, hidden, nearly painless infractions; from the beginning of time to the end, He was guilty of every sin ever committed. And still the great cauldron was far from empty.

"My God, My God, why have you forsaken me?"

Friday, Seventh Hour

As the Master hung on the cross, suffering unspeakably and dying slowly, the world around him remained cloaked in deep darkness and a heavy quiet; for the sun refused to shine on this foul crime, and creation would not lend its collective voice as an accomplice. But the world and its creatures were not the only witnesses that day; mankind everywhere reacted in abject fear to the supernatural blackness that engulfed them on every shore and in every home. Fervent prayers were everywhere raised to gods of stone and wood, and hasty sacrifices were offered to expiate divine anger. But in the land of Judea, among the Master's own people, were those who felt the darkness the deepest.

Peter was lost, numb, and inconsolable. After his flight from the high priest's house the night before, he had run through the tangled, confusing streets of Jerusalem until he dropped in a heap on some side road in a dismal corner of the city and laid there whimpering, curled up in a ball. He was afraid to get up, afraid that someone would find him, afraid that no one would find him. He had no will to seek refuge, no will to go on; all hope was lost, and nothing would ever be the same. If God had any mercy, He would let him die quietly right here so that he would never have to face anyone again.

Pontius Pilate could not get his mind off of the Nazarene. He had never seen anyone take the punishment this man had been given and still hold his tongue. He had been warned by his wife to have nothing to do with him, and he had known from the beginning that the charges against him were flimsy at best. But what could he do? His hands were tied. Sitting alone in his opulent house, in deep blackness and mind-numbing silence, he rehearsed the trial over and over in his mind, looking for ways he might have avoided the outcome. But without any variance, every scenario he examined returned to the moment he had looked into the man's eyes and pronounced judgment. As long as he lived, he would never be able to forget that moment or those eyes. Stranded here in the menacing mid-day darkness, his mind could see nothing but those innocent eyes.

John was still at the cross with the mother of Jesus and Mary Magdalene, the three of them stranded in total darkness. While there had still been a little visibility left from the flashing lightning, he had noticed that no one else had remained except for a single Roman soldier. Now, he could only assume that the soldier was still there. John was terrified, and he could tell by the trembling of the two women under his arms that they were terrified as well. He had considered taking them away, but how could he? With no light whatsoever, he couldn't even see his own hands, so trying to find his way along an unfamiliar and treacherous road was out of the question. The world seemed to be coming to an end. The Master was dying, the sun no longer gave its light, and all sound had died away. In the eerie still darkness, John wondered if he would ever see a sunrise or hear a bird singing again. He knew that he would never smile again.

Caiaphas and Annas had planned to celebrate their victory. But it would be difficult to celebrate in total darkness. No one could join them; no one could serve them. So instead they sat, side by side, on the western steps of the temple. They had been urgently making their way home in the strange waning light, and by the time they had reached the temple gates, they could make it no further. As they had fumbled their way to the steps and sat down, neither of them had spoken; both had been afraid to say anything, afraid to face the obvious connection between the events of the day and the sinister blackness that hung about them like a death shroud. Surely the sun would come back out. This was only an eclipse or something of that nature, and surely things would soon return to normal. There was nothing to fear. Soon the Nazarene would be dead, and the Passover would begin. There was nothing to fear. At least, that is what they both told themselves.

King Herod thought that he had gone blind. He had wakened from a drunken stupor, aroused by shouting and wailing, only to find that he could see nothing. Calling for his servants as he stumbled about in disoriented alarm, he panicked even further when no one came to his aide. He tripped on his robe, and crashed to the cold tile floor. A chilling fear crept up the back of his neck. He called again, this time for his unlawful wife, again to no avail. He was alone; he had to assume he was somehow blind, and at least partially deaf, and no one would help him. It was the judgment of God, he was sure of it, for killing the Baptist. Or was it the Nazarene?

James and most of the remaining disciples were huddled together in the room where the previous night they had eaten the Passover meal with the Lord. They had been hiding here since the trial had begun, frightened away initially by the threatening crowd, and then out of fear of the Jewish leaders and the Romans. Later, when the sunlight began to fail, none of them were willing to venture out to see what was happening. Instead, they shrunk further into the corner of the room, devastated and silent. They were a hopeless and frightened bunch, with nowhere to go, no leader to guide them, and no light by which to see. "If only Peter were here," Thomas whined, "he would know what to do."

In the same city, but among much darker company, the atmosphere was decidedly more upbeat. Never before had rebellious spirits had so good a reason to celebrate. The enclosure, the largest by far that had ever been attempted, had been a complete success; the target disciple had been compromised and used to near perfection; the religious leaders had been easy to manipulate; the foolish king had provided no resistance; the mob had been easily incited; the proud Roman governor had caved and delivered the sentence as expected; and now the entire world had been plunged into darkness. No one could have asked for more. The festivity had been escalating all morning in the comfortable, pleasant blackness, and the commanding officers, from top to bottom were having a difficult time keeping their ranks together. There were just too many of them to control. There were more demons in this one region than ever before assembled anywhere, for any purpose, and they were literally crawling on top of each other, yelling and screaming, laughing and cursing. Since violence and deceit had always been the normal way of life, and since there had never before been such a monumental success, the kingdom of darkness in their moment of triumph naturally resorted to violence. Fights broke out everywhere, bragging turned vicious and deadly, and disorder and chaos spread like wildfire.

But what did it matter? Their mortal enemy was nailed to a Roman cross, brutalized and dying, and completely at their mercy. Right now, nothing else mattered.

He was guilty, guilty, guilty: murder after murder, generation after generation; Political corruption, animalistic brutality, private vice; He did it all, saw it all, became it all. He was responsible for every form of sexual perversion and abuse ever conceived; He performed every act, He gave in to every impulse. He employed every cruelty the mind could imagine, and fostered enslavement to every form of bondage ever conceived. He was guilty of every bad temper, every curse word, and every compromise, from the beginning of time.

He was the one who ate the apple.

He was the one who killed defenseless Abel.

He built the tower of Babel, sinned with impunity in Sodom, and stole His older brother's blessing and birthright.

He lied to His son-in-law, He cheated His father-in-law.

He sold his little brother into slavery.

He oppressed His own people, and slaughtered their firstborn.

He sinned in the wilderness, worshipping idols and fueling complaints against God.

He raised armies, burned villages, killed without mercy, and plundered without restraint. He tortured prisoners, enslaved free men and raped their wives. Nothing was sacred, nothing was off limits. He hated black people, white people, brown people and anyone else in between.

He broke promises, kept score, and got even.

He was ungrateful to His parents.

He was self-absorbed and oblivious to the cares of His children.

He ignored the needs of the poor and scoffed at the homeless.

He was falling into oblivion, abandoned and outcast. And now He was burning up, as if He had been fed to a furnace. His flesh felt as if it was melting and His face as if it was about to flash into flames. And still the vat poured out its hideous flow.

A teenage girl cries herself to sleep because of *His* cruel words.

A soft spoken co-worker is fired for *His* laziness.

A grandmother's heart is broken because of *His* indifference.

A family is devastated by *His* drunkenness.

A father grieves for a daughter *He* has led astray.

There was no crime that He did not commit, no mischief that He left undone, no unkind word that He did not say. And every one of them, without exception, had been carefully stored away in this crucible for this very hour. As the flow of wickedness was poured out upon the Son of God, time lost all meaning. Seconds became years, and minutes became an eternity.

Friday, Eight Hour

In the darkness blanketing the city, the enemy was forging ahead unhindered. Now that the Son of God was on the cross and dying, things were about to change. For centuries and millennia, the prince of darkness had pursued his quest to regain what had been lost in the rebellion: a chance at becoming God himself. Nothing else had ever satisfied, nor had anything ever happened to diminish this defining passion. He would settle for nothing less, and now, finally, that burning ambition was within reach.

In nearly every culture around the world, from the beginning of time, Lucifer and his fellow outcasts from heaven had worked non-stop to deceive and intimidate humans into false worship – worship of they themselves, that is - via worship of the sun and moon and birds and a wide variety of quasi-humans gods and goddesses. In most cases the campaigning and bullying was successful, at least for a season and in some cases even a very long season. But in every case, the worship was never permanent, and it was never enough. What Lucifer wanted, what he had fought for and been exiled from heaven for, was worship from all. His aspiration was and continued to be the throne of heaven, where he would sit as God's replacement.

And now it was so close he could taste it.

Everything was ripe for the overthrow. The Son of God had been isolated and defeated; the world of men had largely been gathered under the rule of one controlled individual, the newest of false deities (who until very recently Lucifer himself had inhabited); and the famed host of heaven, the powerful warriors led by the archangel Michael had disappeared entirely. There would never be a better opportunity.

So the high council was convened to generate a plan. Moving freely in the cloak of worldwide darkness, they gathered openly for the first time ever, without fear of man or angel. At the brief and very upbeat conference, it was determined that while his best commanders spread out across the face of the earth over the next few days, re-deploying their legions in key locations for the takeover, Lucifer would seek an audience in heaven. This time, however, the visit would be different. He would take with him the very best of his troops and stand before the throne, present his demands face to face, and watch with his own eyes as his ancient foe stepped down, trembling in fear. He would have no choice; without his Son to do his bidding, and without his angels to defend him, he would be forced to surrender in humiliation.

But first, the Son had to die.

The deep blackness somehow grew steadily darker and more oppressive. And the searing pain in His hyper-extended arms along with the throbbing, scalding pain in his misshapen hands and bloated feet competed with the horror and agony of asphyxiation, for He had to employ those poor useless limbs to raise up high enough to relieve the pressure on His diaphragm in order to draw a feeble breath. It was all very bewildering: He was still fixed to a Roman cross and slowly dying, but at the same time He was tumbling and freefalling into a dismal, lonely, blistering, bottomless chasm, and all the while the sickening, defiling flow from the foaming vessel poised above Him never wavered, never missed His lips, and He was now bloated with sin and filth.

And the river of sin continued to pour out on Him:
Billions upon billions of angry and thoughtless words;
Haughty looks and calculated lies in numbers too great to imagine;
Scores of holocausts, tens of thousands of bloody massacres;
Endless incest and sodomy and perversion and deviancy;
Oceans of secret compulsions and hidden addictions;
Trillions of betrayals, trillions of rejections;
Vast numbers of robbery and pilfering and larceny of

every conceivable fashion;
Immeasurable amounts of wicked thoughts, condemning attitudes, and hypocritical behavior;
And of injustice, prejudice, intolerance and bigotry;
And of negligence, laziness, carelessness, and recklessness;
And above it all there towered self love and self absorption so vast that it exceeded everything else combined, many times over.

It was He who committed every sin, every single one.
He spoke the angry words and thought the wicked thoughts.
He committed the robbery, He betrayed the friend.
It was He who succumbed to temptation, He who turned away.
Every careless, lazy, reckless or negligent act was His, and His alone.
And the flow continued to surge, deep and unchecked.

□□□□□□

The High Priest and his father-in-law were growing restless in the unnatural darkness. There were arrangements to be made, followers to be rounded up and arrested, and rumors to be stopped. On their way back from Golgotha, before the light was completely gone, there had been widespread panic in the streets. Some had been saying that the darkness was a curse from heaven, and others that it was a sign of the coming end of the world. Still others claimed that the Nazarene had caused it, and that he would come back from the dead to haunt them. These rumors could cause trouble, and had to be stopped.

Caiaphas heard movement off to his left, where Annas had been sitting.

"Where are you going?" he asked, his voice tinged with alarm and sounding very small and distant, even to him. There was no reply at first, so he asked again, raising his voice, "Where are you going?"

"We can't sit here all day. I'm going to find a torch."

Annas was gone for a long time. Caiaphas tried to sit quietly, waiting and watching for the flash of a torch, but his eyes grew tired staring into the darkness, and soon panic began to set in. He was afraid of the strange darkness and afraid of being alone in it. He continued turning his head from side to side, looking and listening, but saw and heard nothing.

Finally, he heard muted rustling of robes beside him.

"Is that you, Annas?"

"It is."

"Well? Where is the torch?"

Again, Annas did not answer immediately. Caiaphas heard him sit down on the steps beside him and could hear his deep breathing.

"What is the matter? Couldn't you find a torch?"

"I found one, but it wouldn't light."

"What do you mean, 'It wouldn't light'?

"I mean it just the way it sounds. There are no lighted lamps or torches anywhere, and I could produce no spark."

"That's impossible."

"Tell me, my dear son-in-law, what does the city look like at night?"

"Why it looks...what do you mean? You know how it looks."

"Yes, but how do I know how it looks?"

"Why are you testing me with riddles, old man? I am in no mood for this."

"You and I both know how the city looks at night because we have both *seen* it. How does it look to you now?"

"I can't see it."

"Precisely; and why can't you see it?" Caiaphas refused to answer, so Annas answered his own question, "We cannot see anything, because there is no light. No light whatsoever: no sun, no moon, no stars, no lamps, no torches. There isn't a single burning lamp anywhere in the city, and no one is able to light one."

"But why, Annas; what is happening?"

And then they felt the ground beneath them rumble.

Annas gave no reply.

He was nearing the end of His life; He no longer had the strength to push up for a breath, and was losing consciousness and motor control. His heart was beating furiously, trying to pump blood to His oxygen-starved extremities. His mind was failing, overloaded with the weight of so much sorrow and sickness and shame. Though He was indeed the infinite Lord of the universe, He was also a man, a mortal with mortal limits, and those limits had long been exceeded. He was breaking down, his body no longer able to cope with the defiling onslaught.

He was falling, falling, falling....

His lips burned, His mouth burned, His chest burned, His eyes burned.

He was all alone, lost and forgotten; He was left out.

He was wickedness, in all of its ugly forms, and He was without help. For Him, there was no savior, no one who would be coming to His rescue: for along with all of the sin and rebellion of mankind, all of the crimes against man and God that He took upon Himself and claimed as His own came the penalty for each one – eternal damnation. For Him there was nothing left but the fearful prospect of judgment and fury, blazing and consuming and infinite.

With the last of His strength, He slowly raised His head and looked up into the blackness above Him, where He saw nothing but a dark, empty cup. He bowed His head, closed His eyes for the last time, and said,

"It is finished,"

and

breathed His last.

Friday, Ninth Hour

The darkness began lifting, and all around the city, activity slowly resumed. The merchants and vendors, who had been interrupted in the final rush before the Sabbath, were the first to venture out into the bizarre twilight. The events of the morning had ruined sales even before the darkness had set in, and although there were no consumers out in the streets yet, it would only be a matter of time. The poor street merchants were determined to be ready to make up for lost time.

Then the soldiers emerged, both Roman and Temple Guard, quietly and discreetly taking up posts that had been deserted in the dark. Officers took stock of their positions, gave orders, and deployed fresh troops for the afternoon watch, though it was still hours away from the normal changing of the guards.

Timid faces appeared in windows and peered up at the mellowing sky. Children escaped from doors, eager to explore the deserted streets; mothers looked out after them, wondering if it was safe to let them go. A few brave souls headed out toward the market district in search of supplies for the Sabbath that they suddenly found they needed. Shops began to re-open; old men eagerly gathered in clusters to exchange stories; tax collectors and businessmen resumed their labors, and a few long flowing robes dashed here and there among the growing crowd.

Yet amidst all the bustle and return to normal routine, something remained missing. At first, no one noticed; but as the afternoon finally gained a rather normal appearance, a few of the more observant residents paused and scratched their heads. Annas, who was still standing at the top of the Temple steps was one of them. As soon as it had become practical in the waning darkness, he had sent Caiaphas off to round up as many of the high council as could be found. There were several crucial matters that needed immediate attention, and Annas had decided that he could not wait for his son-in-law to take the necessary steps. And in spite of his predictably childish objections, Caiaphas had reluctantly given in and stormed off in a huff to do as he was told. But as Annas stood there watching the streets swell with the curious throng, something nibbled at the back of his mind. He took a few steps to the east and looked out over the city wall.

Other than the subdued sound of the crowd in the streets below him, there was no noise. No sheep bleating in the temple pens. No braying of donkeys from their stalls. No hoof beats on the stone pavement. No chirping or calling or singing from birds. In fact, as he scanned the horizon, Annas could see no birds at all. And the sounds that he could hear coming from merchants haggling with customers or old women shouting to one another or from slamming doors seemed hollow and distant, as if his ears were filled with water. Something was still wrong.

Annas turned his back to the crowd and headed quickly through the Women's Court into the Court of Israel, into the Priest's Court and up to the huge gold-covered doors leading into the Temple itself. He paused for some reason, and felt an inexplicable chill raise the hair on the back of his neck. Shaking it off, he reached out and took hold of the doorknob, but again paused.

What was he waiting on?

And better yet, why did he have this sudden impulse to enter the Holy Place?

He pulled on the doorknob, and the massive door slowly swung open.

He peered in.

The towering room was drenched in blackness, perhaps for the first time in decades, for the holy lampstands - carefully tended for generations - had all burned out. Annas panicked. He raced back out into the courtyard and began calling for help. Presently, a minor priest, shaken by the alarm he saw in Annas, procured a torch, handed it to him, and followed behind as Annas once more labored to pull open the huge door.

And there it was, clearly visible in the dancing torchlight: the enormous veil, which separated the Holy Place where men were permitted from the Holy of Holies where men were not, was torn in two, from top to bottom. And there was nothing there.

Annas emitted a strange gurgling sound, dropped the torch and slumped senseless to the floor.

Caiaphas wasn't faring much better. Very few members of the Sanhedrin were to be found, and those who were at home refused to come to the door, much less agree to come with him for another round of meetings. Frustrated, he turned to the handful of nervous old men he had collected, and split up the remaining names among them and sent them off in search for a few more. There was one more item on the list of chores that Annas had given him to do, and for this one he would have to see the governor.

"Why are they worried?" the ranking demonic commander asked, only half listening to the report, distracted as he was with keeping order among the victorious spirits as they continued to celebrate.

"I am not really sure, my lord. There seems to be some lingering concern over the dead body of our enemy."

"Over a dead body? What possible concern could they have with that?"

"There are rumors..."

"I am not interested in rumors. And I do not have time for this foolishness. Leave me."

"But, my lord..."

"Leave me! And do not return until you can tell me something useful."

"Is that you John?"

There was a sudden flurry of robes through the doorway. Inside the dark room, a hasty and bittersweet reunion unfolded. Sad tales were exchanged in hushed voices, while a lookout kept a sharp eye on the street below. The weeping began again as the terrible wounds were opened afresh. The two Mary's were embraced and consoled by several other women who had sought out this place of hiding along with the disciples and close friends.

John pulled his brother aside and asked, "Have you seen Peter?"

James replied, "He is here. After the darkness someone found him hiding in a pile of rubble out in the city somewhere, and brought him here, hoping we could help him."

"Let me see him."

James gripped his arm, and held him back. "Be careful with him, John."

"What's the matter? Has he been hurt?"

"No, brother, as far as we can tell, he isn't injured, but something is wrong. He just sits in the corner with his face in his hands, moaning and rocking back and forth. He won't look at anyone or speak to anyone. I'm not sure he knows where he is or who we are. It's pitiful."

As the two worked their way into the recesses of the apartment, they were joined by Andrew. Presently, the three were standing silently in a dark corner, observing a bundle of arms and legs wrapped tightly in a ball, rocking back and forth, oblivious to their presence.

"What happened to him, John? I've never seen him like this. Our whole lives, he has been the strong one, the one who always came to my rescue. How can something like this happen?

"I don't know. But I think I know how he feels. He may be the only one in the room who has grasped the enormity of what has happened."

"What do we do, John?"

"I don't know."

"Should we leave Jerusalem? Are we safe here?"

"I don't know."

And they all wept as they stood there, silently watching as their world continued to fall apart.

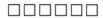

In the bleak anteroom of the Temple, where leading scribes and priests had for generations met and discussed the weighty matters of state on behalf of their Jewish brethren, the atmosphere was bleak indeed. There were clearly forces swirling around them that they could not comprehend and could not admit, even in this room. But having met the bare minimum for a quorum of the ruling Sanhedrin, Caiaphas nonetheless called the meeting to order and to no one's surprise immediately recognized his father-in-law.

"Thank you, my lord Caiaphas. As you are all most certainly aware, the Nazarene has died rather more quickly than we anticipated, and we have been forced to make a few difficult decisions. Due to the coming Sabbath, and upon the advice of the governor, we are placing a Roman guard at the location where his remains will be taken."

There was an uneasy commotion among the old men, and at length one of them spoke up.

"My lord, Annas: why must we involve the Romans again? Is it not enough that we have used these godless gentiles to kill one of our own and...and...brought upon ourselves...

"And brought upon ourselves...what?"

The uneasy commotion returned, and Annas sensed an unspoken undercurrent moving about the room to which neither he nor Caiaphas was a party.

"Speak up, my friends; we must be candid and open with one another."

But there was no response.

"Very well then; let me explain why we have agreed to allow the Roman guard. We have been informed of a plot by the Nazarene's disciples to steal his body."

Bewildered looks raced around the room.

"But why would they do that?"

"Come, come, my friends: has it really been so long? We

are all aware of the rumors surrounding the death of his friend Lazarus of Bethany. Must I spell it out for you?"

"Are you suggesting that he might be...?"

"I am suggesting that his disciples might make the same fraudulent claim in this case if we give them the opportunity. We must not give them that opportunity."

Annas glanced at Caiaphas, who simply nodded in response.

"And there will be a Roman seal on the tomb."

The level of uneasiness rose perceptibly at this revelation, but Annas was ready, and said smoothly over the objections, "We understand your feelings, my friends; really, we feel the same way about desecrating his tomb with a heathen symbol. But we simply have no choice in the matter. The governor felt very strongly that we needed this formal notice to warn any would-be thieves that violation of this particular tomb would be punishable by death."

The silence that followed was heavy and laden with trouble. Finally, someone asked in a subdued voice, "Where will his body be laid, if we may ask?"

Caiaphas answered, "An anonymous friend of the rabbi (Annas winced at the use of this title) has donated a new tomb for the purpose. I am told that it lies quite near the place where he was...well, where his death occurred. His body is being conveyed there as we speak."

The unsettling silence around the room was in no way improved by this information. All faces were downcast or gazing into the distance; no one would look either Caiaphas or Annas in the eyes.

"There is one thing more," Annas said quietly. As he waited, a few faces finally turned reluctantly to look at him.

"We must issue a decree to the population that anyone with information regarding the whereabouts of his disciples is hereby compelled to..."

"So here we are then." The red-faced old Manaseh had risen to his feet so abruptly that his stool had kicked behind him to the floor with a startling crash. He continued amidst a startled tumult, "Are we to round them up and put them all on Roman crosses?" Above a chorus of confusion his voice rang out, "Where will it stop?"

"Please, brothers, hear us out..."

"I will not! I will not play a part in this madness any longer."

He turned and stormed to the door, but before he left the room, he turned back and added, "We have acted foolishly and have unleashed something that we will live to regret. I, for one, regret it already."

At the tomb, the door was closed and sealed. The officer was there; the one who had stood by throughout the whole affair – the arrest, the trials, the beatings, the crucifixion, the hellish lightning, the darkness and earthquakes, and the brave, quiet suffering of the innocent prisoner. He had been there when he had refused the poison offered to alleviate his pain. He had been there when he had cried out in terrible agony. He had been there when he had called out to his mother and friend. And he had been there when he had forgiven his tormentors, and when he had bowed his head and died. And by all that was holy, he would be here to protect his remains as long it is might be necessary. So he stood by a little longer, now joined by an entire squad of his best veterans.

Saturday

The somber, quiet nation observed the Sabbath, as their fathers had done, and as their fathers and grandfathers for many generations back had done. There was no work performed; the thirty-nine categories of work specifically proscribed in writing were carefully honored: there was no sowing, or plowing, reaping, binding sheaves, threshing, winnowing, selecting, grinding, sifting, kneading, baking, shearing wool, washing wool, beating wool, dyeing wool, spinning, weaving, making two loops, weaving two threads, separating two threads, tying, untying, sewing stitches, tearing, trapping, slaughtering, flaying, tanning, scraping hide, marking hides, cutting hide to shape, writing two or more letters, erasing two or more letters, building, demolishing, extinguishing a fire, kindling a fire, putting the finishing touch on an object and transporting an object between the private domain and the public domain, or for a distance of ten feet within the public domain. Instead, there was rest, peaceful and quiet, as the children of Israel waited patiently for sundown, the end of another Sabbath.

At sundown, when there were at last three stars clearly visible in the evening sky, the streets of Jerusalem came back to life. Windows opened, torches were lit, children exploded from the doors, mothers set about to prepare meals, old men gathered, and young men secretly sought out young women. It was the eve of the first day of a new week, and though a strange quiet still blanketed the city, few noticed or cared.

In the deepening twilight, a hooded figure stepped into the crowd, carrying a scroll. He moved softly, the scroll tucked safely beneath his cloak. Without looking back, he made his way through the city without speaking to anyone, and without attracting attention. Presently, he stopped at a dark door, knocked once and waited for a response. After a long pause, he exchanged a few words with someone behind the closed door, and then handed the scroll through a small opening. The figure disappeared into the night.

At the tomb just outside the city, all was quiet. The gates were now closed for the night, and half of the soldiers were relaxing around a small fire eating their evening meal, while the other half stood watch. The officer was still there, still in charge, and still wide awake in spite of his now forty-eight hours of duty.

In the brightly lit home of the high priest, Caiaphas and Annas were discussing their options as they sat for the evening meal together.

"What do you suppose got into the old man?" Caiaphas asked through a mouthful of steaming venison. They had been reviewing the damage wrought by Manaseh the previous day.

Annas shook his head. "It was completely out of character. I have never seen him stand up for anyone before, certainly not for a bunch of Galileans. It didn't make any sense."

"What should we do with him?"

Annas shook his head again. "That is the wrong question. The old man is of no consequence; if we can rally the rest of them, his opinion won't matter – it never has. The one I am worried about is Nicodemus."

"Now that you mention it, I haven't seen Nicodemus since the night before last, here in this very room. He wasn't at any of the trials yesterday morning, or at our meeting last night," Caiaphas murmured, sipping a cup of something hot.

"He is up to something, I can feel it," Annas stated, staring down at his plate of untouched food. "Do you remember what he said when he joined us in this room?"

"That reminds me," the high priest said, pausing with a spoonful of food in mid-air and a dark look spreading across his face, "How do you suppose that he found out about our meeting?"

"Someone told him," Annas replied simply. "Don't you remember? He referred to this someone as 'a frightened old man' who was in possession of delicate information."

"I believe that you are right – he did say something of that sort."

"Do you know of whom Nicodemus was speaking?"

"Me?" Caiaphas responded with an injured voice. "Why do you think I would know?"

"Because he also said that he intended to bring this issue up with you at a later time. I think that perhaps this is what our friend is up to: he possesses information that he believes is damaging...damaging to you, and is organizing some sort of challenge."

"What do you mean 'challenge'?"

Annas looked down and brushed a few crumbs from the table before him. When he looked back up at his brother-in-law, his eyes were troubled. He shrugged his shoulders and said simply, "I don't know."

□□□□□□

"Who was it, James?"

"I'm not sure. His face was covered, but there was something about him that seemed familiar."

The two brothers were sitting at a small table, examining the scroll in the dim candle light. The rest of their friends were crowding around them, still alarmed about the sudden, unexpected knock at the door, and anxious to see what was written on the scroll.

"Well, what does it say?" hissed Thomas from the back row.

"It says 'You are not safe'," read John.

Fresh panic spread around circle.

"That's it? Nothing more?" cried Philip.

"Shhh!"

"Keep it down!"

"What are we going to do?"

"Do you want them to hear us?"

"We are all going to die!"

"Shhh!"

"What does it mean? Are the priests after us, or is it the Romans?"

"Shhh!"

"They are probably searching the entire city, house to house..."

"Will you all be quiet?" James roared.

In the stunned silence that followed, James reached his hand out and moved aside those standing to his left so that he could see his pitiful friend huddled in the corner, still curled up in a ball and rocking back and forth. Still seated at the table, he looked back to his brother who was staring down at the scroll.

"What are we going to do, John?"

"I don't know."

He was once called Lucifer, the light bearer; now he was Satan, the adversary. He is the ruler of this present darkness, the prince of the power of the air, the one who has the power of death and holds the whole world in that power. He believes no one, loves no one, values nothing and honors nothing. He is the original rebel, a liar and a deceiver. He has no controlling morals, uses no restraint, kills and destroys without mercy, and has no remorse; he is the devil.

And the devil had been waiting a long time for the word that he would be admitted into heaven. He was used to this, however; for millennia now he had been visiting the heavenly realm at regular intervals, sometimes upon his own request, and sometimes against his will. Either way, the visit was never pleasant, and he always was forced to wait. He usually spent the time dreaming of revenge, humiliating his ancient enemy, or destroying the host of heaven; he sometimes fantasized in vivid detail what he would do if he were on the throne and ruling the entire universe. This was the vision that gripped him tightly on this particular occasion as he waited, for this was the occasion when the dream would at long last become reality.

An angel suddenly appeared, and the wait was over. The devil recognized the invitation and stepped forward, his entire body pulsing with anticipation. It would only be a few moments now, and then it would all be over. The angel didn't suspect anything.

They were all there; in some cases they had been there for a very long time, though in this place time had no meaning. Abraham was there, and so was Noah, and David, Hezekiah and Malachi; it was a big place, and it was filled with men and women and children of all ages. There was Enoch and Sarah and Joseph and Isaac; Moses and his brother Aaron, Solomon and Ezra, Rachel, Gideon, Naomi and Caleb. They had all died believing the Lord, along with thousands of others whose names were not so familiar. There were royalty and bakers, slaves and shepherds, and husbands and wives from every tribe of Israel, as well as from among the gentiles.

It was a good place, without crime or sorrow; it was a place of comfort and rest without the presence of hardship or toil that had defined the earthly existence of so many of its residents before they came to this place. And while Simeon had been there for only a few years, and Adam and Eve for thousands, no one there grew tired or impatient while they waited. They didn't know what they waited for, and their lack of knowledge in this matter did not bother any of them. They were safe, at peace, and fully confident in God their savior. They were all aware, however, that this place was not their home, and so they continued to wait.

□□□□□□

"There may be a problem, my lord."

"What was that?" asked the ranking demonic commander, who was just returning from his tour of the area.

"We have been following the robed one as you commanded, my lord, and there does seem to be a schism developing," the field officer reported, falling in behind the commander as he strode along.

"And what did the non-participating spy have to say?"

"He has been examined at length, and his story confirms the uh...concern."

"Who examined him?"

"Why, I did, my lord."

Without warning, the ranking commander suddenly turned around and delivered a savage blow to the face of his officer, causing him to stumble to the ground.

"So I am to take your word in this matter, am I? You know that the independent report must remain independent, or it is useless." Turning to a squad of nearby sentries, he barked, "Get him out of my sight!" and the officer was gone.

"Now, bring me that spy. The last thing I need is a problem while the prince is away."

When Nicodemus returned to his house, it was late and dark outside, and even darker inside. He entered the door quietly, laid aside his cloak, and lit a lamp near his bed. Looking up, he was startled to see the old man sitting alone in the corner.

"You gave me a scare, my friend. Why are you here?"

"I can't go back; I am afraid of him. If I go back, he will ask questions and discover that I have been to see you. I have nowhere else to go."

Nicodemus was touched by the old man's plight. He had been a slave as a younger man, and through years of hard and faithful service had won his freedom; but for the past thirty years, since he had learned no other trade, he had remained a household servant, not much better than a slave.

But the man could not stay here; it was too risky for both of them.

"Have you no family?" asked Nicodemus, "No relatives?"

"I have no one. And now what little shelter I had is gone, along with the little hope that was left."

Nicodemus was exhausted. He sat down on the bed and sighed deeply.

"I thought he was the one," whispered the old man.

After a brief moment of quiet, Nicodemus replied, "Me too."

"I took the scroll of Zechariah, you know. He never read it, and he didn't deserve it. It may be years before he discovers that it is missing."

Nicodemus didn't know how to respond, so he said nothing.

"I read the prophecies about the Messiah, and I was sure that the rabbi from Galilee would fulfill them and set us all free. Now he is gone."

The old man began weeping silently, his frail body heaving with emotion.

"What am I going to do?" he asked.

"I don't know."

By the third watch, the disciples had collected all of their meager belongings, and had cleaned up anything that could potentially serve as evidence that they had ever been in the rented room. They were now fugitives, and they had to begin thinking as fugitives. John had gone out secretly and contacted a friend, who had offered a place to hide. It was in a poor section of town, away from traffic, and hard to find. Their plan was to split up and re-group at the safe house before morning. So over a period of several hours, they began leaving, one and two at a time, and scattering throughout the city.

When Judas died, he also went to the place of waiting. So did the two thieves who died on each side of Jesus, and so did thousands of others who died around the world that same day.

Jesus had spoken of this place in his story about the poor beggar, the other Lazarus, who sat daily at the gate of a rich man. The rich man lived sumptuously while ignoring the beggar, and allowed him to die of want and disease; then he died shortly thereafter. Both Lazarus and the rich man were sent to this place: the land of the dead where all men were sent when their earthly existence was through. But there was a catch; the land of the dead was not equal for all who came. Lazarus was comforted, while the rich man was tormented. Furthermore, those who were comforted were separated from those in torment, and there was no way for either to change their prospects. Their treatment in this place was determined by what they did with their life on earth.

After suffering a horrible death and absorbing the guilt of all mankind, Jesus also came to this place.

Lazarus looked up. Off in the distance, he could see the chasm which separated the place where he resided from where he knew those in torment resided. He had seen the chasm many, many times, and had long been aware of the multitude of individuals on the other side. But at this particular moment, he was also aware of something new, a change. He stood, along with those around him, looking intently at the growing source of light above the chasm. Joshua stepped beside him, along with Elijah and Ruth. As they watched in wonder, they became aware of a sound as well: it began as something like a trumpet call, grew louder and more distinct, and soon was a voice which filled the air in that great place from end to end, on both sides of the chasm, and Lazarus clearly heard the voice address him by name. And so did Moses, and Ruth, and Abraham...

"...you are mine; I knew you before the foundations of the earth, and called you by name; I formed you in your mother's womb; I wrote your days in my book before any of them were; the number of my thoughts of you are greater than the sand on the seashore; you are precious in my eyes, and honored, and I love you.

"But you have burdened me with your sins, you have wearied me with your iniquities. You have all gone astray, you are all alike corrupt; there is none that are good among you, no not one.

"I have sworn in my wrath that I will punish the world for its evil: the soul that sins shall die. You have stored up wrath for yourselves on the day of wrath when my righteous judgment shall be revealed.

"So what was I to do? You cannot enter my presence with your sins; you cannot bring your evil and wrongdoing before my eyes. I dwell in unapproachable light and purity, which no man has seen or can see. Yet I have no pleasure in the death of any one; I do not wish that any should perish.

"I asked you to repent and turn away from your iniquities; I asked you to turn and live; 'Come now, let us reason together' I said, 'though your sins be as scarlet, they shall be white as snow.' I made a covenant with you, and promised you life and a future and a heritage; you were to be my people, and I was to be your God.

But still you strayed like sheep, every one turning his own way. If you are to be saved from destruction, if you are to dwell in my holy city, it will not be by your own righteousness.

"Therefore, I myself will search for my sheep, and will seek them out. I will seek the lost, and I will bring back the strayed, and I will bind up the crippled, and I will strengthen the weak.

"I promised you a deliverer, a redeemer:

> 'Behold, I send my messenger to prepare the way before me,
> and the Lord whom you seek will suddenly come to his temple;
> the messenger of the covenant in whom you delight.'

> 'For to us a child is born, to us a son is given;
> and the government will be upon his shoulder,
> and his name will be called "Wonderful Counselor, Mighty God,
> Everlasting Father, Prince of Peace."'

> 'He was despised and rejected by men;
> a man of sorrows and acquainted with grief;

and as one from whom men hide their faces he
was despised,
and we esteemed him not.
Surely he has borne our griefs and carried our
sorrows;
yet we esteemed him stricken, smitten by God
and afflicted.
But he was wounded for our transgressions,
he was bruised for our iniquities;
upon him was the chastisement that made us
whole,
and with his stripes we are healed.
The Lord has laid on him the iniquity of us all.

"I asked you to have faith; I asked you to believe me. Without a redeemer, without someone to pay the penalty for your wickedness and rebellion, you would be lost in your sins and cast into the outer darkness, where there will be weeping and gnashing of teeth forever."

And from the midst of the blinding light above the chasm appeared a man clothed with a long robe and with a golden girdle round his breast; his head and his hair were as white as snow; his eyes were like a flame of fire, his feet were like burnished bronze, refined in a furnace.

Suddenly, every resident, every man, woman and child standing on both sides of the great chasm, bowed down and kneeled before the brilliant figure.

"This is my Son, in whom I am well pleased."

Then the Son, in the midst of the blinding light spoke, and his voice was like the sound of many waters:

"For God so loved the world, that he gave his only Son, that whoever believes in him should not perish but have eternal life. For God sent the Son into the world, not to condemn the world, but that the world might be saved through him. He who believes in him is not condemned; he who does not believe is condemned already, because he has not believed in the name of the only Son of God."

Then Lazarus heard his name again, and so did Moses, and Ruth, and Abraham...

"...believed God, and it was counted to him as righteousness. Well done, good and faithful servant; enter into the joy of your master."

Around the great chamber there began a tremendous rumbling, and a strong wind and deafening roar, and in the blink of an eye, they were all gone: every resident of that place of waiting who had died believing, all of them shouting the name of Jesus their redeemer.

Sunday

At the first hint of color streaking the eastern horizon, the cock crowed heartily and repeatedly, announcing the arrival of a new day. Gabriel stood beside his old friend Michael on the mountaintop, gazing off into the distance, neither of them saying a word. It was a beautiful, cloudless dawn, and the two were struck with deep awe at the majesty and glory the Creator gave his creation. Behind them stood their legions, waiting patiently.

"I would have taken his place you know, if it had been possible."

"You remind me of someone," replied Gabriel with a little smile, still looking out across the broad valley at the brightening sky. In the background he could hear birds singing.

"What is that supposed to mean?" asked Michael, surprised at the change in subject.

"It seems to me that our human friend Simon Peter would have said much the same thing."

"Well, perhaps so, but..."

"And Peter shares something with the savior that you and I do not."

Michael just nodded and smiled, unable to contradict him.

"Peter is a man. Jesus is a man too, so he could take Peter's place facing the wrath of God. But since Jesus is also God, it couldn't work the other way; Jesus didn't need a savior, and Peter couldn't pay for his own sins, let alone someone else's."

"You know what amazes me?" asked Michael quietly, "The fact that he did it in one afternoon. What it would have taken all of humanity all of eternity to absorb, the savior did in three hours."

"You know what amazes me?" countered Gabriel, "The fact that he did it at all. He could have said 'No, they are not worth it.' He could have stepped down from the cross and returned to heaven, never looking back."

"But he didn't. And now it is over."

"No, my friend," Gabriel said with a smile, "It is just beginning. Are you ready to go? We have a thing or two to do before the fireworks begin."

Michael smiled a very big smile, and laughed out loud.

"I have been waiting for this for a long time."

□□□□□□

"What is that?" cried the ranking demonic commander.

□□□□□□

Sitting up suddenly in bed, Herod called out in a panic, "What is that?" The ground was rumbling, and there was a low, steady roar in the air. He jumped to his feet, felt the vibrations growing in the floor, and raced to his door and called for help.

□□□□□□

Out in the early morning streets of Jerusalem, the rumbling and shaking was beginning to take a toll on the buildings and walls. Cracks were showing up in the dried mud structures, spreading and flaking off bits and chunks of mortar. Doors rattled; ladders and loose objects fell. Splits in the ground were opening up, and bricks and stone were falling into the fissures. Mothers screamed for their children. Men ran to and fro in panic, trying to decide what to do.

Annas dressed hurriedly, and raced toward the temple. All around him, clouds of dust were rising into the clear blue sky as the rumbling increased in intensity. Stopping at a corner near the temple grounds to catch his breath, he tilted his head and listened, trying to identify the roaring noise in the background.

It sounds a little like a trumpet of some sort.

He pushed his way through the mounting crowd, and

climbed the steps into the outer courtyard. He paused and looked around. Nothing seemed out of place. Listening again to the noise, he decided that it originated outside the wall of the city. So he ran over to the western wall and raced along it under the portico until he reached the stairwell near the Fortress Antonia which led to the top of the wall. Though he was by now panting and perspiring heavily from the exertion, he climbed the steps rapidly. Finally reaching the top, he looked out over the wall to the north, and the roaring noise hit him in the face, multiplied fourfold up here in the clear.

And then he saw it: out in the hills surrounding the city, great gaping holes had opened up, and out of them were rising bodies – dusty, shrouded, human bodies. The sight was too much for him. Annas slumped to the stone floor, passing out for the second time in three days.

All around the city, in the wake of the earthquake, God's creatures great and small suddenly found their voices. The horses and asses snorted and pranced; the sheep in their fields bleated, the cattle in the stalls bellowed, and the sky was suddenly filled with every bird and hawk and owl imaginable, flapping and soaring and calling, all of them joining the mighty chorus of praise spreading out in all directions, carried on the dancing breeze which stirred every tree and bush in every grove and every blade of grass in every field.

From the graves rose joyous saints, revived from long slumber, dancing and shouting and singing with all of their might, and racing off into the city to testify of God's grace.

The hush was over, and it was a time to celebrate like never before.

At the tomb, all but one soldier had fled. At the first rumbling of the earthquake, the great stone at the sealed entrance had fallen forward with a great crash, smashing the plants and rocks before it into the ground. They had been shocked by this mysterious surprise and by the shaking of the ground and the loud noise rising all around them; but at the appearance of two strange figures emerging from the tomb, the soldiers were struck with terror and fled, leaving their helmets and gear behind them.

Before the officer followed them, with his heart pounding in his chest, he peered into the tomb around the two huge, brilliant white figures. One of them winked at him with a big grin, and said, "He's not here."

"I knew it!" the officer shouted with a big clap of his hands. He had an urge to hug the stranger wearing the grin, but decided against it and ran off toward the city.

"What is happening?" roared the demonic commander. The sky was suddenly flooded with enemy warriors, and chaos had broken out all around him. There was no perimeter defense; there was no longer a perimeter. Demons everywhere were streaking away in flight, put to chase by the blazing, relentless heavenly host.

"What?" cried John.

"We have been to the tomb, and he is not there. He is risen!"

The new hiding place was suddenly alive with activity and animated chatter. The women had been out early to finish embalming the Master's body, since the Sabbath had interrupted them when his body had been laid in the tomb. But now, upon their return, there was a raging debate over the veracity of their story.

"Are you sure?" asked James, the dubious expression on his face speaking volumes.

"The stone was rolled away," stated Mary Magdalene coolly, "The tomb was empty, and we saw an angel of the Lord. He said to tell you that he is risen!"

"I don't believe a word of it," replied Thomas.

As they continued to argue, a lone figure rose to his feet and began walking toward the door.

"Peter!" exclaimed John. But Peter had already gone out through the door, and had begun to run. "Peter; wait for me!"

In heaven, the first thing to be seen, above everything else, is the throne of God. Everything points to it, nothing detracts from it, and it is beyond description. Isaiah and Ezekiel and John all tried to describe the glory and majesty surrounding the throne:

> 'I saw the Lord sitting upon a throne, high and lifted up;
> and his train filled the temple.
> And the foundations of the thresholds shook
> at the voice of him who called,
> and the house was filled with smoke.'

> 'And above the firmament over their heads
> there was a likeness of a throne,
> in appearance like sapphire;
> and seated above the likeness of a throne
> was a likeness as it were of a human form.'

> 'Lo, a throne stood in heaven, with one seated on the throne!
> And he who sat there appeared like jasper and carnelian,
> And round the throne was a rainbow that looked like an emerald.'

Around the throne, on the flashing emerald floor or firmament, stand four individuals so awe-inspiring, so intimidating, that Ezekiel and John could only resort to comparing their features with those of fierce animals. Around these stand twenty-four more thrones with twenty-four elders clad in white seated upon them. And finally, around the twenty-four thrones stand 'thousands of thousands' (or millions) of angels.

It was into this holy, well defended place that Lucifer stepped with his plan to unseat the One on the throne.

He was in. So far: so good. And his legions had been admitted with him, for the first time ever. Lucifer looked up at the gleaming throne with envious eyes; he never tired at looking it, though he loathed the one sitting upon it.

But not for much longer.

He licked his lips, reviewed his plan, and then stepped forward. To his surprise, the ocean of angels silently parted for him, opening a way toward the throne. Again, this was a first. He moved forward briskly, climbing the steep slope and covering the immense distance rapidly. When he reached the twenty-four elders, they parted as well. He was shocked and delighted. He had never been permitted this close to the throne since...

"What is that?" he shrieked, spinning quickly around. The demons following him up the aisle had heard the noise too, and had stopped behind him. It was a low, rumbling sound which seemed to be building. The demons closed ranks around their leader as the sound became deafening, and the atmosphere around them shuddered with it. Lucifer scanned his surroundings in panic, looking for the source of the disturbance, but none of the heavenly inhabitants seemed to notice it. They all just stood there staring at him.

"I demand to know what is going on!" he called out, but his tiny voice was drowned in the crushing weight of the surging noise.

Suddenly, a vast stream of beings roared into view behind him, and banked off to his right, creating a blur of motion circling in a huge arc around the throne. The rumbling was now distinguishable as the combined voices of the intruders, all chanting something at the tops of their voices.

There must be millions.

Out of the blinding stream of motion dropped a single figure, which descended slowly toward the throne.

It can't be.

But it was. The Lord of the universe, the mighty Son of God was back.

And then a second figure dropped, this one heading directly for Lucifer.

"Are you glad to see me?" asked Michael, as he grabbed the astonished deceiver by his shoulders. Suddenly, he and his choice demons were surrounded by a vast army of heavenly warriors, and a brief battle ensued. In the end, Michael personally threw the devil out of heaven.

"Now war arose in heaven, Michael and his angels fighting against the dragon; and the dragon and his angels fought, but they were defeated and there was no longer any place for them in heaven. And the great dragon was thrown down, that ancient serpent, who is called the devil and Satan, the deceiver of the whole world – he was thrown down to the earth, and his angels were thrown down with him.

"And I heard a loud voice in heaven, saying, 'Now the salvation and the power and the kingdom of our God and the authority of his Christ have come, for the accuser of our brethren has been thrown down, who accuses them day and night before our God...'"

"'Rejoice then, O heaven and you that dwell therein! But woe to you, O earth and sea, for the devil has come down to you in great wrath, because he knows that his time is short!'"

Revelation 12:7 – 10, 12

Made in the USA
Charleston, SC
13 September 2016